THE EVENT THAT
CHANGED EVERYTHING

THE EVENT THAT CHANGED EVERYTHING

A NOVEL ABOUT COOKS, CHEF'S, RESTAURANT
LIFE, FARMING, RELATIONSHIPS AND
ENVIRONMENTAL CONSCIOUSNESS

Paul Sorgule

THE EVENT THAT CHANGED EVERYTHING
A NOVEL ABOUT COOKS, CHEF'S, RESTAURANT LIFE, FARMING,
RELATIONSHIPS AND ENVIRONMENTAL CONSCIOUSNESS

iUniverse books may be ordered through booksellers or by contacting:

iUniverse
1663 Liberty Drive
Bloomington, IN 47403
www.iuniverse.com
1-800-Authors (1-800-288-4677)

ISBN: 978-1-4917-5510-5 (sc)
ISBN: 978-1-4917-5509-9 (e)

Library of Congress Control Number: 2014921635

Printed in the United States of America.

iUniverse rev. date: 01/09/2015

DEDICATION

This book is dedicated to my wife Sharon and my children Erika, Jessica and Leif as well as their wonderful spouses Matt, David and Stephanie. I feel incredibly fortunate to have them in my life. Finally, to all of the chefs, cooks, bakers, pastry chefs, farmers, cheese makers, ranchers, educators, students and food professionals with whom I have had the pleasure to work with over the last 45 years.

SPECIAL THANKS

To my advance readers: Nancy-Matheson Burns, Chef Jamie Keating, Chef Charles Carroll, Chef Curtiss Hemm, Kevin O'Donnell, Sharon Sorgule, Erika Sorgule, and Jessica Sorgule and JoAnne Bestine.

To Chef John Folse for allowing me use his name and Restaurant R'evolution in the chapters focused on New Orleans and Baton Rouge.

To my copy editors: Bob (Bo Jest) Seidenstein for his honest and gentle critique. And to Rebecca Steffan for the final edit.

To Sara J. Henry whose writing inspired me to finish this second book and attempt a work of fiction.

FOREWORD

In an era of fast food and instant gratification, we are consumed with digesting endless streams of trivial information simply because we can with the invention of the smartphone. One might suggest or even argue that we should take the time to slow down and savor life a little more, as we would a well-balanced pinot noir. This book is a story crafted with all the care of a beautiful wine from a person who has made a life in the hospitality industry. Through discipline and time-tested methods anyone who has ever worked in a kitchen would respect, this story has matured over time, just like that well-crafted wine.

Paul Sorgule takes his passion for food and beverage, his long resume of experience, and inspires us by allowing the readers to see the inside of a kitchen through his eyes, stirring a recipe of life-like characters as only a great chef can. For anyone who has worked in the food industry, this book will take you back in time to the place where you waited tables, sweated over the hot stove or smelled the perfume of that certain waitress from long ago. This book will spark memories that capture the energy and craziness of the hospitality business. For those of you who may not have had the opportunity to experience a professional kitchen it gives a very accurate snapshot with an eye for the details, similar to a good chef who always focuses on the "center of the plate".

The author has been a mentor to many in the hospitality industry as a teacher, competitor, chef and friend. Through his experiences he once again, in the third person, mentors the reader unknowingly with the story line and real life anecdotes of the restaurant world. While this is not a cookbook it could be a lightly illuminated road map for someone entering in the field.

It clearly summarizes what many of us already know about this business, "Good food is the foundation of genuine happiness." Auguste Escoffier

Kevin G. O'Donnell
Hunger Mountain Coop – Montpelier, Vermont
Vermont Fresh Network
Former Vice President – New England Culinary Institute
Former Manager of The Inn at Shelburne
Farms and the Inn at Grafton
July 2014

TESTIMONIALS

"This is a tenacious tale of two culinarians, both cursed and blessed while being committed to the responsibility we burden ourselves with as chefs in search of creating the Total Dining Experience. I found myself reflecting on my own personal journey of 30 years. A must read for all who are trying to find their way."

Chef Jamie Keating, CEC
Chef/Proprietor: Epic Restaurant
Georgia, USA

"Paul is a zealous culinarian and professional educator who has been a lifelong mentor and contributor to the world of food. His work is his vocation and his passion. I thoroughly enjoyed reading The Event this summer. Sorgule's love for the Vermont/Adirondack Farm to Table Community shines through on every page. I appreciated the back-of-the-house character development, and felt Jake and Carla could very well have been students' of Paul's. After teaching and inspiring a generation of chefs, Sorgule now shares his passion with a new audience. Bravo, Chef Paul!"

Nancy Matheson-Burns
President, Dole and Bailey Provisioners
Boston, MA

"Through *The Event*, Chef Sorgule takes us on a journey that examines the physical and emotional transactions experienced by those within the hospitality industry. These transactions are highlighted through a series of environmental changes that push the boundaries of our current and transitioning food system, farming practices, and the ecosystem that it supports or destroys.

Chef Sorgule not only shares his passion for food and cooking with the reader, he spells out the reasons why we collectively need to nurture, grow and support contemporary artisan agriculture and cooking. We can no longer trust our food system with the health and welfare of our family, friends, and customers.

As we follow the journey of a few young chefs, *The Event* showcases why chefs have been leading the grassroots movement toward a renewed focus on local, farm to table, artisan foods. I am certain *The Event* will move you closer to your food, table, and into the kitchen."

Chef Curtiss Hemm
Founder and President
Pink Ribbon Cooking www.pinkribboncooking.com

PART ONE

The Event Strikes in New York Food, Wine, Cooks and Sudden Death

"Yet, as only New Yorkers know, if you can get through
the twilight, you'll live through the night."
Dorothy Parker

...and then again – maybe not

CHAPTER ONE

A RESTAURANT'S WORST NIGHTMARE
OCTOBER 16, 2015

Jake stumbled to the bathroom of his New York studio apartment with crusty eyes and a pounding headache. It was just past noon on Friday, the first time in four days he had been able to sleep. This was only possible with the help of way too much alcohol the night before. Now he would pay the price. As his eyes came into focus Jake looked in the mirror and wondered how he'd gotten to this point. This was the first Friday in longer than he could remember that he would not be going into work. Not going to work, all because of *The Event*.

A line cook's life is different than the norm. Jake's every moment was dictated by the job, a job, even given all of its challenges, which he loved. On this morning, as was the case since Monday night, his schedule was empty. Empty in more ways than one. *The Event* had instantly changed his life and he hadn't even begun to wrap his head around it. Monday had been his day off, the only one scheduled for the week, and after taking care of some long overdue chores he was settling in for a simple meal and Netflix video. When his cell phone rang, his world turned upside down.

"Jake, this is Chef Andre. I would normally take care of this face-to-face, but given the seriousness of the situation I wanted to call you right away. Let me get right to the point - there's been a suspected outbreak of E.coli traced back to our restaurant. Jake, I don't know how to say this, but four people have died and six others are in the hospital as a result."

The silence that followed was haunting. At first, Jake was in shock. Gradually, he felt a series of emotions creep up from the depths of his soul. Jake was at first overcome with sorrow and remorse. Was he responsible for the death of four people? He began to weep, gasping for air and finding it difficult to focus, he became fully aware of his heart pounding in his chest and forced himself to take a breath. Was he weeping for the poor individuals who died? Was he panicked for the restaurant, his crew, and his own potential responsibility for this? Was he just in shock and this was a way to keep from passing out?

What came next left him alone and confused. "Jake, I'm calling to let you know that I'll have to let you and your team go in an effort to save the restaurant. Someone needs to be responsible for this. You can pick up your last check any time this week or we'll send it in the mail. Take care Jake, you're a great cook, I'm sorry this happened." Jake ended the call and set his iPhone down. For the first time since he was 16, Jake was without a job, alone in New York, and possibly responsible for the death of four restaurant guests. How did this happen?

Looking in the mirror Jake knew drinking was not the answer, although it did allow him to get 10 hours of sleep. He hoped that after a shower and a decent breakfast he would be able to clear his head and start to figure this whole thing out. Jake made a cup of strong French roast coffee in his Keurig, fried two eggs with wheat toast, peeled back a banana and proceeded to flush the cobwebs from his brain. There must be an answer to this; he was responsible for not just himself, but his team as well.

Jake knew the answers would not come to him without help so he quickly dialed the four other members of his line team: Shelly, Marco, Kelly and Rob and suggested they meet for coffee at Abraco on 7th Street in the East Village. This was a favorite, no frills espresso bar cooks liked to patronize. The call to arms: figure out what had happened and strategize on next steps. While walking to the meeting he was already beginning to wonder if this was an isolated incident or part of *The Event* the news had been covering for the past six months. *The Event* wasn't something that occurred, but rather something that was evolving and growing as if an out of control virus. In any case, isolated incident or part of the growing event, Jake felt responsible for finding the answers. Enough drowning his sorrows in an alcohol bath, it was time for action.

Jake was always a stickler for food safety and kitchen sanitation, and his team members shared his obsession. As he turned onto 7th Street Jake kept running through every step in the food handling process from the past week. He couldn't pick out any potential miss-step; nothing from the normal routine of checking in product, recording HACCP information, proper washing and cooking techniques, sanitation of work stations and tools, hand washing, etc. It was all in order. Maybe the team would have a different recollection, he thought to himself. He knew that the Health Department would be all over the restaurant, taking swatches, starting cultures, testing products in coolers and looking for any common denominators among the sick and deceased. Maybe, just maybe, the team would be exonerated and that would be that. But maybe wasn't good enough, not when lives were lost, careers were in shambles and the restaurant's future was in serious jeopardy.

As he entered Abraco, Jake took a deep breath. Now he had to face his teammates, his friends. The others were already there and shared the same somber look. The reaction when Jake entered was like a long lost family getting together for the first time in years. They jumped up from their seats and hugged Jake, tears running down everyone's faces. They knew words would be hard to come by, but they were in this together and somehow they would find answers to this tragedy.

Everyone ordered an espresso and sat down to begin working through the issue at hand. Jake pulled out a pad and pen and took charge of the discussion as only he knew how. First, make a list of factors and begin to address each one systematically. This is how a sous chef works, this was his routine, and this was what his team expected.

"We need to catalog what we know and what we don't know. I think we should approach this situation just like we would an insanely busy night in the restaurant. Let's list potential problems, extraordinary situations, positive and negative opportunities, likely causes, probable effects and potential solutions." This is what the team was use to. This methodical approach gave them all a level of comfort, a feeling they might get to the bottom of this just as they had with crazy nights in the restaurant. "If nothing else, this will help to take our minds off the tragedy, those families grieving the loss of loved ones, our careers and the fate of the restaurant - at least for a moment."

After three hours and far too many espressos, they had an outline and assignments. Jake was determined and the team was focused. Now it was time to act. What they did not anticipate was how deep the issues were and how much worse the situation would become. *The Event* kept spreading its viral tentacles and would soon extend way beyond their individual situations.

CHAPTER TWO

WE DON'T KNOW WHAT WE DON'T KNOW

The five cooks left Abraco, turned in different directions, down 7th street and began to approach their assignments. The plan at this point was to stay in touch via cell phones and meet up again for dinner at Jake's apartment. Jake returned to his apartment first to collect his thoughts and pick up his laptop. He sat down and reviewed what they knew thus far:

- Four people had died, apparently from E.coli
- Six others were hospitalized
- A common denominator seemed to be Restaurant Lust, where the 10 people had dined recently
- E.coli was present on the surface of primal cuts of meat and could be killed with enough heat. Typically, this was not a problem, except with ground beef where the bacteria would be spread through the meat, requiring hamburgers to be fully cooked to destroy E.coli. Since their restaurant did not serve ground beef, Jake was confused as to the source of the problem. There had been some cases where produce had been reported contaminated as the bacteria originates in some animal feces used for fertilizer, but those cases were rarely widespread
- The press would be all over the restaurant today resulting in a public relations nightmare and the probable closing (at least temporarily) of the restaurant
- The Health Department along with the police would be on premise looking at everything
- The restaurant had chosen to terminate his team in an effort to take a proactive approach
- The restaurant recently completed its annual health inspection and received a great report with a score of 95 out of 100
- His entire staff had completed and passed the ServeSafe Sanitation Program
- He was a tyrant when it came to food safety and sanitation so he knew that every precaution was always taken to ensure the safety of the restaurant's guests
- The restaurant used the most reputable vendors for their supplies

Jake was torn between an absolute sense of horror at the death of four innocent people and anger at Lust's management, which had jumped to conclusions and thus fired his staff without any evidence of wrongdoing. He had a deep feeling there was more to this story, something that would not only clear them of any responsibility, but also bring to light an issue with terrible consequences. He and his team were committed to finding the answer, it was all they had to hang on to, and it might allow them to sleep at night.

Jake's assignment was to visit with the chef (Andre Brousseau) and determine what, if anything else, was known. He quickened his pace as he came within two blocks of the restaurant. When he turned the corner he was shocked to see pandemonium surrounding the business. Police tape blocked the entrance, three police cruisers were out front, as was the Department of Health van, and more press with cameras than he could count. Through the front window he could see the chef and owner talking with a Department of Health representative and the restaurant's public relations person. Chef Andre saw Jake through the window and waved him inside. Jake wormed through the crowd and entered before the press could figure out his relationship to the property. To his surprise, the chef walked over and hugged Jake, patted him on the back and said: "grab a cup of coffee Jake, we need to talk."

Jake made himself a double espresso and pulled up a stool at the bar. Chef Andre joined him and started the conversation.

"Jake, I'm sorry you are going through this, but I have some good news and some not so good news to share. First and foremost, you and your team are not responsible for what happened. As it turns out, the coroner's office determined it wasn't E.coli that killed those customers and made the others sick. In fact, it's some new strain of deadly bacteria they aren't able to identify." Jake, of course felt an immediate sense of personal relief. Chef Andre continued, "What's worse however, is that five additional deaths in the city have been reported as a result of this mysterious bacteria and there are at least three-dozen others in the hospital with similar symptoms. The CDC is now involved and will be in town shortly to start a full investigation. The Health Department official I was just talking with told me in strict confidence that other cities across the U.S. have begun reporting cases - some fatal. This is really big." Now, as Jake had feared, the scope of the issue was far greater than anyone had initially imagined.

"At this moment please know how sorry I am that the restaurant let you and your team go. We would like to make amends, however, at least for the time being, the restaurant will remain closed. If you and your team will accept our apology we'd like to give all of you your jobs back as soon as we're able to reopen."

Jake was grateful that the responsibility had shifted away from him and his team, but fear quickly encompassed his every thought. What could it be? Why was this happening and why as quickly as it had? Jake shook the chef's hand and thanked him. "My team and I are available to help in any way we can." Jake finished his espresso and left the restaurant in a bit of a mental fog. If the CDC was involved, it was likely that the comments from the Health Department official were true, and that this incident was just the tip of the iceberg. Jake pulled out his iPhone and sent a text message to his team giving them a brief overview and suggesting they meet in Union Square the next day instead of his apartment as originally planned. Everyone enjoyed the Green Market, so this was a great place to hopefully bring a ray of sunshine to a very gloomy day. They all confirmed a meeting at 10 a.m.

CHAPTER THREE

THE EVENT TAKES A TURN FOR THE WORSE
OCTOBER 17, 2015

Jake turned the corner and passed Union Square Café, it was mysteriously closed. He looked across the street to the Union Square Park for Green Market activity, but instead of the bustling crowds of shoppers there were a few empty tents and no sign of farmers, local producers or paying guests. The place was empty.

Shelly, Marco, Kelly and Rob were already there and just as dumbfounded as their boss. Marco shouted across the street to Jake, "What the hell is going on!" Jake was at a loss for words. Was this all connected? Had the market been canceled for another reason? Was it a coincidence that the Union Square Restaurant (one of New York's busiest) was closed? Was this a dream he would soon wake up from?

The team of five stood in silence for a few more moments until Shelly broke the ice: "Do you think this is related to *The Event* in the news for the past six months? Is it possible the worst case scenario the media talked about is coming true?"

Jake began "From what I know, we have been cleared of responsibility in the deaths, as has the restaurant. There were more deaths in New York from a strain of unknown bacteria and all indications are, that similar instances are being reported from other cities across the country." He sat down on a park bench, "We need to review everything we have heard about *The Event*." Rob, the tech guy in the group, pulled out his iPad and Googled *The Event*.

The Event was a noticeable change in the environment and the food supply over the past six months. Actually, many believed that the numerous environmental changes were driven by an avoidance of the tell tale signs that had been occurring over the past few decades. But during the last six months, it had become more and more apparent that a dramatic evolution was taking place.

The article Rob had found went on to describe the beginnings of *The Event* in 2011, a time of dramatic weather patterns, melting polar ice caps, increased tornadic activity, floods, deep-freeze temperatures in the winter, forest fires and even above average volcanic activity throughout the world. With a country committed to centralized farming, these weather changes had been causing sporadic problems with crop growth and in turn animal yield. Jake had noticed this, as some products had been difficult to come by for the restaurant, the size of the eye on primal meat cuts was noticeably smaller, and as the chef constantly stated "Prices of product are going through the roof."

For years, farmers had been growing crops from genetically modified seed (GMO's), ranchers' added antibiotics to animal care, and increased the use of growth hormones to compensate for yield depletion. The corn feed given to livestock was comprised of genetically modified seed, and there was some question about what else was in the mix (everyone remembered what had happened to the entire herd in England a decade or so ago). The argument that the use of GMO's would haunt us in the future, that corn was not a natural food source for animals designed to feed on grass, and that antibiotic use on livestock would have dire long-term implications on human resistance in the future continued for years. Even though the government had banned the automatic use of antibiotics on livestock in 2014, the impact was only now being felt as new antibiotic resistant ailments were cropping up.

Even with all of these warning signs, no one had anticipated what would happen over the past six months. *The Event* started with a series of catastrophic weather events and an outbreak of Salmonella so severe, so widespread, the CDC was unable to identify a single source and control it. At last count, over 300,000 people in the U.S. alone were affected (and those were only the ones who wound up under hospital care) with nearly 1,200 related deaths. The only thing they could tell was that it appeared to be related to eggs; even after most farms had switched to the process of irradiation. For some reason, the outbreak subsided on its own, maybe due to a dramatic decrease in egg consumption by the American public. This was the biggest food-related scare people had experienced in U.S. history.

Just when things were settling down, cattle in the Midwest began dying in large numbers. By mid-July nearly 150,000 cattle had simply dropped over dead or were euthanized. There was no indication of a common disease at first, but many believed it was Mad Cow Disease since all had experienced some form of sudden and in many cases, fatal brain hemorrhage. Combined with ongoing deaths among bee colonies and a strange resurgence of trichinosis among a large section of the hog population, it was becoming apparent the food supply in America was facing serious problems.

The media had labeled this *The Event*, an escalating attack on the food supply of America causing other countries to stop importing products raised or grown within U.S. borders. This was an attack significantly impacting the economy and the health of Americans.

Restaurants had been affected too. Chain restaurants were scaling back their menus to reflect what was available, and what people felt safe eating, wholesale costs-to-operations were skyrocketing, prices to customers were nearly double what they had been a few months earlier, and thousands of restaurants simply closed their doors, leaving one of America's largest employers in a shambles. To a large degree New York restaurants had been getting by because customers simply paid the higher prices, and in many cases were not prepared to cook on their own. New York was doing OK until this latest series of deaths without a known cause.

Jake, like many other talented chefs and cooks in the Big Apple, suddenly found himself without a job and no clear vision of when things might return to a semblance of normalcy.

Shelly walked across the street to a newsstand to pick up a copy of the *Daily News.* After a cursory review of the front page she returned to the group with a stunned look on her face. Handing over the paper to Jake, she sat on the park bench while the rest of the team huddled around the latest news.

Shelly joined Jake on the bench as he put his face in his hands. "How did I arrive at this point in my life?" He closed his eyes and began to reflect back on his journey from the early days in Buffalo.

PART TWO

Buffalo, New York
The Early Years

"If anything is good for pounding humility into you
permanently, it's the restaurant business"
Anthony Bourdain

CHAPTER FOUR

BACK IN TIME

Jake grew up in Buffalo, New York on the shores of Lake Erie. He attended Kensington High School, lived in what was an ordinary neighborhood, in a city that over the years had been maligned by the press and every comedian on the face of the earth. Yes, his hometown had severe winter weather; yes, the Buffalo Bills had a long history of not quite making it all the way; and yes, with the demise of Bethlehem Steel, GM, and Bell Aircraft plants, the economy in this city had suffered greatly. However, talk to any Buffalonian and they will stand tall and refer to their city as if it were the greatest place on earth.

Jake's first real job at 16 was washing dishes in a small diner two miles from his home. He worked weekends and summers throughout high school and was able to save enough money to afford an aging used car and a savings account for "the right future move." Jake enjoyed being in restaurants and working with people whom he considered to be a cross between pirates and saints. This was a place that set him at ease unlike high school where he found little of interest. Since he was blessed with a pretty sharp mind Jake was able to skate through school without much effort. At least in the diner he was able to see the results of his work and felt comfortable being around the crew, who were totally transparent.

Buffalo, at the time, was not breaking new ground in the culinary world, but, Jake was able to learn some of the basics from the lead cook at the diner. He now knew how to hold a knife, cook an egg a variety of ways, and time his preparations so the food was hot and fresh. He also developed an obsession for cleanliness. On the weekends he split his time between washing dishes, busing tables, prepping for the line and helping out with the breakfast rush. He did work an occasional night after school and could easily keep up with burgers, club sandwiches and fries. Once in a while, he even wound up working solo when the lead cook was sick. Jake had become important to the diner and as such, felt a real sense of worth -he mattered.

Near the end of his senior year, Jake felt plenty of pressure to apply to colleges, but, he was mentally and emotionally done with school. He wanted to be on his own and start searching for whatever it was he was meant to do. With plenty of resistance, his parents finally admitted it was time for Jake to find an apartment and make his way. Jake had saved enough money to pay first month's rent and a security deposit; so he signed a lease on a small apartment in the Elmwood District of town.

Elmwood was fairly active with lots of bars and restaurants and plenty of people Jake's age. Buffalo State College was just down the street, so even though Jake chose to avoid higher education, he was immersed in the environment of college life.

Jake was getting restless at the diner even after they promoted him to night cook and bumped his pay up to a respectable rate. He had mastered everything on the limited menu and although he was not sure yet what he wanted to do with his life, he felt that cooking was a great bridge to something else. He set out to find a restaurant with a bit more finesse, a place with swagger and classical technique, a restaurant willing to continue his education in food.

After a few interviews he was offered a job as commis (assistant) at The Cloister on Delaware Avenue. At the time, this was one of Buffalo's most popular restaurants and incredibly busy. From the moment he walked into the kitchen Jake knew this was the place for him. A whole new world was opening up; dramatically different from the single stove and grill top of the diner. The kitchen was large from his perspective, with a battery of ranges stretching fifty feet from end to end. There were 18 open burners, a French top range, sizeable char-grill and three deep fryers. Opposite the ranges were stations with lowboy coolers, roll tops for various ingredients and what he learned was the "pass" with heat lamps to keep the plates of food piping hot. In the back of the kitchen were steam kettles, convective steamers, more French tops, sinks, prep tables and huge walk-in coolers. This was a real kitchen and suddenly Jake felt totally inadequate and unprepared. As he took it all in, the chef walked over and introduced himself as Philippe.

Philippe had been around. At one point he was the Executive Sous Chef (a new term for Jake's vocabulary meaning second to the chef) at the Queen Elizabeth Hotel in Montreal. This was a Hilton Hotel servicing multiple in-house restaurants and an enormous number of banquets. He had been at the Cloister for two years helping to make the restaurant as popular as it was today. He gave Jake a tour, pointing out departments, equipment and product along the way. The chef introduced Jake to various people in the kitchen without much fanfare. As is typical, Jake was greeted mostly with a nod or a few grunts. Finding his place would take some time, he would need to earn their trust and show them that he wanted to learn and work hard. "Jake, this restaurant will typically serve between 400 and 500 guests every night and as many as 800 on Saturdays." These were numbers that were difficult for Jake to comprehend.

"Jake, take these copies of the menus and our employee handbook. Study them on your own time so you are familiar with what we do and what the restaurant requires." The chef showed Jake where to punch in, pick up his uniforms and then he dropped him off at the staff locker room. "Get dressed and report back to the kitchen as soon as you are ready." The adventure was about to begin. Jake was now ready to start the process of becoming a line cook at a reputable restaurant.

As Jake entered the kitchen in full uniform he realized that what he thought he knew no longer mattered. It was obvious from the first minute he entered his new home that everyone around him was well-seasoned and had the chops to show him up at every turn.

Jake had two knives to his name: a Sabatier 10-inch French knife with a few years of wear and tear and an inexpensive paring knife he had lifted from his parents' kitchen drawer a few years back. Most of the cooks in this kitchen had toolboxes filled with knives and other gadgets foreign to Jake. It was 7 a.m. and the kitchen was already buzzing, even though lunch wouldn't begin for another five hours.

Jake was assigned to evening prep and would work from 7 a.m. to 5 p.m. making sure the mise en place for the evening shift was ready. He would be working alongside Teresa, a forty-something cook who, for over forty years, had worked in various restaurants in the Buffalo area. She looked up at Jake and gave a half smile while extending her hand for a cursory welcome shake. "Welcome to hell!" This was not quite the greeting that Jake was looking for, but he figured she was probably exaggerating.

"Sharpen your knives, grab a cutting board, wash your hands and I'll get you started." Jake did as directed and returned in a minute. He had never learned to sharpen his knives properly and when Teresa looked at his French knife she shook her head, pulled out a wet stone and proceeded to show Jake how to draw the blade across the stone to maximize the edge. "Make sure you keep the angle of the blade as I showed you and after a few draws on both sides of the knife, stroke the edge on a steel to get rid of any burrs." The sexual innuendo went right over Jake's head even after he noticed Teresa's smirk while demonstrating the process. He immediately felt comfortable with Teresa, who would be his teacher during this first phase of training.

Teresa grabbed the clipboard holding the day's extensive prep list and began to go through their assignments for the day. She asked Jake which items he was comfortable with and placed his initials next to them. Jake was given a quick tour of the coolers and storeroom and then he was off and running. Peel 50 pounds of fingerling carrots, split three cases of salt potatoes for the lobster entrée, scrub and poke ten trays of 80-count russets for the prime rib, clarify two cases of butter and chop and wash a case of curly parsley. After a brief demo on how she wanted each accomplished, Jake went to work. What Jake lacked in culinary knowledge he made up for with speed. Although Teresa needed to correct a few of his methods, he was able to complete everything by 10. Teresa was impressed but didn't let on that Jake was working out.

Teresa added a few more complicated tasks to Jake's list: mise all ingredients for a veal stock including roasting veal bones (something Jake had never done), prepare a mirepoix (whatever that was), caramelize it, deglaze the pan, add tomato paste to the bones, and transfer everything to one of the gigantic steam kettles in the prep area. Teresa explained everything with the patience of a saint and walked Jake through the process until the kettle was simmering with a stock that wouldn't be ready until later in the evening.

Next: prepare the ribs for tonight. The Cloister was famous for their ribs; in fact, nearly 60% of their nightly business was prime rib.

Jake was shown how to trim the fat cap, tie the ribs, season and prepare them for roasting. The ribs would be placed in a hot oven for the first 45 minutes to caramelize the exterior, the temperature would be dropped down to 325 degrees and the roasting would continue until an internal temperature of 125 degrees was reached. Jake would then remove the strings securing the roast, cut back the fat cap, and lay the cap back on the roast until service (this helps to keep in the moisture and protect the eye of the meat). Finally, Jake was to transfer the beef to warming units. He was told there would be some carry over cooking and the line wanted ribs to be at around 130-132 degrees internal temp for service. This was critical and Teresa emphasized the temperature numerous times during the shift. The ribs would take around 2 ½ hours to get to this point, so once they were in the oven Jake was free to move on to another task.

He was taken aback when Teresa told him he would be preparing 15 roasts for this evening. This represented 270 orders of prime rib for tonight. The restaurant expected to serve 400 guests by the close of business.

By the time Jake finished with the ribs it was 2 p.m. and the evening crew of line pirates was arriving. Teresa introduced Jake as they passed and each gave him a high-five as they moved to their stations. There were four hot line cooks and two working Garde Manger to handle cold apps, salads and desserts.

This crew seemed different from the morning and lunch staff. They had some swagger, were fairly young (all in their early twenties) and very quick on their feet. Within a few minutes they were all set at their stations and busy with smaller, specific mise en place like snipping herbs, reducing sauces, mincing shallots, pre-marking steaks on the grill, blanching vegetables, and setting tools in place. It appeared to Jake that they were scientific about their set-up; arranging and re-arranging, pacing out the steps from stove to coolers and steam table, folding towels and setting up their lowboys. These cooks were preparing for battle.

As Jake finished the rest of his prep including a few favors the pirates asked him to do, and began scrubbing the tables and sinks in his area, Teresa called him over, "I just reviewed tomorrow's business with the chef and completed the first draft of tomorrow's prep sheets. Nice job today," she said this with a high-five and then dropped the prep clipboard on the table.

"This is the start of tomorrow's mise en place. At the end of the night the evening sous chef will adjust and probably add a few items, but this gives us an idea of how to mentally prepare. Tomorrow will be VERY busy so I can't babysit you again. Whatever I showed you today must be second nature tomorrow. Don't bombard me with questions because I won't have time. Do not make mistakes." Jake nodded in agreement. "Even though your shift starts at seven I'd encourage you to come in early, off the clock, to get a jump on things. With the reservations currently on the books we may hit 650 covers tomorrow and everyone will depend on us to be on our game."

"Thanks Teresa. I think I will stick around for a bit to watch the line cooks during the first part of service." Teresa smiled again and thought to herself, this guy might have the right stuff after all.

CHAPTER FIVE

GAME TIME

At 6 p.m. sharp the tickets started coming into the kitchen. Jake had never seen a professional line work before so he asked the sous chef if he could hang out and watch. The chef agreed, but said, "Don't be surprised if I call you into action if necessary." As the tickets arrived, the chef began calling out specific dishes to each station, and they responded to confirm that it was received. Two guys worked the grill and carving station for rib (Jake's rib), one crazy looking pirate was on sauté dishes and a woman (about Jake's age) worked like a magician on the fry station and hot appetizers. By 6:20 they were all engaged and the chef was told the 160-seat dining room was already full.

Jake watched in amazement as salmon and shrimp were flying off pans from the sauté station (that crazy looking cook was actually incredibly well organized and totally in sync with the orders). As anticipated, it seemed like every order had prime ribs on it. The cook on the carving station drew his knife through the meat like it was butter. He gracefully ladled an ounce of au jus on top and served it with a crisp, warm popover. Jake's baked potatoes and the vegetable of the day were served as sides. Carla, the cook on hot apps was a machine, handling the five hot appetizers on the menu, pommes frites, onion rings for steaks and the house onion soup without ever missing a beat. Jake had no idea how they were able to keep it all together. It looked to him like art in motion. It was intense but, looked like fun. It was a thing of beauty.

By this time it was 7:30 p.m., and Jake had been in the kitchen for nearly 13 hours, and yet it seemed like time had flown by. He was pumped. This is what cooking was all about. He wanted more than anything else to be one of those line cooks. Whatever he had to do to get to this position, Jake was ready. Starting tomorrow he would commit to being on his game, every day, every shift. He wanted to learn as much as he could, as fast as he could. Jake had a line position in his sights.

He thanked the chef, who nodded, but was in his zone. The chef on hot apps smiled at Jake as he started out the door. Now he had two things in his sight; the line position and maybe, at some point, a girlfriend. Wouldn't it be great to date someone who shared the same passion for food and who understood what it would take to be great in the kitchen?

CHAPTER SIX

DAY TWO – TIME TO START PROVING HIMSELF

To Jake, this was the first day of the rest of his life. He was on a mission; nothing was going to hold him back. He fell instantly in love with this new kitchen experience and saw in the mirror a person who could one day be a chef, maybe even own his own restaurant. For the first time in his life he was totally motivated. He woke up at 5 a.m., showered and shaved, drank two cups of coffee, ate a piece of toast, grabbed his two knives and headed out the door. He arrived at the Cloister by 6 a.m. – one hour before his shift was to start, put on a clean uniform and walked into the kitchen at 6:10.

To his surprise Teresa was already there and hard at work. She looked up and said, "You're late." Jake wasn't sure if she was serious or joking, but simply said, "Sorry, it won't happen again." Jake was starting to get the idea that to be a serious cook was to totally commit to the craft.

Jake moved quickly as he set up his board, washed his hands again and sharpened his knives the way Teresa had shown him the day before. He grabbed the prep clipboard and noticed Teresa had already put his name beside a handful of items. He was determined to move forward without asking too many questions. The list was similar to yesterday, but the quantities were greater. Potatoes, parsley, ribs, stock, vegetable prep were all there. He knew those could be handled well and without asking for help. There was also a new section with meat fabrication. He froze when he saw this. Teresa identified trimming 12 tenders for filet mignon, six 1 x 1 strip loins for New York steaks and shaping ground sirloin for burgers used in the bar. He knew he would need direction and help on these, but decided to hold off until he had a good portion of his regular prep complete.

As Jake was preparing his mise en place for veal and chicken stock, Chef Philippe walked by. He looked at what Jake was doing, "It is important for you to caramelize the mirepoix for the veal stock. Caramelization enhances the flavor and adds an important essence of sweetness to the finished product. Additionally, this browning will help to give the stock its characteristic color." Philippe smiled slightly and said, "So I hear you stayed around last night to watch part of service." Jake responded with the appropriate "Yes chef, it was fantastic. "Philippe nodded and walked away.

Teresa picked up her head "Jake, how are you doing on your list?" He replied, "I'm ahead of schedule, but will need some direction with the butchery on the prep list." Teresa gave a nod, "After lunch we can work on that together as long as everything else is done."

Teresa stopped for a moment and asked Jake if he had eaten any breakfast. "Coffee and toast." Teresa put down her knife, went to the hot line and proceeded to fry a couple eggs. She returned with breakfast of eggs, bacon, toast and a grilled tomato. "Stop what you are doing, sit down for ten minutes and have breakfast. You'll need the energy to get through the day and I don't relish having to pick you up off the floor." "Thanks." He moved to the corner and wolfed down the meal. Jake hadn't realized just how hungry he was. Revitalized, he returned to his board and picked up the pace. It was already 9 a.m. and the list in front of him was starting to look impossible.

By 11 the ribs were ready for the oven (20 of them today), vegetables were prepped, stocks were simmering and only chopped parsley remained. By 11:45 the basic prep was complete. Sweat was pouring off his forehead from humidity in the kitchen and the intensity of the work. In a manner of minutes Jake's station was cleaned and his knives re-sharpened. He stood in line with the morning crew for a staff meal of red beans and rice, eating quickly again, followed by drinking nearly two quarts of water. A few minutes after twelve he returned to the prep area. "Teresa, all of my regular prep is done. I am ready to tackle the butchery with you." Teresa turned with a smile, "Grab a red cutting board for meat, make sure your boning knife is razor sharp, put on a cutter's glove and bring out a dozen tenderloins from the meat cooler. I will be with you in a minute." She demonstrated breakdown of the first one and fabricated another tenderloin while Jake shadowed her motions. She was good. Teresa trimmed the silver skin, removed the chain, cut the tenderloin into seven-ounce filets and reserved the scrap pieces for some type of chef's special all within about five minutes. She used a scale, but every steak she cut was spot on. Jake's first tenderloin took about 20 minutes, he cut into the eye of the meat a bit and his steaks were not consistent. Nevertheless he moved on to a second as he looked at the pile of tenders next to his station.

By the time he'd moved on to his fifth tenderloin Jake had cut his time down to about 15 minutes and was starting to feel confident until the chef turned the corner and stood next to him. The chef picked up three random steaks and weighed each one. The first was 8 ½ ounces, the second was 6 and the final one was pushing 9 ounces. He pounded his fist on the table and yelled, "Are you trying to put the restaurant out of business?" Turning his rage on Teresa, "How could you allow this to happen?" The chef stared at Jake, "I will not allow you to cut another steak." He turned and walked out of the kitchen. Jake stood in shock feeling embarrassed, confused, incompetent, and responsible for Teresa being chewed out. Before he could say anything Teresa cut him off, "Don't worry, you'll get better. I'll talk with the chef. In the meantime, why don't you just trim the silver skin and move the tenderloins back to the cooler. I'll cut the steaks a bit later."

Jake felt like everyone in the kitchen was staring at him. He suddenly started to doubt his dream and felt as if he had just taken two steps backward. Actually, most of the other cooks didn't pay any attention to the chef's outburst and one even walked by Jake, patted him on the back and simply said, "Rock on."

Wow, he wondered how he could go from being so pumped one minute to being totally despondent the next. Jake wondered if he should worry about his job. He tried to stay focused and returned to trimming the silver skin. Teresa had let him borrow her flexible boning knife for the task. It was as sharp as a razor making the job much easier than he thought it would be.

His hands were shaking from the episode with the chef and his mind wandered a bit while he went through a variety of future scenarios in his head. This momentary lapse in attention resulted in the blade of the knife slicing through his index finger. First there was shock then he grabbed his finger with his apron as blood began running down his hand. It didn't hurt at first; in fact his first reaction was to see if anyone had seen him make this foolish mistake. He couldn't decide what to do so he wrapped the hand in a side towel and started towards the employee rest room. Then he went down - apparently the sight of his own blood was too much for him to take. A few seconds later he opened his eyes to see the chef on one knee putting a rolled up towel under his head. Smiling the chef said, "I will wrap your finger, but you will need stitches. As soon as you're able, I'll have one of our servers drive you to the emergency room." After a few hours wait, Jake ended up with six stitches and a pocket full of painkillers.

When Jake returned to the kitchen around 5 p.m. he was greeted with a round of applause from the crew. "Hey Jake, now you're christened as one of us," said one of the evening line cooks. The chef patted him on the back and Teresa let him know she had finished all of the prep, and not to worry about anything else for the day. Totally embarrassed, Jake had mixed emotions from his second day on the job; elated one minute and ready to quit the next; on his way to becoming a line cook when he arrived, to wondering how he would function tomorrow. In the emergency room before the end of the day and now acknowledgement from the team that he had somehow passed a test everyone goes through. On top of everything else his finger hurt like hell and the painkillers from the hospital weren't cutting it.

Teresa brought Jake a cup of espresso, "I'll drive you home since I am done for the day. The chef said you should take tomorrow off to recoup, but be ready to come back 100% after that." Jake thanked her, hung his head, knocked back the espresso and accepted the ride from Teresa.

Home again, Jake said nothing to his neighbors as he walked to his apartment, swallowed a couple painkillers, decided he would wrestle with the issues of the day tomorrow and quickly fell into a deep sleep.

CHAPTER SEVEN

IS THIS REALLY THE CAREER FOR ME?

The next morning Jake's head was pounding, he was sick to his stomach, and felt like he was suffering from a bad hangover. He woke much later than normal, his hand was throbbing, he was seriously hungry, and was quite depressed. Is this what it would be like from now on? Did he have what it takes? What would it be like when he arrived at work tomorrow?

Jake threw on some clothes and went for a walk. The fresh air always seemed to clear his head. He walked by his high school, past the diner where his kitchen life first began, past the restaurants and bars down Elmwood: Mr. Goodbar's, No-Name, Bullfeather's, Cole's and Merlin's. He walked into a Starbuck's and ordered an espresso (this could be his new drink of choice), tipped it back and ordered another. He looked at the baristas behind the counter and watched their skill at frothing a cappuccino. He watched local business people in their suits stopping in for a coffee, never letting their iPhones depart from their ears, assessed the cars driving down Elmwood Avenue and tried to guess what each car owner did for a living. Then it hit him; "I don't want to get a job to live, I want to live to get the job that fulfills me. I want a profession that makes me feel, makes me

29

get up in the morning ready to explore, ready to learn, ready to create. There isn't any job out there that offers all of this better than cooking." From that moment, Jake decided to let yesterday be, and to not dwell on what had happened but rather focus on what could be. Maybe it was the espresso, but he felt a surge of positive energy return. He would approach tomorrow as if it were the first day all over again.

His pace quickened on the way back to the apartment. Jake stopped to pick up a few groceries and decided to make himself a nice dinner for a change. He could barely afford it, but bought some fresh fish and vegetables and decided to make a seafood gumbo from the only cookbook he owned: Paul Prudhomme's first book, a gift from his mother when he started his job at the diner. The meal was good, but he made a mental note to try making it again when his skills improved.

Jake got a good night's sleep and arrived the next morning at the Cloister by 5:45. He was dressed and in the kitchen before 6, managing to arrive a few minutes before Teresa. When she arrived she walked over and gave him a hug. "Welcome back, Jake, glad to see you're on time today."

The next week was challenging for Jake. His stitches impacted some of the work he could do and slowed him down a bit. Teresa limited his work to the standard prep Jake was comfortable with. He didn't pick up any new skills, but he did survive, and no one mentioned either the chef's outburst or his injury. Everyone knew what it took for Jake to come back after that horrendous day in the kitchen. At the end of the week Chef Philippe called Jake into his office. He had his sous chef bring in a round of cappuccinos, "Jake, have a seat."

"How did your week go? I have been watching you and thought that it was time to ask what your goals are for the future." Jake began, "First, chef, I want to apologize for what happened." Chef Philippe stopped him; "Jake, we don't live in yesterday, we live in today and tomorrow. What is important to me is how you move forward. I saw with great admiration how you returned to the job ready to stick it out and learn. Many young cooks would have left and never returned. You showed me some real mettle and I am impressed. Do you want to be a serious cook?" Jake responded; "Chef, I want that more than anything else and I'll do whatever I need to do to make it happen." Chef Philippe shook his hand and said, "I will be hard on you, but if you are serious then you could work through all of the stations in the restaurant."

Jake thought as he left the office, "I'm back in the game and I want to make Chef and Teresa proud."

As she left for the day Teresa gave him a thumbs up. Once again, Jake asked if he could stick around and watch evening service. The sous chef said that he would only allow it if Jake would shadow Carla, his appetizer cook, on the line and give her a hand. Jake was beaming as he approached Carla and asked what he could do to help. Carla was nearly done with her mise en place but still needed to snip and separate fresh herbs for garnishes and blanch the pommes frites in oil before service. After a quick demo Jake was left on his own. Carla was happy with the results as the first orders began to tick in. Jake knew he would be in the thick of it within a few minutes. Carla let him handle the fryer all night, taking care of pommes frites and onion rings for steaks and chops. Jake kept up and only burned himself a few times with spattering oil from the friolater. It was 10:30 when the last orders went out. Jake stayed to help Carla clean up and was ready to leave at around 11:15. Both the sous chef and Carla said he did great and thanked him. Jake had to be back in the kitchen in just a few hours so he started to walk home. Carla left at the same time and offered to drive him the 15 blocks to his apartment. He accepted and said very little on the way home. As he left the car, he turned to Carla and asked if she would like to grab a cup of coffee some time when they weren't working. Carla said "Sure".

How quickly things change. Jake was back on a high. Words of support from the chef, an opportunity to experience the line, and something like a date with Carla, the girl who had it all together.

He didn't feel tired, but knew he had better catch a few hours sleep before it started all over again.

CHAPTER EIGHT

FROM THE FRYING PAN INTO THE FIRE

Jake arrived at work at 5:30 the next morning, put on some fresh chef whites and headed for the kitchen. He pulled down the prep board, set up his station and began to bang out the normal mise en place. The next time he looked up it was nearly 7:00 and Teresa had not arrived yet. This was strange, but he was looking forward to telling her that she was late when she did arrive. At 7:30 the chef arrived and Jake decided to go to his office to express his concern that Teresa still hadn't made it to work.

The chef turned to Jake with a stressed look on his face and quietly said Teresa had been in an auto accident and had suffered a broken pelvis. She would be out for an indefinite period of time. It was obvious the chef was concerned about the loss of an important employee, but Jake also sensed he was sad to know his friend and teammate was hurt. Chef Philippe said, "Jake, I need you to step up to the plate. I don't have time to find another prep cook and Teresa will likely be out for a few months. You know what needs to be done, I trust you can do it and this is a chance for you to really shine. We can't miss a beat. If you get in the weeds I can always jump in, but I need to feel you are comfortable with the challenge." Without hesitation Jake responded, "Yes chef." After less than a month on the job Jake was flying solo. The chef depended on him to meet his expectations. This was scary, but there was no choice.

Jake got through the day without a hitch, even handling the meat fabrication. He didn't finish by five, but was cleaning up at 6:30 that night. He made his production sheet for the next day, talked briefly with Carla and then headed off to Buffalo General Hospital to see Teresa.

Teresa told Jake that she was touched to have him stop by and that the chef had already been here to visit. She was out of surgery, in a fair amount of pain, covered in black and blue marks, but thankful to be alive. What Jake had not realized was Teresa was a single mom with two kids (boys) ages 12 and 15. They would be staying with her sister for the next month while Teresa was in the hospital and going through physical therapy. Jake gave her a hug as she fought back the tears. When she composed herself Teresa said, "Jake, I know a lot is on your shoulders now, but I'm confident you can handle the work. Make me proud." "Teresa, please let me know if I can help with your boys or anything else." Teresa smiled, "Thanks so much, I might just take you up on that."

For Jake, the next four months were a blur. The restaurant was extremely busy even through one of the worst winters Buffalo had seen in decades. Snowfall totals for the winter exceeded 30 feet! Despite this, Jake, like all true Buffalonians never missed a beat. Life goes on.

Jake was averaging 65 hours a week at the restaurant (not including the hours he didn't punch in for), and throughout this time he mastered all of the prep at the Cloister. The chef was particularly impressed with Jake's sense of taste. He had a very acute palate and could identify very subtle flavor nuances, and make corrections to produce truly extraordinary food. This, the chef knew, was a gift most cooks are not blessed with. In response, Philippe promoted an eager dishwasher named Julio to be Jake's assistant. Julio came to Buffalo via Mexico City and after two years earned his citizenship. He spoke broken English but was learning fast. Julio wanted to be a cook so the chef gave him a chance to learn the ropes. Jake was now a teacher as well as a respected prep cook at the Cloister.

Jake visited Teresa often while she was in the hospital as well as after she returned home. He would occasionally cook for her and spend some of his free time hanging out with her sons, offering help whenever he could. Jake had become part of Teresa's family now and she welcomed his kindness through a difficult time in her life.

While working through the changes at the Cloister, Jake and Carla started dating. Even though the chef knew in-house romances always spelled problems at some point, he liked both Jake and Carla and adopted them as his special project. Their schedules rarely matched up, but since Jake started early, and Carla punched in at two in the afternoon, they were able to spend some morning time together on Jake's day off and an occasional evening on Carla's day off.

Chef Philippe took a real interest in developing his two young cooks. On occasion he would take them to local food events, and one evening the chef took Jake as his guest to a black tie fundraiser at the Statler Hilton Hotel. Jake had never worn a tuxedo before so this was a huge deal.

The grand ballroom at the Statler sat 1,200 and on this evening it was filled with every celeb Buffalo could dig up. The keynote speaker was the son of Jimmy Griffin, Buffalo's former mayor, who had everyone laughing within minutes. The food was good, not life changing, but the orchestration of an event of this size was amazing to Jake. Service was "Russian Style," meaning wait staff transferred items from platters to individual plates including saucing the entree. The highlight was dessert when the ballroom lights were turned off and wait staff paraded flaming platters of Baked Alaska around the perimeter of the dining room before serving portions tableside. In Jake's eyes, the whole evening was incredible.

Chef Philippe was friends with the chef of the Statler, Vinnie Pecoraro, and after dinner managed to get Jake a tour of the massive kitchen. There had to be 30 cooks in the kitchen half the size of a football field. Separate departments included a butcher shop, pastry department (temperature controlled), saucier with a bank of 100 gallon kettles, an island of 12 French top ranges, a Garde Manger area as large as the entire kitchen at the Cloister and 800 square feet of caged-in space to house the hotel's silver chafers, platters, flatware and burnishing machine. The entire evening was an education for Jake.

In November, Jake accompanied the chef to New York City (Jake's first time out of Western New York) for the annual International Hotel Show. Jake visited the booths of vendors offering new products, talked with restaurant equipment manufacturers, marveled at the artistic displays of food at the Society Philanthropique Culinary Salon and had his first four-star dinner at Gotham Bar and Grill. He met the chef/owner Alfred Portale, who Jake learned was originally from Buffalo. Chef Portale gave both Chef Philippe and Jake a tour of his kitchen (smaller than the one at the Cloister) and introduced him to the most ethnically diverse team of cooks he had ever seen. Jake, once again, felt inadequate and wondered to himself how he would fare in this kitchen. Everyone that he met was masterful at his or her craft, totally confident and able to present food on plates like a painter would present art. Everything was delicious and visually stunning.

The next day Jake and Chef Philippe returned to Buffalo by train talking non-stop about food. He learned that Chef Philippe was born in a town called Sancerre in central France, had attended the Cordon Bleu in Paris, and worked in the vineyards of Burgundy, as well as, various one-star restaurants in Dijon and Cosne. He took English as a second language while in the French equivalent of high school and when he finished his apprenticeships in Cosne and Dijon, moved to Montreal, Canada at 26 on a work visa. He took the job of Executive Sous Chef at the Queen Elizabeth Hotel and began working for the Hilton chain.

Philippe spent four-years at the QE before he was transferred at the age of thirty to the Statler Hilton in Buffalo to serve as their Executive Chef. He actually hired Vinnie Pecoraro as his Executive Sous Chef. After three years, he became a U.S. citizen with the help of the Hilton administration, and decided to accept the Executive Chef position at the Cloister. Vinnie took over at the Statler, thus completing the story that had brought Jake to a black tie dinner in the grand ballroom of the Statler Hilton. At 36, Chef Philippe was young, but seasoned enough to be one of Buffalo's elite culinarians. Jake was in awe of his mentor.

The staff of the Cloister had a field day ribbing Jake about being the chef's pet and at times their jokes were pretty tasteless. Nevertheless, Jake was in his own zone and knew his mentor was the key to his future success as a cook. Maybe someday, Jake thought, he would become a chef in his own right.

Life was good. Jake and Carla were a number, his cooking skills were improving every day, his understanding of food benchmarks was evolving, and his confidence was stronger than ever. The restaurant was doing extremely well and Jake's family was proud of where he was going.

CHAPTER NINE

CARLA

Jake had never had a real girlfriend. He dated girls in high school and had monumental crushes on a few, but being a cook was not really conducive to having a serious relationship with anyone. Carla was his first girlfriend and he was head over heels.

Carla's father was from Venezuela and her mother was Irish, born and raised in the First Ward of Buffalo. Her parents met when their families were on a long-awaited cruise in the Gulf of Mexico. The two teenagers fell in love, and after a few years reunited at the ages of 19 and 20 and were married soon after. Her father became a U.S. citizen and wound up as an employee at Bell Aircraft in Buffalo.

Carla was beautiful, taking on the physical traits of a South American with the red hair and freckles of her Irish heritage. Like Jake, she was very intelligent, but uninspired by high school. She began cooking at 16 while going to school and started working full-time at the Cloister when she was 18. After 18 months she earned her first line position at the restaurant. Carla had a unique eye for structure and was very detail oriented. She loved desserts and thought maybe one day she could become a baker or even a pastry chef at a great hotel.

Jake and Carla had a lot in common; they knew Buffalo, loved kitchen work, and enjoyed cooking and eating more than anything else. Whenever they had a chance, they tried out a new restaurant in Buffalo, occasionally slipping over to Toronto for something different. Since the drinking age in Canada was 18, they both began to build an understanding of wine, something foreign to most people at the time, but essential if they were ever going to work in fine dining restaurants. They kept records and personal reviews of everything they ate, every restaurant they dined at, every chef they read about and every bottle of wine they shared. Jake and Carla lived food and food experiences.

Chef Philippe continually resisted warning them about the dangers of an in-house romance. They seemed so good together and their work actually improved as a result of the romance, so the chef turned a blind eye. At times Philippe even encouraged Jake and Carla by providing opportunities for them to share great experiences. A call to chef friends would always yield the best seats in a restaurant and a few extra courses for free. When vendors brought new wines to the restaurant for a tasting

Philippe would set aside half bottles for Jake and Carla to take home.

Once he even gave them two tickets to a Buffalo Bills game when the home team was playing the Miami Dolphins. Jake and Carla arrived early and joined the tailgating fun, tossing around the football, grilling some famous Buffalo sausages and watching Jim Kelly and crew trounce Dan Marino and his fish. Life was great.

Jake and Carla spent a few nights together and always came to work the next day with that blush of something very personal, but totally transparent. The crew was relentless in their ribbing - talking about what might have happened, Jake's likely performance and Carla's loose behavior. It was all good fun. The two did not move in together, although they talked about it. Things were too good right now and they were reluctant to move forward for fear of changing the dynamic.

Then, beginning in early spring Carla began to seem a little distant. Jake tried to avoid confronting her, but finally in late May, over dinner and a great bottle of wine, he asked what was wrong. "Jake, I've been accepted into the Culinary Institute of America's Pastry Program beginning in October. It's something that I've always wanted and my grandparents have left me the money to afford the tuition. Chef Philippe put in a good word for me and I received my acceptance letter. I love you, but I really want to do this, so I accepted." Silence.

On one hand, Jake was excited for Carla, but on the other he couldn't comprehend what this would mean for their relationship. One moment he felt anger towards Carla and Chef Philippe for keeping this secret, and in the next hopelessly lost at how his life was about to change. As the silence stretched, he tried to find a way to see the positive, but it did not look good.

Instead he hugged Carla, said congratulations and blurted out, "I could move with you, we could find a place near the school and I could find a job in a local restaurant." Carla smiled, a tear falling down her cheek; she knew, as did Jake, this plan wouldn't work. Not now. "We will see" was all she could come up with.

They still had the summer to work and enjoy their time together. As the days moved on, they struggled to find every opportunity to share in various experiences, most having something to do with food.

Since Carla was leaving in the fall, Chef Philippe told Jake he would be moving up to the evening line. He would train with Carla during the summer in addition to his duties as lead prep cook until he was confident enough to take over. It helped that Teresa returned to her position in early June. She was still going through physical therapy and could only work part-time, but felt certain that by the fall she would be back to normal.

In September when business slowed, Chef Philippe agreed to give Jake and Carla a week's vacation together. They decided to go camping in the Adirondacks and right after Labor Day left for Saranac Lake and Lake Placid. This would be their last real time together before Carla left, and they wanted to make the most of it. They borrowed a tent and sleeping bags from friends, bought hiking boots and some outdoor cooking equipment, loaded the car and set off for one more adventure.

CHAPTER TEN

THE ADIRONDACKS

Carla had been to the Adirondacks with her family when she was 12. Camping was something she enjoyed so Carla was really looking forward to this trip. Jake had never been to Northern

New York, but had friends who went there as Scouts. He was looking forward to spending a solid week with Carla and really didn't care where they went.

The couple arrived in Saranac Lake around noon. They planned on spending the night in a hotel, renting canoes the next morning, and paddling out to the campsite they had reserved on Lower Saranac Lake. They checked into Gauthier's Motel, and walked into town. The downtown was quaint and not very exciting, but it seemed to have an aura of the community. They stumbled through a huge antique store making them wonder how anyone could keep track of the incredible inventory of other people's junk. They met the owner, Scott, and spent about an hour trying to leave without buying something.

Across from the shop was a French bistro called The Left Bank Café. They grabbed a cup of coffee and a crepe while sitting on the deck watching the Saranac River flow under their feet. It was a bit cooler here than in Buffalo, but the first signs of fall colors made up for having to put on a sweater.

After picking up a map of the lakes and campsites on Lower Saranac, and finding out where they could rent canoes, Jake and Carla returned to their room and fell asleep in each other's arms. Jake spent a few minutes looking at Carla, already in deep sleep, and wondered again how he was going to get by without her. She was his only balance in life. Without Carla his life would revolve solely around work.

Jake and Carla woke up at 7 a.m., drove to the Adirondack Outfitters shop and rented two fiberglass canoes. They tied down the canoes and headed to the Lower Saranac boat launch at Crescent Bay. The canoes were packed with a small tent, sleeping bags, cooking gear, a flashlight, some dry firewood and enough food for four days. The site they reserved was called Norway Point, close to the entrance of the Middle Lake and quite a haul in their canoes. They were tired by the time they arrived, but knew it was best to set up the campsite while they still had the energy.

Fortunately, the four days on the Lower Lake offered cool, sunny afternoons and nights that were cold, but made comfortable by a crackling fire and connecting sleeping bags. Their time was spent swimming, hiking in the woods, cooking rustic meals over an open fire, reading books, and talking about anything and everything. The two got to know each other even better than before and both were feeling the strains of their impending separation. It felt to both like they were meant to be together.

As they broke down camp and rowed back to the boat launch under the growing veil of colorful autumn leaves and perfectly still water, both vowed to keep their relationship alive. "Jake, we have such a special relationship; I will miss you, but I intend to make this work." "Carla, I can visit whenever I get two days off in a row. The CIA is only five hours from Buffalo. Maybe you can arrange your internship at a property in Western New York; I'll bet Chef Philippe could help." As their canoe slid through the still waters of the Lower Lake, Carla and Jake even talked about finding their eventual home in the Adirondacks. The area was so beautiful.

Chef Philippe knew the owner of the Mirror Lake Inn in Lake Placid and arranged for a great deal at this pristine resort. Their room was in the Colonial House and had a veranda facing Mirror Lake and Whiteface Mountain. They had dinner and a great bottle of wine in The View Restaurant and walked hand in hand back to their room. It had been a perfect week.

The drive back to Buffalo was bittersweet. The weather changed and they drove seven hours in heavy rain and much cooler temperatures. Tomorrow, they would be back to work for Carla's last week at the Cloister. She wanted some time to prepare for her new adventure and a few days once she arrived in Hyde Park to settle into her apartment before classes began.

The week was torture for Jake. The team at the Cloister went out of their way to joke with Carla, "Those chefs at the CIA are going to show you how little you know. Are you sure you have the backbone to make it through?" They kept it up for the entire week, "You could learn just as much staying right here. Chef Philippe has the patience to deal with all of your mistakes."

Carla knew they were only kidding. She had proven many times over that she could hold her own with anyone on the line. It was the team's way of saying they would miss her, and none more than Jake.

A few days after her last at the Cloister, Carla packed her car, said goodbye to Jake and drove off with tears flowing freely down her cheeks. It was hard, but it was her dream and nothing was going to hold her back.

With the Adirondacks behind him, a determination to keep their relationship alive, and lots of time on his hands, Jake dove into his work as never before. He spent three days a week doing prep work during Teresa's days off, three 14-hour days on the line, and he helped Chef Philippe with special projects in the kitchen. Jake was re-energized and focused on his short-term goal to master every line position at the Cloister, and his future as a chef and restaurant owner. It would take time, but Jake knew it was in the cards for him and Carla.

Carla settled in very quickly at the Culinary Institute (CIA) and in a short amount of time became a star pastry student. It was week four when she realized that pastry was her destiny. In Chef Higgins plated dessert class it didn't take long before other students were asking her for advice. Carla was going to be a pastry chef and this was the start of her new life.

Jake managed to visit a few weekends in the winter, but driving in the snow quickly made that impossible. As summer approached he knew it would be difficult to get away. Carla had to make a decision about her internship soon. With her natural talent and impressive skills it was inevitable that great opportunities would be coming her way. In May she called, "Jake, I've been offered an incredible opportunity to complete my internship with Chef John Folse in New Orleans. I know I promised to stay close to home, but I really can't turn down the opportunity to be in New Orleans and learn from the father of Cajun/Creole cooking." Jake was heartbroken, but knew that with his busy summer at the restaurant he would never be able to spend time with Carla anyway, so he wished her well and saw an important part of his life begin to dissolve.

PART THREE

THE BIG EASY

"New Orleans food is as delicious as the
less criminal forms of sin."
Mark Twain

CHAPTER ELEVEN

New Orleans – The Big Easy Isn't So Easy

Carla arrived in New Orleans in late May to start her internship at Restaurant R'evolution. The restaurant was a collaborative venture between Chefs John Folse and Rick Tramonto and had all the makings of a benchmark for others in New Orleans to follow. Chef Folse was, after all, the new Godfather of Louisiana Cuisine and Rick Tramonto was known as one of the nation's food stars after his time at Tru in Chicago.

Carla would be one of four working in the pastry shop and as the CIA had prepared her, she expected to be relegated to the more menial tasks, at least initially. She had originally planned on living in Baton Rouge and commuting to work, but after learning that this plan would involve a 90-minute drive each way she found a studio apartment just off of Canal Street on the fringe of the French Quarter. The neighborhood wasn't great, but it was what she could afford. Located on the third floor of an apartment building, Carla felt reasonably safe. As it happens, another intern from the CIA had a studio just a block away, so Carla felt she had a local connection in case of emergency.

Arriving at the kitchen she was greeted by Alex, the Chef de Cuisine who brought Carla to the pastry shop. "Carla, since we serve lunch, dinner and a large Sunday brunch there will rarely be more than two of you in the pastry shop. You will be busy." This meant she would be much more involved in the full dessert menu than originally anticipated. The menu was small with lots of room for creative specials. She was pleased to see the desserts, like the savory menu, were reflective of the Louisiana melting pot of influences from Native American, Acadian French,

Spanish, African, German, and English and Italian cultures. By the time Carla returned north she felt that she would be a master of beignets.

The pastry shop, as was the case with many great restaurants, was small and efficient. The pastry chef Lorraine was a seasoned veteran of New Orleans restaurants even though she was only in her mid-thirties. She welcomed Carla and said, "Hang on to your hat." They would be working every day at breakneck speed to get everything done. "John Folse is involved with many culinary projects including restaurants, a packaged food facility, cheese making, oversight of a culinary school, and numerous humanitarian projects." As the consummate resource for everything Louisiana Cuisine, Folse was always in the public eye. Carla would see Chef Folse on occasion, but he would rarely be working at Restaurant R'evolution. The same was true with Chef Tramonto.

Carla fell into the groove almost immediately. Her previous training had served her well. By the end of week one she was already handling the majority of items on the daily prep sheet without issue.

Like Chef Philippe in Buffalo, Lorraine took Carla under her wing, and was determined to have this new pastry intern maximize her New Orleans experience over the next four months. This would include building an appreciation for the culture of the unique city, from the dialect to its restaurants, the fishing community and, of course, the music.

New Orleans was also hot, really hot. Unlike Buffalo where a handful of 90 degree days found natives complaining non-stop, in New Orleans a 90 degree day was a cool break from the real heat. Additionally, in the summer it seemed to rain for about 20 minutes every day. The rain on hot pavement immediately created steam and the lingering humidity made chef uniforms stick to bodies throughout a shift. Working with sugar and chocolate in this heat and humidity was one of the biggest challenges Carla faced throughout her time in the pastry shop.

Even though the shop was temperature controlled, the humidity plagued everything they did. Sugar work would weep, meringue would bead up, chocolate would melt and ice cream didn't stand a chance.

At the beginning of week two Carla had a day off and called Jake back in Buffalo. Jake was obviously thrilled to talk to her, it had been two weeks since they had communicated and Carla was full of enthusiasm for her temporary home, the people of Louisiana, the food that she had experienced so far, and how well she was being treated by her pastry chef. "Jake, you have to find a way to come down and visit. You will love it here and I really miss you."

Jake missed Carla as well, and said he would find a way to visit as soon as he was able to break away (although he knew it was not likely since they were into their busiest time of the year). He updated Carla on what was happening at the Cloister, telling her that over the past few months he moved through every line position at the restaurant, and felt very comfortable with grill and sauté. He knew that he could work every position in the restaurant as well as anybody. Jake was the shining star in the eyes of his co-workers and Chef Philippe. He did add, "The only problem is that I am beginning to feel bored." Jake was mentally almost ready to move on, to find the next phase of his career. He missed Carla, her warm smile, her freckles, her kind words and desire to listen to what he had to say. He missed their time together and continued to treasure memories of their week in the Adirondacks before Carla had left for school. "We need to find a way to get together." Jake's voice cracked as he finished his thoughts, told her to be careful and arranged another phone call at the same time next week.

Jake hung up after nearly an hour that seemed like a few minutes. He had been so busy that he had set aside how much he missed being with his partner. Now a rush of feelings came back to him. As he relived their conversation he kept thinking about the Cloister. What had been a fabulous experience was now becoming routine. He really needed to move on from the comfort of a job that meant the world to him, his current cluster of friends, and even from Buffalo where he was born, raised and trained. After all, he hadn't left his hometown for more than a week at a time. He made his decision; he needed to see Carla and wanted desperately to define the next steps of his career.

When he arrived at the Cloister the next day Jake asked Chef Philippe if they could talk. "Chef I love how you have supported me, and I've learned so much under your wing, but I am feeling like it might be time for me to do something different. In addition, I really miss Carla and the balance she brought to my life." His mentor and friend listened intently. When Jake was done, Chef Philippe spoke, "Jake, I've known for a few months you were almost ready to move on. You're one of the most naturally talented cooks I have ever worked with, a friend and quite frankly, almost a son to me. The most important job a chef has is to develop his people and prepare them to move on. As hard as it will be for me to see you go, I know it must happen. I have a chef friend in New Orleans who I would be happy to call, his name is Jamie Hirsch and he has a restaurant called "Spice". Like John Folse, the chef of the restaurant where Carla works, he's one of the major players in the Louisiana food scene. He owes me a favor, so if you like I'll put in a good word. The only condition is that I need you to stay here through the end of the summer."

Jake was excited and relieved that his culinary idol was fine with this life-changing decision. "Yes, please call and I will certainly stay through August if there is an opportunity in New Orleans." As he left the office Jake felt the same rush of adrenaline that had pushed him through the early days at the Cloister. This felt right. Finally, he would be moving out on his own, taking risks, cutting the apron strings of Buffalo, and reigniting the spark of romance he and Carla shared.

He immediately went to talk with Teresa who had been his supporter from day one. "Teresa, you have been the best teacher I ever had. I have grown so much in my time at the Cloister, but,

I need to move to a new opportunity at the end of this season and chef has been kind enough to help." She hugged him and cried. Jake was a part of her family now and just like any family transition this would be tough for her. She smiled and said, "Good luck my dear friend, you're going to be a great chef some day; a chef who'll make a difference. Now, get your ass in gear and start working. You still have three months of torture at the Cloister."

Jake worked the shift with a spring in his step. It was the most memorable evening service he could remember. His food looked great, the line worked like a well-oiled machine, the sous chef complimented everyone on a terrific night and even bought the team an end-of-shift drink to celebrate.

It was nearly midnight when Jake got back to his apartment, but he knew Carla would still be awake after her shift. He called and told her the news, "I have made a decision to move to New Orleans right after Labor Day. I am excited to start a new phase in my career and am so excited to be with you again." Carla was thrilled, but reminded Jake she would only be there until the end of September, when she would return to the CIA. Jake knew this, but felt a month with Carla was a step in the right direction. He would move into her studio apartment till the end of September and then take the space over once she left. He was so pumped he couldn't sleep that night. At the same time, 1,500 miles away, Carla, was wide-awake thinking about reuniting with the person who made her feel complete.

When Jake arrived at work the next day Chef Philippe stopped him, "Jake, I talked with Chef Hirsch last night and a position in the kitchen is waiting for you when you arrive in New Orleans." Jake hugged the chef and thanked him again, "You are one of the most important, and influential people in my life. I can't thank you enough."

The date was set, Jake would leave for New Orleans on September 4th to start the next phase of his career and join Carla in one of America's culinary Meccas.

CHAPTER TWELVE

You Don't Know as Much as You Thought You Did
September 2010

September 1, 2010 was Jake's last night at the Cloister. After service the entire team in the kitchen, along with service staff and even the chef, took Jake out to Cole's for a few drinks and a sad farewell. Cole's was one of Jake and Carla's favorite neighborhood watering holes and although they weren't big drinkers, they would often end their shift with a beer or two at this Elmwood Avenue landmark. The owners had gotten to know the couple fairly well so when the crew arrived there was a large banner above the bar wishing Jake the best of luck in the Big Easy. It was a fun way to spend his last official night in Buffalo.

A few of the cooks cracked jokes about the mistakes Jake made along the way, but the toast from Chef Philippe said it all. "To Jake, one hell of a cook, a passionate advocate for working in kitchens, a good friend to all of us and a caring human being. We wish you the best of luck and expect we will all be invited to your own restaurant whenever the time comes."

Everyone clinked mugs and gave Jake a healthy dose of high fives. When the crowd parted Jake noticed another friend had arrived; it was Teresa. "She never went out at night, yet here she was." Teresa held a wrapped gift for her pupil. There was silence in the room as Jake opened it revealing a case with a full set of Henkel knives. They were the most beautiful tools he had ever seen. Jake was speechless. As he gingerly handled each knife he noticed every member of the kitchen team had autographed the inside of the case under the heading, Chef Jake.

Jake worked hard to hold back his emotions. His eyes welled up and his mouth was suddenly dry as he felt a love for these people who had become family. They were some of the best people he had ever met; they were true friends and teammates. He really couldn't get many words out but managed to say, "Thank you, everyone. I promise not to disappoint any of you." The entire bar cheered as the owner poured another round of drinks before the crowd dispersed. Jake went home to start packing.

Jake would be leaving for Louisiana in two days and wanted to quickly pack up his important possessions, close out his bank account and spend a final day with his parents; who would miss him, but felt proud of their son who had charted his own course. They both loved Carla and hoped the couple would marry at some point.

On September 4, as planned, Jake pulled out of his parent's driveway with a full car and started his trek to New Orleans. Three days later, he parked his car, stepped outside and took in the hot humid air, enticing smells, and the feeling of being in a city he had dreamt about over the past three months.

Carla ran down the stairs of her third floor studio apartment and threw her arms around Jake. They hugged, smiled, kissed and hugged some more. She took him by the hand and said, "You can unpack later, and I want to show you the French Quarter." Their first stop was the Gumbo Shack where Jake experienced a true taste of Louisiana. They ate delicious gumbo flavored with okra, chicken and pork, file and a good dose of New Orleans spice, drank frosty mugs of beer and kept their eyes locked on each other for the entire time. Jake had never felt this alive. It must be right.

Jake wasn't scheduled to be at John Hirsch's restaurant for another three days so he put himself in Carla's hands to acclimate to his new home. They barely took the time to sleep. The couple visited fishermen in the Bayou, caught informal concerts by Dr. John, Leon Russell and The Neville Brothers, had Eggs Benedict at Commander's Palace, frequented the Gumbo Shack, filled themselves with beignets and on the last evening before he started work, the two were treated to dinner at R'evolution, compliments of John Folse. Carla and Jake were happy beyond words, but now both had to return to work.

Jake appeared at the back door of Spice Restaurant a day early. He asked for Jamie Hirsch and was told he wouldn't be in until the afternoon. The morning sous chef welcomed him and offered to give Jake a tour. What struck Jake immediately were the smells of the kitchen. This was totally new, a revelation of intensity both in spicy heat and the earthiness of the herbs foreign to kitchens in Buffalo. As the sous chef walked him through the sparkling kitchen Jake was struck by the freshness of ingredients, especially the fish and shellfish, the methods of cooking going on around him, the diversity of cultures in the kitchen and the heat.

Jake was offered an espresso (even more intense down in the Bayou) and was shown the schedule for the week. Jake smiled when he saw his name already on the list. "Jake, you will start off on morning prep." Surprisingly, his shift started at 4 a.m. When he looked a bit confused the sous chef said, "All cooks start their first week on the foraging shift. You will meet in work clothes, not chef whites, with Chef Hirsch to travel to the fish and produce markets and handpick the ingredients used each day. Chef Hirsch wants all cooks to get as close to the source as possible to learn respect for the ingredients from day one."

Finally, the chef gave Jake a package that included five sets of chef whites, each with his name embroidered on the pocket. Jake felt instant pride in the operation and satisfaction with his career. This first impression from a new employer was something he would take with him when he was in a chef's position someday. He felt respected, and he hadn't even met the chef.

Chef Hirsch arrived at 1 p.m. and extended his hand to Jake. He began, "You came highly recommended by Chef Philippe, a dear friend of mine. You are very fortunate to have worked with him." He spent a few minutes talking about his food philosophy, "Jake, there are a few things I consider my stakes in the ground. I am totally committed to buying from local and regional sources, supporting farmers and producers, helping my staff grow and presenting the most authentic Louisiana food I can. Work in Spice's kitchen will not be easy. It is critical for you to win the trust of other cooks." The chef went on for a few more minutes talking specifically about the menu and how they approach dishes. "I have high expectations of all my cooks. You will go through a period of acclimation, but will eventually work on the line." Jake's schedule will be 50 hours a week and, as was the case at the Cloister, the chef noted most people chose to come in additional hours on their own to stay ahead and learn from each other. This was never a problem for Jake, "I am very grateful for the opportunity to work at Spice and am anxious to learn all I can while contributing to the restaurant's success."

When the formalities of the interview had ended Chef Hirsch asked for something Jake had not expected. "Jake, since you're here a day early, I want to assess your cooking skills and most importantly your palate. I've asked Jason, our sous chef to put together a basket of ingredients, set aside a prep table and give you access to burners on the line. You'll have two hours to show me how you work, how you use ingredients, what your plates look like and most importantly what your food tastes like. Take a few minutes to get into uniform and get to work. If you haven't brought your knives today you can borrow mine. Jason will watch you while you work and I'll assess your product in two hours. I'd encourage you to interact with the other cooks and start the process of bonding. Show me what you've got."

Jake took a deep breath, hurried to the staff locker room and changed quickly into whites. He picked up an apron, a few side towels, and within minutes was standing next to Jason. The chef gave him a market basket of crayfish, Pompano (a fish he had never seen before) a fresh spicy sausage called chorizo and a handful of vegetables. Immediately Jake thought about the gumbo he made a couple years back in his Buffalo apartment and decided to re-create this. After all, it was New Orleans, he had a general idea how to proceed and had consumed about a gallon of gumbo during his last three days with Carla.

At first, Jake struggled to locate the right pans, hand tools, spices and vegetables, but eventually began interacting with the cooks. They were accommodating, but in some cases he had a tough time breaking through their Louisiana dialect. It appeared to be a mix of broken English, French and Spanish put into slow motion due to the heat. Finally, he had his mise en place and started to sweat the vegetables (onions, garlic, jalapeno, okra, celery, scallions) and added the chorizo. In a separate pot he sautéed the crawfish in the shells and then added white wine and some chicken stock. After 30 minutes he strained the stock and pulled the tail meat out of the crawfish and set it aside. Jake filleted (actually hacked would be a better term) the pompano and cut the fish in 1-inch cubes. He dredged the fish in seasoned floured and browned the pieces in a small amount of olive oil. Eventually Jake added the sautéed vegetables to the stock, brought it to a boil and then reduced the heat to a simmer.

The right mix of seasoning was not familiar to him, but he pulled together what he knew using red pepper flakes, file powder, salt and bay leaves. He added this to the stock while it was reducing, tossed in some fresh, diced tomato and the chorizo. With ten minutes to spare he added the crawfish tails and pompano and thickened the gumbo with a lightly browned roux. With a minute to spare he tasted the gumbo and nearly dropped the spoon – it had too much heat, but it was too late to do anything about it.

Chef Hirsch came to Jake's table at that moment and asked if he was ready. Jake said it was done, but he was afraid he had blown it. Chef Hirsch looked at him and then asked the other cooks to join in the tasting of Jake's gumbo.

Jason told Hirsch that Jake had worked clean, was organized, his knife skills were adequate and he had interacted well with the staff; now for the tasting.

Some of the cooks smirked; others tasted and grabbed glasses of milk to cool down the burn. Chef Hirsch did not even pick up a spoon. His words were kind, informative and serious.

"Jake, gumbo is the signature dish of New Orleans. Some cooks spend a lifetime trying to get it right, so I'm not sure whether to congratulate you for trying or curse you for having the balls to try and show this team how a northerner thinks gumbo should taste. In either case, I don't have to taste this to know what's wrong. After my critique I'd encourage you to get individual feedback from these cooks who grew up on Cajun food." Chef Hirsch went on, "First, taste before you add heat. The chorizo that you used was already very spicy so adding red pepper flakes was adding insult to injury. Second, why would anyone use a beautiful and fairly expensive fish like Pompano in a stew, and third – this is very important - the thickening agent in gumbo is a combination of file and the waxy starch from the okra. We don't use a roux in our gumbo. Now, welcome to New Orleans, where your tastes will evolve and your success as a cook will depend on your ability to understand flavor, flavor, and flavor. Chef Philippe told me you were organized, hardworking, dedicated and fast. All of those things are important, but in New Orleans people want flavor first and foremost. Our charge is to help you grow in this regard. Whatever you thought you knew about flavor before coming to New Orleans, just forget it. Your education begins tomorrow. I will see you at 4 a.m."

Jake packed up his uniforms and left feeling a little bit like he did on day two at the Cloister. But if time had taught him anything it was that the bumps in the road only make you stronger. He shook it off and focused on the positive; he was going to really learn how to cook.

Chef Hirsch would be spending each morning of this first week showing him how to pick the best ingredients for his restaurant. Chef Hirsch's intent was to prepare him to work the line in as short a period of time as possible and he was already recognized as a member of the team; his name was, after all on his uniforms!

When he arrived back at the apartment Carla was already home from work. "So, my first day was much different than I expected. Chef Hirsch gave me a market basket and asked me to cook. I didn't do very well, made lots of mistakes and felt embarrassed at my poor showing." Having said this, he went on, "They were all very kind and great at making me feel welcome. I already have uniforms and a schedule for the week. I will be going to local markets all week with Chef Hirsch. I can't wait."

Carla was actually impressed with the approach that Hirsch has taken with a new employee. "Jake, why don't you set up an appointment to meet Chef John Folse? His encyclopedic knowledge of Louisiana cooking could help you get a feel for how to integrate the ingredients, traditions and flavors of Cajun/ Creole and Acadian French cuisine." She would ask Chef Folse the next time he stopped in the restaurant.

Jake and Carla had an early dinner and went to bed. Jake would need to be up at 3 a.m. and her shift started just three hours later. Tonight, both would sleep well. They were back into the swing of things, back together. "Since both of our schedules are early, let's plan to spend a few hours each night exploring another part of Louisiana culture together." Their time together would be short. Carla would be packing up for the CIA in two short weeks.

CHAPTER THIRTEEN

GETTING TO THE SOURCE

The first morning of work at Spice Restaurant, 4:30 a.m., found Jake at the fish market in New Orleans. It was still dark but already the air was warm and sticky. The market was buzzing with chefs and small wagon jobbers who delivered fish to restaurants throughout the city. Chefs who made it to the fish market before 5 a.m. always landed the best product of the day. Chef Hirsch or another representative from Spice was there nearly every day.

The fish was incredible; so fresh and so plentiful. Iced bins were overflowing with grouper, pompano and dorado (all on the Spice menu) and beautiful oysters, jumbo shrimp, octopus and squid (standards on the menu at "Ocean," another Jamie Hirsch restaurant). The chef showed Jake how to select fish based on freshness. "Look for clear bulbous eyes, well defined and deep red gills, the firmness of the flesh and of course, smell. Fresh fish does not smell strong it should have a slightly sweet aroma."

As Hirsch moved through the market, fishmongers acknowledged him with a smile. Obviously, Jamie Hirsch was well known in this market. He handpicked the fish he wanted, had them earmarked for specific restaurants in his portfolio and assigned them for delivery later in the morning. It was a ritual the chef really seemed to enjoy.

Once he finished in the fish market, Chef Hirsch moved on to another section of the city where produce from various farms in the region was set up for sale and distribution. They arrived around 6:15 (Hirsch said they were actually a bit late) and proceeded to go through a similar system of hand selection and earmarking different items for his restaurants. Leeks, beautiful fingerling carrots, baby vegetables, a vast selection of fresh herbs, okra, the last of the summer tomatoes and corn, and easily twenty different varieties of potatoes left Jake in awe of the quality and variety.

Chef Hirsch introduced him to farmers who were proudly selling their goods picked earlier that morning. This experience, although he did not realize it at the time, would establish the food philosophy Jake would hold close to heart for the rest of his career; fresh and local would be his mantra.

During their foraging trip each morning that first week, Jake learned about Chef Hirsch's history and how he came to be one of the premier chefs in the country. Like Carla, he was a product of the Culinary Institute of America, had established New Orleans as the place he would call home, won the James Beard Award for Best Chef in the Southeast, opened four restaurants to date, and was an author. He was also the energy behind numerous regional organizations, which helped those who were dedicated to improving New Orleans with grants, scholarships and advice. Jake was suddenly struck with how lucky he was to be able to have this one-on-one time with such a remarkable and extremely busy chef. He would later note that his time with Chef Hirsch would be much more limited as this entrepreneur bounced from restaurant to restaurant, and event to event. In the meantime, he would take full advantage of this special time. It was the best education he could ask for.

When their week of foraging ended Jake had a much deeper appreciation for the raw materials he would be working with at the restaurant, the farmers and fishermen who made it all happen, and the bounty Louisiana provided. It was the best way to start his training and introduction to Cajun/Creole cooking.

Jake shared all of this with Carla, who quite frankly was a little jealous of the experience he was having. But, through his detailed nightly review Carla was able to learn nearly as much as

Jake. What fun they were having together, becoming even closer than before. As their final week was coming up both knew it would be incredibly difficult to say goodbye.

As they ate their way through New Orleans during his foraging week, Jake would constantly ask waiters which farm or what market the produce and fish on the menu came from. He wanted to see the connections, the level of commitment chefs had to the ingredients they used and just how far-reaching the connections were between New Orleans chefs and product sourcing. Jake was beginning to get the big picture and sense the food movement that was well underway.

Jake's second week on the job was a shock. As he arrived for work, Jason told him not to bother putting on his crisp, new, monogrammed chefs jacket, but rather to just grab an apron. His second week on the job at Spice would be spent washing dishes. Jake looked puzzled. He was a cook, after all, not a dishwasher. He didn't leave the Cloister and move to a new city to wash dishes. The sous chef explained that all new employees spent a week in the dish pit. This was where Jake would learn the lay of the kitchen, appreciate the importance of the dishwasher position, be able to observe the flow of service and earn the respect of every cook, dishwasher and server in the restaurant. This was where the kitchen team would either accept Jake, or not. This was his real orientation and the moment that would define whether or not he would succeed at Spice. He took a deep breath, and decided he would be the best dishwasher Spice had ever seen. With a smile on his face, he dove in.

In the evenings Jake and Carla found time to talk seriously about their future. They knew they were soul mates and would be together. The question was how to make things work over the next 8 months while Carla finished her education. It would be far more difficult for Jake to visit from New Orleans, and there would be no break from her studies once classes began. They decided to take some of their savings and purchase laptop computers for teleconferencing. They would use Skype to keep in touch, and

Jake would arrange for a few days off around Christmas to join Carla in Buffalo with their families.

Their last passionate night together was bittersweet. They had a wonderful meal at Spice Restaurant, drank a bit too much wine and put together a photo book of their time in New Orleans that Carla could take with her up north. The next morning, they said their sad goodbyes as Carla packed her car and left for the three-day drive to the CIA. It would be a long three months before they would see each other again.

CHAPTER FOURTEEN

THE EDUCATION CONTINUES

Earlier the previous week, Jake met with John Folse. Carla was hoping that Chef Folse could help Jake establish himself in the New Orleans food scene. The two hit it off very well and Jake was instantly struck by how warm and supportive this giant of the food industry was. Chef Folse offered to continue Jake's exposure to local farmers and fisherman and teach him about the history of the area. "Thanks Chef." They would meet again on Jake's next day off to tour Chef Folse's manufacturing plant in Donaldsonville, Louisiana. It was a whole new facet of foodservice that Jake had never been exposed to.

Jake visited with Chef Folse at his manufacturing facility where he discovered the other side of the Cajun Chef's empire. Jake was amazed that Folse had adapted historically pure Louisiana recipes into large-scale production. His company was preparing soups, sauces, entrees and other food-service grade ingredients for use in restaurants, hotels and even retail applications for the home. The USDA-certified and inspected plant was immaculate, impressive in its production capacity and to Jake's surprise, true to the integrity of the dishes that made Folse's reputation what it was.

"Jake, it is critical for a chef to know the history of a dish and the culture it represents. In my mind, it would be impossible to create a dish without this understanding. There is something about living a dish that allows its authenticity and uniqueness to shine." Chef Folse went on for quite some time. "Great cooking is all about the intangibles. These come from the experiences a cook, chef or restaurant has with that history, the people and their lives." Jake was again impressed with the chef's encyclopedic knowledge of all that was present in the Bayou, something Folse was obviously obsessive about and proud to share. "Keep in mind Cajun/Creole cooking is one of America's truly authentic cuisines. It is a melting pot of Native American, Acadian French, Spanish, African, German, and English and Italian influences. To be a great Louisiana cook you must appreciate this heritage."

Over the next three months Jake spent a few more days visiting with Folse, meeting the characters he felt were essential to Jake's education in real Louisiana cooking, and breaking bread with him at some of the most obscure, but superb hole-in-the-wall restaurants in New Orleans and Baton Rouge. This was a special education Jake knew would shape his style of cooking and food philosophy.

Jake and Carla were immersed in their respective educations. Carla was building her baking and pastry skills under the guidance of the talented instructional staff at the CIA, and Jake was becoming a transplanted Cajun with help from the staff at Spice and occasional one-on-one sessions with Chef John Folse.

Carla was doing so well at the CIA that many of the faculty in baking and pastry were proclaiming her gifted with the potential to make a significant mark in her field. Even with the intensity of her courses, she was able to pick-up a part-time job working in an artisan bread shop in Poughkeepsie one day a week. As much as she loved pastry and plating desserts Carla was intrigued by bread and how therapeutic it was to work with dough, a living organism. She even began thinking that making bread could be her future career.

Jake and Carla stayed in touch using Skype, filling each other in on what they were learning and how much they were enjoying their experiences. They began planning their Christmas in Buffalo. Jake had made arrangements to be absent from work from Christmas Eve until the 28th; when he would need to return for New Year's Eve events at the restaurant. Carla had a short holiday break from school. So Jake would fly home, while Carla took the train to avoid driving in the Western New York winter snow.

Jake was doing well in the kitchen at Spice. He moved from the first week of dishwashing to prep, as he had at the Cloister. He was able to master the prep and the flavor profiles used at Spice. As in the past, Jake arrived very early (off the clock) and stayed late to watch the line and to see how they orchestrated final prep and presentation. Jason mentioned after the holidays that he would be giving Jake his first shot on the line. Next to his visit with Carla, this was the most exciting news in his life.

The team at Spice accepted Jake, even with his funny northern accent. Collectively they felt responsible for his education as a future Cajun cook and complemented the education he was getting from Chef Folse, Chef Hirsch and Jason at Spice. Although Jake could never afford to go to culinary school, he didn't feel like his food training suffered. Who could ever top the personal education he was receiving in New Orleans?

As the weeks flew by, Jake became more and more confident. After his rocky start with the market basket test, Jake developed a taste for Louisiana cooking and even began to impress the cooks at Spice who were born and raised in the Big Easy.

Jake could not sleep the evening of December 23. He finished his last shift, packed his suitcase, hastily wrapped his Christmas presents for Carla and his family, and sat up in bed waiting for 6 a.m. when he would leave for the airport.

In Hyde Park, 1,300 miles north, Carla was equally excited about returning home and being with Jake. She had made arrangements for her family to pick Jake up at the airport about two hours before her train pulled into the station.

As is typical, Buffalo was predicted to get hit with a snow storm over the next few days so Carla was glad to be coming home early. Christmas would certainly be white in Western, New York.

CHAPTER FIFTEEN

CHRISTMAS IN BUFFALO

Jake arrived at Buffalo International Airport on time. Fortunately, he was able to book a direct flight from New Orleans and had avoided any delays or missed connections. The short time he would have in Buffalo was too precious to spend stuck in airports.

After picking up his suitcase at baggage claim he saw Carla's parents waiting for him. It had been quite some time since he had visited, but their smiling faces put him instantly at ease. They hugged him and talked non-stop on the way to their home. Jake and Carla's father would return to the train station in another hour to meet Carla and make the reunion complete.

Plans were to have Christmas Eve dinner with Carla's family and Christmas morning with Jake's family. The rest of the time would be all about Jake and Carla.

Buffalo had an eight-inch dump of snow on Christmas morning, making the landscape spectacular. As was always the case in Buffalo, this did not slow down the locals. Jake bought a few artisan pastry and bread books for Carla including an autographed book from Chef Jamie Hirsch. Carla had a friend build a beautiful wooden case for Jake's kitchen tools and made a book of photos from their early days at the Cloister. Included in the book was a gift certificate for dinner on December 26th at the Cloister. She made sure that Chef Philippe would be there as well. Both were thrilled with their gifts and spent most of their time with eyes locked on each other. The chemistry between the two of them was evident.

Carla and Jake's parents were happy to have them home, even if it was only for a short time. They were confident that these two young cooks would eventually marry and raise a house full of grandkids for them to enjoy. Christmas in Buffalo was off to a great start.

On the 26th after a day full of sledding at Chestnut Ridge, the couple arrived at the Cloister for dinner. Before they had even looked at the menu, Chef Philippe was at their table. Even though the dining room was full, Chef did not hesitate to hug them both and in the French style, kiss them on both cheeks. There was no question Chef really adored these two. He made some suggestions for dinner, asked the waiter to bring them a bottle of wine on him and asked them to stop in the kitchen afterward.

The service was great as special attention was paid to the former stars of the Cloister kitchen, but ironically, the food was only OK. There wasn't anything wrong, it just seemed ordinary to Jake and Carla. The Cloister was, after all, a steak, chop, salmon fillet and prime rib house. The customers always seemed happy and the restaurant was constantly busy, but the food did not speak to them anymore. Both had moved on to embrace flavors and presentations that far exceeded the formula at the Cloister, and the use of local ingredients and farmer relationships was not at all evident in the Buffalo landmark. The couple suddenly realized that they had grown as culinarians, and had outgrown the type of restaurant represented by the Cloister. They were a bit embarrassed for their first mentor, he was the reason they were where they were today.

After dinner they toured the kitchen giving high fives to all of their old friends before settling in the chef's office with espressos. Philippe wanted to hear all about their experiences with his friend Jamie Hirsch. Jake recapped his time in the markets, lessons from John Folse, his week as a dishwasher and his sheer enjoyment of Louisiana's flavors. He beamed as he talked about each item on the menu at Spice, how the line worked, the beauty of each intricately designed plate and how significant the farmer/fisherman to chef relationship was in New Orleans. Philippe listened intently to Jake and then Carla as she expressed her joy in working with bread and the new skills she had picked up regarding plated restaurant-style desserts.

When they finished, there was a brief moment of silence and a worn look on Chef Philippe's face. He began, "I have not told this to anyone else, but as much success as the Cloister has experienced while I have been chef, I am not content. Your experiences have only heightened my feeling that it may soon be time for me to move on as well. The food here is good, but not reflective of who I am."

"I think my work here may be done and it is time for someone else to take the helm. I am not completely sure when it will happen or exactly where I might go, however, I have been reading much about Vermont and how, as you have said, the connections with the source are so critical. My dream is to someday have a very small place of my own where I might grow vegetables, raise cattle for the restaurant, milk the cows and care for chickens. The restaurant would be the vehicle for demonstrating to a select group of guests just how beautiful and delicious fresh ingredients can be. It may just be a dream, but it is what keeps me up at night. This is my excitement now, the dream that inspires me to get up in the morning. Someday it will happen."

Carla and Jake were not surprised; they were actually relieved to hear that Philippe was not satisfied with his food. Their mentor still had the spark of passion that inspired them. They wished him well, "Please stay in touch with us Chef and keep Carla and me in mind for any of your future endeavors." They finished their second espresso and walked out of the Cloister - the last time they would ever visit that part of their past.

The final days Carla and Jake spent together in Buffalo were a whirlwind of visiting fellow chefs, having a few drinks at Cole's, and talking about their future together. Jake said he would fly up for Carla's graduation in May and in the meantime would keep an eye open for opportunities in New Orleans that would suit her skills, passion and desire. They spent their last night in a friend's cabin on Darien Lake. In each other's arms by a crackling fire was the perfect way to end their short visit, and make a memory to hang onto until the spring. In the morning, Carla rode in the cab with Jake to the airport for their final goodbye and then continued on to the train station.

Buffalo would always be their home, but living and working there was just a memory now. They would probably return every year for holidays, family events and maybe an occasional Bills game, but both knew that their careers would take them to other places they had only dreamt about a few years prior.

CHAPTER SIXTEEN

SETTING THE STAGE IN NEW ORLEANS

It had been quite a few years since Hurricane Katrina laid waste to New Orleans. After the storm, and the breach of the break walls designed to protect New Orleans, the city had appeared dead. Thousands lost their lives, were injured, homes and businesses destroyed, and the fishing was devastated by oil spills and the flooding of the Bayou. The Army Corps of Engineers was desperately trying to reinforce the broken levy walls so they could drain the city and rebuild its infrastructure. As the city was positioned to start rebuilding, a few determined restaurateurs led the charge for a new and refreshed New Orleans. Jamie Hirsch and John Folse were two of them. They were determined to come back, and as a result became ambassadors of hope in the Big Easy.

After years of work, New Orleans was back. Mardi Gras was as vibrant as before, and the Jazz Festival bigger than ever. Music flowed through the streets, the French Quarter was alive with excitement, and Louisiana Cuisine returned stronger and better.

Jake was there to ride the wave of positive vibes drifting through the city. He was now one of the strongest members of the Spice team, and, having mastered each station on the hot line, now served as the restaurants roundsman. He could work any shift, any position and do so with the skill of any cook who worked for Hirsch.

It was eight months since he had first walked through the doors of Spice and embarrassed himself with a sub-standard version of gumbo. Now he was building menu features every night, showing the chops of a true Louisiana cook as if he were born and raised on Bourbon Street. Since Christmas, he had thrown himself 200 percent into the job. Jake's education continued due to his insatiable thirst to work and learn everything he could about the Spice menu and the vendors who provided the raw materials used in every preparation.

He made arrangements to take three days off in May to attend Carla's graduation and swore no matter what, he would be there. Carla continued to excel and was a shoe-in for the Roth Award as the most outstanding graduate at the CIA. Her level of confidence was high and her ancillary skills as an artisan bread baker had improved substantially. As much as she would miss the energy of the CIA, she was ready to start working full-time again.

In early May, two weeks before graduation, Chef Hirsch asked Jake to join him for lunch at one of his other restaurants, Seine, a bistro on River Street famous for French fare and delicious local shellfish. Over an enormous platter of oysters, clams and Louisiana shrimp, the two talked about how far Jake had come in a mere eight months. Jake reiterated how he had changed as a cook and how much he had learned from Hirsch, John Folse and the team at Spice. Near the end of lunch, Chef Hirsch got to the point, "Jake, I see in you a real star, a person with the right priorities, a passion for food and food knowledge, a natural talent and the respect of your fellow workers. I am truly impressed. Last week Jason gave his notice. He'll be moving on to one of the large hotels in New Orleans as their Executive Chef. I'm very happy for him, he is a great chef and is ready for the move. But, this leaves a serious hole in the staffing at Spice and I need to find the right individual to take the helm. You are still young, but experienced beyond your years. I would like to offer the position to you." Jake was in shock and for a moment that seemed like an eternity he did not speak. Instead he took a drink of sweet tea and cleared his throat.

He wanted to plan out his words and do justice to the moment, so he began, "Chef, I am a bit lost for words. Never in my wildest dreams would I have imagined this moment. I am torn between bursting with excitement, and a bit of self-doubt. Of course I'm honored and desperately want the job, and will give every ounce of energy and dedication to the position, and to your company if you trust my ability."

He looked Jake in the eye and said firmly, "Jake do not ever express self-doubt. Doubt will kill even the most talented chef. You must be as confident as the quarterback of an NFL team in the playoffs, down by seven points with two minutes left in the game and possession of the ball. Of course you can do it, I would never ask you if I were not confident. If you, however, have serious doubts then do not accept. If you are confident then say yes and never express those doubts to me or anyone on the staff again." Jake looked up, smiled and simply said, "Yes, Chef."

They shook hands and the deal was done. "Jake, you will begin by shadowing Jason for the next three weeks, until his departure. I will inform the staff of the changes in a day or two at a full team meeting and send a press release with your bio to the regional media and to your hometown paper immediately."

Suddenly, panic came over Jake, as he remembered Carla's graduation. He had made a promise, and he had to keep it. Carla was too important to him and even though she would understand, he would not allow himself to waiver from that promise. "Chef, I hate to bring this up, but there is one problem. Carla, my girlfriend is graduating from the CIA in two weeks and I promised her I'd be there. It's very important to her and I must be there. If this changes your offer, I understand, but I have to be there." Hirsch smiled and said, "John Folse told me great things about Carla's pastry skills and ironically I am an alumnus of the CIA and was scheduled to be the commencement speaker for the graduation ceremony. Of course, you can go. In fact we could have dinner together one night in the American Bounty Restaurant at the CIA." He finished with, "Jake, there is one final condition. You can go to the graduation as long as you convince Carla to come on as pastry chef for one of my other restaurants." Jake thanked him, beaming with pride, "I'll see what I can do, Chef."

Jake went to New Orleans to enhance his skills and set a path for his career. Everything was moving forward much faster than he had ever dared to hope. He would not let Chef Hirsch down.

When he returned to his apartment he called Carla on her cell. She did not pick up, so he left a message saying that it was urgent she return his call. Thirty minutes later she called in a panic, "What's wrong!" Jake told her about his promotion and she was so excited she dropped her phone. "I am so happy for you. I know this means you will miss graduation, but please don't worry about that." "On the contrary, I will be coming with your commencement speaker. We will be having dinner with him in the America Bounty afterward." Carla was thrilled, "Jake, I love you and am so proud of what you've accomplished." Jake built up to the last bit of great news, "Oh, one more thing, Chef Hirsch said I could only come to graduation if you would accept a position as a pastry chef in his organization." Carla cried with joy and thought how lucky she and Jake were to do what they love, and be together. "My answer Jake is yes, yes, yes!"

CHAPTER SEVENTEEN

THE WORK BEGINS

Graduation was a very proud moment for Jake and Carla. As anticipated, she won the Roth Award as the most outstanding graduate in her class, a recognition not only addressing her talent, but also her commitment to building a skill set beyond what was offered in class.

Chef Hirsch offered a brilliant commencement speech that earned a standing ovation from the class of future chefs and pastry chefs. Following the reception, Hirsch, Jake, Carla and Carla's family were treated like royalty as they dined in the American Bounty Restaurant. Carla relished the opportunity to be on the other side of service in this famous CIA training restaurant. The entire group was enamored with Chef Hirsch, and his stories of life in New Orleans. Everyone was riveted by his detailed synopsis of the devastation the area experienced as a result of Katrina.

The next morning Jake and Chef Hirsch returned to New Orleans. Once back, Jake would have only a few more days with Jason before he would be on his own and in control of kitchen operations for the first time ever.

Carla returned to her home in Buffalo for a week with family before heading off, once again, to New Orleans and the next phase of her career - a pastry chef for Chef Hirsch and another chance to reunite with Jake. Once settled, she and Jake would be looking for a larger apartment, one they could now afford with their new positions.

Conversations with her family ran the gamut from Buffalo transitions after losing so many jobs and residents when industry faded, to updates on old friends and relatives. Discussions shifted to some interesting reflections on the dramatic changes in weather patterns across the country and the impact it was having on everything from travel to food prices. Based on her talks with faculty, students and Jake over the past two years, Carla pointed out that weather, in combination with farming practices had a cause-and-effect relationship. Controversial use of growth hormones in animals, genetic engineering of crops, and centralized farming were depleting the nutrients in soil creating a potentially serious, long-term negative impact on the integrity of the U.S. food supply. This was a new subject for her parents, one they dismissed as something extremists were using to get attention. Carla was somewhat taken back by her family's lack of interest in what she considered a potentially huge dilemma.

At the end of the week, she was exhausted from her attempts to make her parents understand the explosive environmental issues before them. She simply shrugged her shoulders, and guessed that any further discussion would continue to fall on deaf ears. She focused on packing, preparing her car for another long journey and mentally conditioning herself for the impending transition from student to a professional pastry chef. At the end of the week she said her goodbyes and set off on another journey south.

It was early June and already the temperatures around the Mason Dixon line were in the eighties. Moving from spring in the Hudson Valley of New York where temperatures were barely at the 50-degree mark, this took some getting used to again. Carla had to spend an extra day in Beaufort when travel became impossible due to very severe thunderstorms and highly unusual hailstorms that yielded golf ball size projectiles. The windshield of her car was cracked during the storm and she counted two-dozen dents in her hood and roof from hail. She had never experienced anything like this and would never have guessed that it could happen in June with temperatures in the mid-eighties.

After a four-day drive she arrived in New Orleans with an interesting story for Jake about her unusual weather encounter.

She threw her arms around Jake who had been waiting for her safe arrival. "Carla, we are finally together. This time there are no anticipated separations in the foreseeable future. I am so glad you are here."

Carla unpacked, but kept many things in boxes, realizing that when they had the time, they would be moving to a larger place. When they had time was the defining statement.

Jake was settling into his new role. The staff at Spice welcomed him as their new sous chef, all except Phil, one of his line cooks who had apparently always thought he'd be next in line for the position. This would prove to be a real challenge for Jake – his first as a manager. Aside from this, he was comfortable with ordering, menu management, expediting on the evening line, and even found himself adept at talking with service staff and guests.

Jake had numerous one-on-one meetings with the disgruntled line cook, but every time he thought they were making progress, Phil would do something to try to make Jake look inept. After reviewing the situation with Chef Hirsch, Jake decided to offer Phil an ultimatum: either join the team or move on. Phil chose to move on and did so in a dramatic fashion by trying to throw a punch in Jake's direction. The other line cooks wrestled him down and he left in a fury, cursing at the top of his lungs as he walked out the back door. Jake was shaken up, not for fear of an ill-placed punch (he could have handled the line cook if need be), but more from the realization that someone whom he had worked with expressed so much hate for him in his new role as sous chef.

Carla was assigned as pastry chef in a different Hirsch restaurant, Spice Chop House in the New Orleans Hilton Hotel. The restaurant differed from the original Spice in its connection to the steak houses of New York City. There were still some traditional New Orleans plates on the menu, such as Shrimp Etouffee, but it didn't have the same feel as Spice. On the plus side, there was still a commitment to farmer relationships and local ingredients and the dessert menu was fluid. She would have almost total control over what was offered every day and night on the menu. This would give Carla a chance to focus on her creativity and make desserts a drawing card for the restaurant.

Jake and Carla would have similar crazy schedules but both would have some control over when they worked. Jake made the kitchen schedule at Spice, and although the pastry team of three at Spice Chop House was small, Carla was still responsible for assigning shifts. They managed, for the most part, to schedule Mondays off each week giving them a chance to spend some time together. Aside from Monday, Jake and Carla were easily working

70-80 hours per week. They were young and didn't mind except on those weeks when, for a number of reasons, Mondays off didn't happen.

The months before summer, unlike the rest of the world, were actually busier than July and August, when the heat would reach over 100 degrees nearly every day. This typically kept tourists away from New Orleans and locals glued to their air conditioners. In mid-July, Jake and Carla managed to take two days off to move to a larger apartment. Their new place had a nice kitchen, living room, full bathroom and two bedrooms. Most important was off-street parking for both of their vehicles and a pool shared by all of the residents in the complex. Rent was more than twice what they were paying at the studio apartment, but they could afford it now.

Carla's touch with desserts was quickly building a different reputation for Spice Chop House, as guests began asking what was on the dessert menu even before they ordered their meals. Late night in the restaurant also saw many grazing diners arriving from meals elsewhere for an after-dinner drink and dessert at the bar. Carla desperately wanted to make her own artisan breads (currently purchased from another bakery in town), but the kitchen was simply too small for the equipment. Her hands were tied.

The local media in New Orleans covered the press release about Jake's new position at Spice, but since the food scene was so diverse in this city it did not make much fanfare. However, when presented in the Buffalo Evening News, the small but tight-knit restaurant community was standing on their feet. Buffalo boy makes it big in New Orleans! It helped that Jake's and Carla's parents sent copies to everyone they knew and Chef Philippe proudly posted it on the Cloister website. Jake was appreciative of the support he received. In the meantime, business at Spice was strong and aside from the one incident with Phil, Jake did not miss a beat with the change in leadership. Chef Hirsch was very comfortable with his two new hires and at the end of their first six months in their respective roles, he presented them with a substantial bonus, enough for Carla to get her car fixed and pay off a good portion of her college debt. Jake put his bonus in a savings account reserved for the day when his own restaurant might become a reality.

Things were good and aside from the very, almost unusually hot summer, and the escalating cost of raw materials used in the restaurants, Jake and Carla were settled in and content with jobs and life in general.

CHAPTER EIGHTEEN

ANOTHER HURRICANE SEASON TO REMEMBER

After Katrina, New Orleans was gun shy. All indications were that this year could be a record breaker for tropical storms and as a result, Louisiana was prepared to batten down the hatches. As it turned out, the overall number of hurricanes and tornadoes in the U.S. during 2012 were fewer than 2005 and 2011 (crazy years of activity), but more severe due to the path the powerful storms took. In many cases, these storms seemed to target areas of denser population than in the past. New Orleans dodged the bullet, but relinquished the anger of Mother Nature to the midwest. There was also devastation to the Northeast caused by Hurricane Sandy (by all calculations one of the worst storms in at least 100 years). The media was all over these events. Reporters switched from referring to them as anomalies in exchange for fear mongering about Global Climate Change caused by human energy consumption and ignorance of the irreversible tragedy of human excess. The debates continued on television, in the papers, through online chatter and of course, in Congress. Everyone had his or her own opinion but what seemed most disturbing to Jake and Carla was the disregard of the scientific facts being presented.

FEMA funds were running dry as disaster after disaster became almost commonplace. The cost of Hurricane Sandy alone was estimated at $50 billion and the loss of human lives second to only Hurricane Agnes in 1972. New Orleans was still working on the infrastructure damage caused by Katrina and everyone was well aware that another such storm in the area might be impossible to recover from.

Time-lapse photography demonstrated, without a doubt, that the polar ice caps were melting at an alarming rate raising the ocean water levels to the point where a subsequent Sandy-type storm could actually wipe out lower Manhattan and other coastal areas. This is the part of the U.S. with the heaviest population density. In the Midwest, super tornadoes were becoming the norm, leveling entire sections of towns and even appearing in highly populated urban centers including Chicago. This was a new phenomenon, one that could not be ignored, yet many in positions of power still tried to pass it off as nothing unusual and unrelated to anything to do with human impact.

In the meantime, extended periods of drought increased the number of forest fires, devastating certain crop yields from the grain belt. This would drive up the cost of supplies in the U.S. food distribution chain. The drought combined with Santa Anna winds meant that forest fires were now threatening cities that had always seemed to avoid the evil hand of out-of-control fires. Western wildfires in 2012 destroyed 9.2 million acres of forest, farm and residential land.

The total cost of climate disasters in the United States in 2012 exceeded $116 billion. Not only was this number hard to comprehend, it was depleting America's monetary reserves, both on the federal and state level. It seemed every week that another part of the country was applying to the U.S. Government for disaster relief, and Red Cross requests for support from the population were commonplace.

Jake and Carla discussed this frequently and began to read more and more about potential causes and the ultimate projected outcomes. It was a scary time and when they uncovered the depth of the problem it set the stage for a period of advocacy consuming most of their free time and driving many of their decisions at work.

Jake was certain the outlook, as grim as it appeared in the media, was far worse than what was being revealed. He wanted to believe that the government was hard at work thwarting the inevitable disaster before them, but as quickly as a sign appeared, it disappeared from the public's consciousness within a few days. Ignorance, in all cases is not bliss, yet Jake became increasingly fearful that many people remained ignorant.

What would subsequent years bring in terms of natural disasters and the impact they would have on the American way of life? Jake felt he couldn't just sit back and watch, he had to do something. He joined organizations like Chef's Collaborative because of their commitment to sustainability issues, talked with Chef Hirsch about replacing kitchen equipment with more energy-efficient units, started buying environmentally friendly cleaning supplies, and actually sold his car, committing to walk or bike to work every day. Carla and he could certainly get by with one vehicle. It was not much, but it was his part in an effort to change the habits of others.

There was no question that restaurants would be feeling the pain of climate change on yields and subsequent prices. Vendors were already beginning to plant the seeds regarding product availability and a challenging price structure.

CHAPTER NINETEEN

ESCALATING FOOD PRICES HIT THE RESTAURANT INDUSTRY

The long-term effect of weather change over the past few years was having a severe impact on the restaurant industry.

The stage was set more than a century prior when the job opportunities created by the industrial revolution drove farmers away from diversified, decentralized practices. As consumerism and a more affluent population created an increased need for crops, America began converting millions of acres of land to the focused growing of a limited number of specific crops by region. This focused effort was designed to maximize yield and profitability and support an infrastructure of distribution, allowing every part of the country to have whatever crops they wanted, any time of the year. Purchasing strawberries in February for New York City? Not a problem. Looking for access to asparagus year-round? Of course that can happen. Beautiful mixed greens from coast-to-coast even in the dead of winter? Absolutely. It was an idyllic situation for consumers, who quickly learned to expect this in their grocery stores and restaurants. Quality and price were a challenge for businesses since this type of availability and distribution resulted in numerous compromises.

Carla was the first to be affected by the long-term impact of recent climate changes, or anomalies as some politicians would have the public believe. The droughts in the Midwest had a significant impact on crop yields and, in anticipation, the price of flour rose substantially. Since pastry shops primarily use flour, sugar, eggs and butter, this created a dilemma pertaining to what she could produce in her kitchen. Dessert prices rose, alternative recipes needed development and she would restructure her menu to reflect the change. Not a huge deal, but an increase in dessert prices from $8 to $9, or $10, would mean a slow-down in dessert sales and a challenging sell for the service staff. The ripple effect was always a tightrope walk when pricing and luxury courses were involved. As much as people want desserts, they certainly do not need them.

At Spice Restaurant and Spice Chop House, beef was the next victim. With grain yield down, prices of crops rose, including animal feed. Since the vast majority of cattle in the U.S. were grain and corn fed this meant profit margins for cattle growers were in jeopardy. Decreasing feed and increasing the use of growth hormones prior to slaughter were a partial answer, but since the costs were high and yields were still off budget, prices needed to be increased. Rising costs forced restaurants to increase their selling prices, reduce portion sizes and quality or eliminate items from their menus. In the end, consumers would either continue to buy with less satisfaction, choose an alternative restaurant, or stop dining out altogether. Everyone was scrambling to find a strategy that would work for the restaurant and the guest. It was not easy.

The fishing industry in Louisiana was almost back to normal after the damage from one of the largest oil spills in history when the impact of Katrina and then Hurricane Isaac churned things up again. Suddenly all the precious Gulf seafood that was the mainstay of many New Orleans restaurants was either cost prohibitive or unavailable. At one point, buying from local vendors was the fun part of Jake's job, now it was a real pain, and sometimes impossible. His menu had to move to a more fluid format with many seafood items simply listed as catch of the day.

As time went on, everything was affected: eggs, dairy and produce. Even coffee took a hit. Not so much from weather as from political strife in areas that were the primary sources of beans. The world food supply was closing in and appeared to

Paul Sorgule

be in real jeopardy. The hardest part was Jake, Carla and every other chef in the country could do nothing about it except adjust.

As Jake continued reading about the long-term impact of current practices he realized that for farmers to continue to meet product demand and maintain some level of profitability they had to work on new ways to maximize yield, minimize the impact of insects and drought, and ensure that the land kept producing. Any square foot of farmland not contributing to profit every year was suddenly a liability. Large machinery replaced much of the hand labor associated with farming, but this equipment was extremely expensive. In many cases, the farmer had no choice but to partner with a larger conglomerate and use seed, chemical fertilizers and insecticides designed to protect his investment and squeeze out a minimal profit. Genetically modified seeds engineered to protect against certain pests and maximize yield were purchased (or basically rented) from large seed producers. These seeds would later become part of the global collapse of farming and a worldwide change in the survival of the human species. For now, this not only seemed like the farmer's salvation, it was their only hope. Jake wondered what impact these changes would have on the integrity of the foods he was using and the long-term health and well- being of his guests.

Jake and Carla became consumed with the realities of the larger picture, detracting, to a degree, from their passion for cooking and baking. They began to see a larger purpose to their lives involving education and advocacy. This became their mission in and out of work.

CHAPTER TWENTY

RAISING THE BAR, BUILDING THE BRAND AND CHANGING DIRECTIONS

One evening in early May when Carla was walking home from work, she was robbed at gunpoint and knocked out with what was believed to be the butt end of a Glock. Jake got the call from the hospital just as he was finishing up for the night. He hailed a cab and was at the emergency room within minutes. His heart was pounding as he ran to the emergency room desk. He could barely focus or speak clearly. The nurse directed him to one of the curtained rooms where Carla was recovering. She had needed to get six stitches on the back of her head. When Carla saw him she said "Jake," and burst into tears. He hugged her harder than he ever had and wept as well. "Carla, I was so scared when I got the call. I am so sorry this happened to you."

"I'll be OK, but the doctor said I have a mild concussion and will be kept overnight for observation." Her head hurt like hell and she could not stop shaking. The mugger ran off with her wallet, which had about fifty bucks cash in it. She felt totally violated and now fearful of the city which had previously seemed fun, exciting and harmless.

Carla was moved to a private room for the evening, and Jake asked if he could stay the night and sleep in the chair beside her bed. The hospital agreed, but reminded him that she would need to be observed by a nurse throughout the evening.

It was one year since Jake and Carla had started their new positions in New Orleans. Carla had, in spite of the escalating costs of raw materials, managed to create a remarkable image for her restaurant. Chef Hirsch had recognized this early on by adding another pastry cook to Carla's staff roster and asking her to spend time consulting with his other restaurants about their dessert programs. By the time Carla began her second year with Hirsch he had created a new corporate position of Company Director of Pastry and Specialty Desserts just for her. Each restaurant's pastry chef now reported to Carla and they collectively revamped all of the baking and pastry menus within the company. Although her position required her to work a normal five-day shift, she saw her role differently. Carla spent her days fulfilling her company responsibilities, and rotated six nights per week in each restaurant. She was happy and Chef Hirsch was thrilled.

Jake was on an equally fast track, but his focus was still exclusively Spice restaurant. In April Jake was nominated as one of five finalists for Southeast Rising Star chef by Food and Wine Magazine (Chef Hirsch had started the ball rolling on this nomination). It wasn't likely he would win this soon in his career, but Jake knew that this was a tremendous boost to his culinary brand.

The only downside was that Jake and Carla rarely saw each other anymore except to share a cup of coffee in the morning while watching CNN. Neither Jake nor Carla had time to breathe let alone nurture their relationship.

As he sat half-awake in the hospital, Jake's mind drifted from work to how little time he had spent with the most important person in his life. It was an epiphany, a moment that would change his outlook on the direction he would take in the future. He and Carla were on the fast track with their careers and he suddenly wondered if that was so important. He vowed things would change.

The next morning Carla and Jake joked a bit about the food in the hospital, it needed a chef's touch. Carla had a CT scan to make sure there weren't any potential long-term issues. A detective from the New Orleans Police Department stopped by to take her statement, and get a description of her assailant. Around 11 a.m. she was released, and Jake brought her home in a cab. He called the restaurant early to let them know that he was taking the day off to care for Carla. They were, of course, concerned for her well-being and told Jake to take a few days off, they would get by.

Over the next three days at home Jake waited on Carla and took care of her every need. They talked about positive things and how much they missed spending quality time together. By day three Carla was well enough, but needed to take another day off to be in top shape before returning to work. As Jake was about to leave for the restaurant he turned to Carla, took her hands in his, "I want us to consider making a change. You are more important to me than my career and I think we should consider making a move and build some balance back into our lives." Carla agreed, "I'll give it some thought. We can talk more this evening."

The crew at Spice was happy to see Jake back, but they were concerned about how the attack had affected Carla. Chef Hirsch stopped by to check on Jake, and the two sat in his office to talk. "Carla and I will be fine." But, Chef Hirsch could see in Jake's eyes that everything was different now. He wouldn't be shocked if Jake decided to change directions with his career. It was just a matter of time.

Jake and Carla got back into the groove of work fairly quickly, with a few immediate modifications to their routine. Jake would not allow Carla to walk home after work and insisted she take a cab each evening and call him as she was leaving the restaurant. Additionally, both returned to a schedule that included one common day off each week. Unlike their previous pattern of finding something interesting to do in New Orleans, they spent more time talking, cooking for each other and researching their next move.

In July, Carla's parents said they intended to spend Thanksgiving in New Orleans so that they could be together as a family. It would be the first time they had seen Carla since the attack. They were distraught over it, but both Carla and Jake assured them that she was fine. Still, the past few months were upsetting for Carla's family. They were worried about where the couple lived, and the life they were living.

Jake and Carla were both working on Thanksgiving, so the plan was to celebrate as a family the day after in their cramped apartment kitchen. Carla was looking forward to her parents' visit, even with the challenges surrounding hosting them at a busy time of the year.

When her parents called they also relayed some upsetting news. The Cloister, where it all began for the couple, had closed its doors. They were out of business and no one had any idea why. They had not heard what happened to Chef Philippe, but everyone felt that he would be fine, especially considering the connections he had in the restaurant business.

Jake immediately tried calling Philippe, only to discover that his home phone had been disconnected. Although Chef Philippe was still reasonably young, he had never bought into the cell phone lifestyle, making it very difficult to track him down.

CHAPTER TWENTY ONE

WEATHER ANOMALY OR A SIGN OF SIGNIFICANT CHANGE?

Typically, the first week of October, in New Orleans would bring temperatures in the low 70's. But when Jake and Carla woke, the thermometer outside their kitchen window was stuck at 31 degrees. They hadn't seen temperatures like this since Christmas in Buffalo last year. New Orleans was in a state of shock as it experienced a phenomenon that meteorologists termed a "Polar Vortex." Everyone had been watching the computer modeling of the weather pattern as it neared the city, but now they were experiencing it. Keeping in mind this part of the country is never prepared for anything except hurricanes, floods and excessive heat, panic ensued.

Jake and Carla found it a bit amusing how people were suddenly hunkered down like they were riding out the end of the world. People called into work to say they could not make it, schools were closed, and the mayor of New Orleans was on the morning news pleading with people to stay inside and only go out if it was an emergency. The night before, there was a run on grocery and hardware stores. By morning, it was hard to find a quart of milk or loaf of bread anywhere in the city.

Jake and Carla were confident their staff would still show up to work, but they were not so sure how many people would be leaving their homes to dine out. With the mayor's plea in mind, they decided to close the restaurants for the day. Jake was on the phone all morning calling his staff and letting them know they had the day off. He still needed to walk into work to check on coolers, receive any deliveries already scheduled, and check on the security of the operation. After a few hours taking care of those tasks, he returned home to a perfect meal prepared by Carla. Even though the power was still on throughout the city they ate by candlelight.

When the next two days brought the same, and at some point even colder temperatures, everyone started to take notice. This seemed to be more than an anomaly. As hard as it was for New Orleans to adapt to this, the temperatures in the Northeast were hovering around zero, totally unexpected for the first week in October. The addition of rain had resulted in horrendous ice storms, crippling airports and roadways, and causing severe power outages from Maine to the Carolinas. Schools were closed all week and dozens of people had lost their lives from weather-related accidents and hypothermia. It was still fall, but a good portion of the country was in a deep freeze.

Debate resumed about climate change, often referred to as global warming, which is a confusing phrase to use when people were suffering from extreme cold. The political left and right had opposing views about the reality of change and the impact mankind has on weather patterns. Even so, more and more people were acknowledging the scientific facts: the polar ice caps were melting, ocean levels were rising, severe and unusual weather was becoming commonplace, and holy crap it was 30 degrees in New Orleans!

After two days, even though temperatures were still 30 degrees colder than normal, New Orleans was starting to come out from under the covers. Jake and Carla were back at work and customers began to return to their dining out routines. By the end of the week temperatures were back to 75, 45 degrees warmer than a few days prior.

A few days later, everyone put the strange weather out of his or her consciousness, and meteorologists moved on to talking about the last tropical storm of the season. Still a few were scratching their heads and looking for more information about the cause.

Weather patterns continued as normal for the remainder of the fall. In late November, Carla's parents arrived. Their time was short, but their visit was nice. They stayed at the Hilton Hotel and were able to see the restaurant where Carla began her position in New Orleans. They dined there, and at Jake's Spice Restaurant, and enjoyed a wonderful, traditional Thanksgiving at their daughter's apartment.

At one point Carla's father pulled Jake aside and to his surprise, asked him what his intentions were with Carla. Jake was not prepared to answer this question, although he thought often about tying the knot at some point. Her father said, "Jake, Carla is very special and her happiness is the most important thing to us. I trust you'll do the right thing by her. And believe me when I say that if she winds up hurt, I will be, let's say extremely disappointed in you." Jake nodded and shook his hand.

Christmas was arriving soon and Jake and Carla would be back in Buffalo for a few days. Jake took Carla by surprise as he said, "While we are in Buffalo, I want to talk with a few friends about opportunities in the Northeast."

PART FOUR

NEW BEGINNINGS
THE MOUNTAINS ARE
CALLING YOUR NAME

"Thousands of tired, nerve-shaken, over-civilized people are beginning to find out that going to the mountains is going home; that wildness is a necessity; and that mountain parks and reservations are useful not only as fountains of timber and irrigating rivers but as fountain of life."
John Muir, "The Wild Parks and Forest Reservations of the West," Atlantic Monthly, January 18, 1898

CHAPTER TWENTY TWO

CHRISTMAS IN BUFFALO 2012

The usual festivities seemed different this year. Jake and Carla knew one way or another, they were beginning their last full year in New Orleans. They had no idea what was next, but felt it was time to move on.

Both Jake and Carla's families were grateful they could spend the holidays with them and felt especially blessed Carla survived her mugging with only a few stitches. Although little was said, both families hoped this would be a sign that the couple needed to move to a safer environment.

Since they no longer had the opportunity to connect with their old team at the Cloister, Jake suggested they take two days, drive up to Lake Placid and try cross-country skiing. There was a break in the weather, and the drive would be clear sailing. When they called for reservations at a hotel, they were disappointed to hear every hotel in town was full for the week. Jake managed to line up a motel in Saranac Lake, so after packing a few things they were off.

Carla forgot how long the ride was and decided to take a break in Watertown for lunch. While there Jake picked up a copy of Adirondack Life Magazine and thumbed through stories of ice fishing on Lake Clear, snowshoeing down the Jack Rabbit Trail, cutting ice blocks from Pontiac Bay for the February Winter Carnival, and of locals training for the upcoming Winter Olympics in Sochi, Russia 2014. When he reached the classifieds in the back, he stopped at a restaurant for sale in Saranac Lake. It was a property he and Carla had visited when camping a while back, a Mexican Restaurant popular with the locals. He remembered the food being acceptable, the drinks strong, the service friendly and the overall feel of the place fun. He was surprised to see it was for sale.

Back in the car he started brainstorming with Carla about owning a restaurant in the Adirondacks - quite possibly the furthest place imaginable from New Orleans with weather from another planet. As strange as the idea was on the surface, they actually began to feel excited. Suddenly, the purpose of the trip shifted from an attempt at cross-country skiing to finding a way to become restaurateurs.

Carla recently finished a novel by Sara Henry called, "A Cold and Lonely Place" that ironically took place in Saranac Lake. She wondered if the title was a warning. As they passed through the vacated towns of Star Lake and Cranberry Lake it almost felt like they were entering a forgotten area. The snow was beautiful, the skies were clear, the evergreen trees were weeping with the weight of snow and an occasional family of deer gave them a brief scare as they leapt across guard rails from one side of the road, to the other. Over the next 60 miles they only saw five other cars on the road. When they arrived in Saranac Lake it was mid-afternoon, eight hours since they had left from Buffalo.

Jake pulled into Gauthier's Motel in Saranac Lake, turned off the car and stepped out into ten below zero weather. "Holy crap it's cold. I can feel the hair in my nostrils freeze." Carla agreed the air was certainly crisp, but at the same time it felt clean, fresh and invigorating. Across the street Jake and Carla saw the closed and lonely looking shell of Casa del Sol restaurant. "The last time we were in this town that restaurant was full and vibrant. It seems almost creepy to see it now, lifeless and deteriorating."

Jake and Carla checked into Gauthier's and asked the owner, "What's the story with the restaurant across the street?" The motel owner was quick to respond, "Well, after the original Casa owner passed away, his wife continued to run the operation for a few years. She sold it to a local restaurateur who kept the original concept, but with the downturn in the economy in 2008 and the significant number of competitors in the area, he was unable to keep it going, so it closed. It is now owned, after auction, by a local developer who really wants to return it to its original glory and find an operator who'll work with him to make that happen." They thanked the owner and decided to walk across the street to see what they could.

The restaurant was vacant, but they jotted down the number of the developer posted outside. Back at the motel, Carla and Jake decided to take a ride to Lake Placid for an early dinner. They pulled into the a grocery store plaza and chose to eat at Caffe' Rustica.

Kevin, the owner, was behind the bar and Greg, the lead line cook was stoking the wood-fired oven. "Let's eat at the bar where we can watch Greg prepare our meal and maybe chat a bit with Kevin about Casa." These two would likely have their pulse on the community. Once Kevin discovered Jake and Carla were in the business, the information flowed pretty easily. Greg piped in, "People really miss Casa. I think it was popular because of the neighborhood feel, maybe even more than the food." Kevin agreed, "It's so important to have a restaurant where you can always run into people you know and the owner is always there. Having the staff know their customers by name and smile when they arrive is the most important attribute of a successful business in a small, tight-knit community like Saranac Lake."

The food was very good at Caffe' Rustica. Carla and Jake shared a wood-fired pizza and a delicious salad, toasted with a bottle of Sangiovese, finished with a cup of coffee and thanked Kevin and Greg. As they were leaving, the restaurant was beginning to pick up. It looked as though Rustica would be busy tonight. The couple drove downtown and decided to walk the length of Main Street a bit before settling in for the night. A light snow was falling and the streets were lit with antique style sidewalk lights and the glow from the specialty shops lining Main Street. Jake and Carla were arm and arm, snow flying in their faces, a glow in their cheeks from finishing the bottle of

Sangiovese and smiles from ear to ear. This was a place worth living in. This was going to be their new home.

Jake's cell phone vibrated, it was the developer who owned Casa del Sol. They made arrangements to meet at the restaurant next morning for coffee, a tour, and friendly discussion about possibilities. As Jake ended the conversation he turned to Carla and said, "This could be it, the moment that truly changes our lives." Carla shared in Jake's optimism and felt the rush of adrenaline that accompanies any exciting and unnerving opportunity.

The ride back to Gauthier's was a scary. The road only had a dusting of snow, but Jake was not used to winter driving anymore and with a little too much wine from dinner, he played it safe and drove well under the speed limit. They arrived safe, and turned in for the evening enjoying the warmth of their relationship and thoughts of getting even closer if they could work out a deal for Casa.

Carla woke before Jake, around 5 a.m. and after a shower sat down to write out her thoughts for the meeting happening in just a few hours. By the time Jake woke up she already had a plan outlined. While reviewing the plan Jake couldn't help but admire his beautiful, smart, talented and supportive partner. He felt lucky to call Carla his girlfriend and confidant. This was a woman he probably didn't deserve. He loved her.

Jake showered, shaved and mentally prepared for this meeting that was so important to their future. Neither he nor Carla had the money to buy or even substantially invest in a restaurant. They would have to convince the owner they brought something special to the table, something so enticing it was worth supporting and investing in. Jake and Carla were ready to sell their potential as a team.

The restaurant was in rough shape. Nearly a year after closing, much of the infrastructure was in need of major repair as a result. Floors were uneven and in need of replacement, the hood system no longer met building codes, years of grease build-up and a lack of maintenance had left the kitchen ranges unusable, on top of that the wiring and plumbing were inadequate and not installed to code.

Gary, the owner was pleasant and enthusiastic. He did most of the initial talking, "I bought this restaurant for the community. I have many found memories of great times in Casa as do most of the residents of Saranac Lake. This was a restaurant where you could always find a friend. The town deserves to have it back." He talked strongly about wanting to bring back the feel of the place and restart the love affair the town had with this neighborhood establishment. The owner was not a restaurant person, but was ready and willing to rebuild the operation to suit the needs of the right person who would live up to his expectations. He even referenced many of his personal experiences holding court with friends in the dining room and pointed to tables he had reserved for large parties of friends. There was definitely an emotional tie to a place, and a place in time.

When he finished, he turned to Jake and Carla and said, "So, tell me about yourselves and why you're interested?" Jake began "Carla and I first met working in a restaurant in Buffalo. We spent a couple years in a busy operation building our skills and speed. Carla went on to study pastry at the Culinary Institute of America while I finished up in Buffalo. We moved to New Orleans as Carla finished her degree and now we work for Chef Hirsch at some of the most authentic and noteworthy Cajun/Creole restaurants in Louisiana." Carla interjected, "Jake is the number two person at Spice Restaurant. He's received numerous accolades in the Louisiana community for his food. I am responsible for all of the pastries, breads and plated desserts for Chef Hirsh' cluster of restaurants." They went on talking about their style of cooking and philosophy about food, much of this just went over the owner's head, but when Jake talked about their week in the Adirondacks camping out before Carla left for school, his eyes lit up. Listening to Jake and Carla talking about their instant love for the area was paramount to saying positive things about the owner's family. Adirondack residents are deeply proud of their home.

From that point on, Carla and Jake outlined their thoughts on creating a neighborhood restaurant that emphasized the food they loved. The melting pot food of Louisiana had some similar traits to the powerful flavors of the Mexican food previously served at Casa del Sol. Gary invited them to his house for dinner to continue the conversation. "We will be happy to take you up on the invitation under one condition, Jake and I will bring the supplies and cook for you and your wife. This will be a chance to show our style of cooking and complete the vision we have for a restaurant."

Jake and Carla were now in their element. This might be one of the most important meals they had ever prepared. The rewards could be great, but failure to bring home their concept might end the conversation about the restaurant and the subsequent discussion about the owner investing in them. They spent the next two hours planning a menu, shopping at Price Chopper in Lake Placid and a small health food store in Saranac Lake called Nori's. They decided on the following:

* A Fennel and Orange Salad
* Shrimp Etouffee served on a Polenta Cake
* Cajun Roast Pork Loin with Spicy Slaw, Remoulade and Fresh Flour Tortilla (An interesting twist to demonstrate the fusion possibilities with Mexican Food)
* Carla would make a Banana Peanut Butter Pie with Meringue and Fresh Peanut Brittle

They arrived mid-day at the owner's house in nearby Bloomingdale and after acclimating to the kitchen told Gary and his wife, Sarah, to relax while they took charge. The aromas in the kitchen were intoxicating and unique to this part of the country. Both Gary and Sarah spent most of the time watching these two professionals perform. It was obvious that they were accomplished and having fun.

At around 7 o'clock everyone sat down to dinner and more conversation about what Casa could become. "Although Cajun/Creole food is not Mexican, there is a mutual appreciation for chili peppers and the right use of spice. If you like Mexican, you will love Cajun/Creole." By the end of the evening Gary was sold. He saw his restaurant in the hands of two incredible chefs and a couple who would be totally committed to doing it right. As they cleaned and packed up, Carla and Jake agreed to work on formalizing their thoughts after they returned to New Orleans. Specifically, how the kitchen and dining room should be designed to complement what they would want to do. The owner would in turn prepare a contract, lease and conditions of occupancy and send it to them within 60 days. They shook hands (formal enough for the Adirondacks) and left knowing their mission was accomplished.

The following morning Jake and Carla left for Buffalo for a final night with their families before packing up to return to their jobs in New Orleans. Telling Chef Hirsch would be difficult and they would certainly give him plenty of time to find replacements.

Two days later they were back in their apartment in New Orleans, with seventy-degree temperatures and business as usual, at least on the surface.

CHAPTER TWENTY THREE

THE ADIRONDACK EXPERIENCE – A SAFE HAVEN

The next three weeks in New Orleans were difficult for Jake and Carla. They were physically in Louisiana, but emotionally in the Adirondacks opening a new restaurant. They hadn't received any news from the developer of the building still referred to as Casa, but Carla and Jake had spent every free moment outside of work building the concept and menu for their new venture in the frigid north.

Chef Hirsch hadn't been told anything yet, Jake was holding off until he knew they had a deal. Thirty days after returning to New Orleans, Jake and Carla received a FedEx package from Saranac Lake with a lease agreement and conditions of occupancy. In the document was a statement giving them complete control of the restaurant concept. The lease agreement was very favorable, requiring a fixed monthly fee plus 3% of gross. This would give the couple some breathing room during slower months and yield greater return for the owner when business was good. Jake and Carla would need to come up with $25,000 of good faith money as a contribution to the substantial funds needed to equip the kitchen and they were on their own to arrange for a personal bank loan for initial operating expenses. Although the agreement seemed very favorable, Jake and Carla had no idea how they would come up with the money and doubted any bank would provide such a big personal loan to two unknowns.

Jake was struck with a sense of hopelessness, but Carla rose to the occasion, "There must be a way to figure this out if we just think creatively. Why not contact our parents to see if they would be interested in an investment?" Jake reluctantly agreed to see if they could help.

Both parents were so relieved that Jake and Carla might leave New Orleans, tempering their constant fear for the couple living in a potentially dangerous place, that they agreed to see what they could do. After meeting over dinner in Buffalo, Carla and Jake's parents decided to provide the $25,000 for the "good faith" contribution and not require repayment for two years. As difficult as it had been to ask, Jake knew that one obstacle was removed from their dream.

Feeling confident and sensing it was time to move on, Jake and Carla met with Chef Hirsch the next morning and told him everything. "Chef, Carla and I are so grateful for the opportunities you have provided. Your restaurants are outstanding, the crews are talented and focused and we have become advocates for Louisiana food as a result. This is very hard for us, but it is an opportunity we just don't want to pass up." Jake and Carla said they would stay on for three months while a search took place for their replacements, and help transition those individuals into their important roles. "We are so sorry to do this to you and hope you will understand." What happened next took the couple by surprise.

Chef Hirsch stood and hugged them both. He began "Jake, when you first took on the role of chef in this restaurant I told you to never doubt yourself. And I might now add, don't ever apologize for making a decision that is in your best interest. Both you and Carla have worked extremely hard and I am the one who is grateful for everything you've done for my restaurants and your employees. This is your time and I applaud you for taking the risk and doing what you want to do. I know you'll be successful and will continue to make us proud in New Orleans." This was what Jake and Carla had hoped for, an understanding mentor. "Now, I can help you in a few ways. First, you're young and will likely not have the credit history to allow a bank to invest in your start-up capital. I'll cosign the loan. I'm sure any bank will take that as adequate, if not, I will talk my bank into making the loan. Secondly, I'll bring up my core players when you are close to start-up as an opening team and spend a week to help draw press and get you up and running. This is my way of saying thanks."

Carla and Jake were shocked and both showed mixed emotions, a cross between laughing and crying. A tear rolled down Carla's check while all Jake could say was, "Wow Chef." Hirsch was generous beyond belief. Jake and Carla shook his hand, and reiterated they would give him 100% until departing for the Adirondacks.

That night after service, when Carla and Jake returned to their apartment they signed the letter of agreement and the lease, made a copy on their home printer and packaged it for return to Saranac Lake. The following morning they sent it via FedEx, hugging each other as they turned it over to the clerk.

The next three months were a roller coaster. Between the businesses of the Hirsch restaurants, to back-and-forth discussions with the developer in Saranac Lake and negotiations with banks, the couple barely had time to breathe. A new chef was promoted to Jake's position from within the company and Carla selected the pastry chef from Spice to take on her role. Two new pastry hires would vie for the Spice position, leaving the final decision up to the new chef. The couple did an outstanding job of preparing their replacements and at the end of April they packed up their belongings, rented a moving van from U-Haul and left for the Adirondacks.

Jake and Carla managed to build a restaurant concept and likely menu for their new venture, but knew it would probably evolve once arriving at their destination. Preliminary thoughts on the restaurant renovation and kitchen equipment had been sent two months prior, but since they were 1,400 miles away they needed to trust that work on Casa del Sol was progressing. In order to take advantage of the busiest season in the Adirondacks the intent was to open in mid-June. There was an unmanageable amount of work yet to be done, but they were up for the challenge. As Chef Hirsch said, this was their time.

They drove through Georgia and the Carolinas, Virginia and Pennsylvania arriving in Buffalo on the third day for an overnight with their families. They left the van in Buffalo and drove to Saranac Lake in search of an apartment. Jake's parents agreed to bring the van up once the couple found a place to stay.

Exhausted, Carla and Jake arrived in Saranac Lake. They stayed once again at Gauthier's, had a quick bite to eat and then settled in for the evening. Tomorrow they would be signing the final loan papers with the bank, taking possession of the restaurant and starting the hunt for a suitable place to live. As much as it would be convenient to stay right in town, the couple had been talking about a place with a little land.

Sunrise the next morning was spectacular. They looked out their motel room window across Lake Flower and saw a single loon guarding the lake. It was so calm it reflected a mirror image of the shoreline trees. Carla and Jake knew this was the right move. They quickly got ready for the day and anxiously walked across the street to see what they could of the restaurant they would soon call home.

It was only 8 a.m., but the landlord's crew was busy at work. Jake and Carla walked in beaming with excitement. The place looked great. The dining room floors had been refinished, the wall colors were exactly right. The exterior of the building had been restored, and was fresh with whitewash and terra cotta tile roof. A sign out front stated that a new neighborhood restaurant would be coming soon.

Walking in the kitchen, the place where they would spend most of their waking hours, was not quite as exciting. The space had been stripped down, quarry tile floors re-grouted, and a new drop ceiling installed. The hood over the hot line had been refreshed and the walk-in coolers were clean and ready to go. All of the other old equipment had been removed, and the balance of the kitchen was empty. Rewiring was in progress with Romex cables hanging from the ceiling at various spots throughout the empty space. The kitchen was ready for Jake and Carla to fill in the blanks.

Jake touched base with the clerk of the works and told him that they would return a bit later to review everything with the owner.

After a brief formality at the bank they left with a personal loan approval, business account, personal checking account and joint savings. Everything was falling into place.

They picked up a copy of the Adirondack Daily Enterprise while stopping into the Blue Moon Café for a late breakfast. They were hoping to get some leads on an apartment or even a house to rent. Ken, the owner, was walking through the dining room greeting his guests and stopped at their table. "Hi. Are you folks here on vacation?" He introduced himself and welcomed them. "We're moving up from New Orleans to open a new business in what was Casa del Sol. We just arrived and are looking for a place to live." Ken congratulated the couple, "The town has been waiting for Casa to re-open. I can't wait to hear your ideas." He mentioned he knew of a place on Turtle Pond that had about a half-acre of land, and was available for rent or sale. He looked up the phone number of the owner and wished them luck.

The property was great, although the house was a bit large for their needs. It bordered State land and offered access to the water. Protected from activity and noise by trees and a still water pond, the house was just a five-minute walk to the restaurant. The owner met them and after a tour they inquired about price. The house was within their budget. Jake and Carla signed a lease and took possession of their first house, now part of the big plan. They were ready to begin the adventure.

Jake's parents said they would be up with their van full of possessions the following weekend, which meant Jake and Carla would be spending the next few days at Gauthier's. This gave them the rest of the week to jump right into the restaurant project.

They met with the owner, took possession of the restaurant and spent a bit of time reviewing their concept with him. They were thrilled that he gave them full autonomy on design and concept, so it was only fitting he had a sneak peak at the direction they were moving in.

The restaurant was to be called Bayou indicating the Louisiana-style of cooking taking place inside while referencing the body of water the restaurant was near. The concept would be informal, with a community table in the center of the dining room, surrounded by smaller tables for private dining. Music would be Zydeco-style, with the intent of creating a warm, fun atmosphere for local and visiting patrons. Although it was not Mexican, as was the case with Casa, the feel of the operation would be very much the same. The landlord sensed the concept was right for Saranac Lake and said that he would do everything in his power to help introduce the couple and their creations to the people of his community.

Jake and Carla hadn't finalized the menu. Much would depend on their ability to purchase the necessary ingredients, trial and error on building the flavor profile, tasting final recipes, and making sure the items fit into a pricing structure that would work in Saranac Lake. They wanted to make sure the restaurant was accessible to anyone and everyone.

At this point the menu would likely include a handful of stand-alone appetizers, a core of standard menu items offered in two sizes: small plates and, full portions. The idea of small plates was to encourage people to order multiple items and share them with others at their table. This would help to stimulate conversation about the food and create a lively atmosphere in the restaurant.

At this point, the following items were on the drawing board:

BAYOU MENU IN THE WORKS

Jake's now perfected Seafood Gumbo
Shrimp Etouffee
Jambalaya
Crawfish Boil
Fried Oyster Po Boy
Fried Green Tomatoes with Remoulade
Crawfish Enchilada
Blackened Rainbow Trout with Spicy Slaw
Cajun Style Shaved Roast Pork Loin with Mole
Roast Chicken with Polenta and Fried Green Beans
Oven Roasted Queen Snapper with Fresh
Herbs and Preserved Lemons
Skirt Steak with Chimichurri
Carla's Peanut Butter/Banana Pie with
Meringue and Peanut Brittle
Sweet Potato Pecan Pie
New Orleans Style Chocolate Bread Pudding with Hard Sauce
Praline Crème Brule
Beignets with Powdered Sugar and Crème Anglaise

Jake and Carla reviewed the timeline on renovations, selected equipment, and determined the location of each piece. They scheduled a meeting with an Adirondack artisan potter for the design of some specialty china pieces and a rep from Fortessa China for the primary selection of plates, flatware and sturdy glassware.

It was now the end of April and it appeared like everything would be in place for an early June opening. Ranges, refrigeration, a smoker, as well as pots and pans would arrive in mid-May and be installed soon after. Tables and chairs were being made by a friend of the landlord, and should be ready by the end of May, with china and glassware coming in around the same time.

Since time was tight, Carla and Jake decided to test all of their recipes at home once the kitchen on Turtle Pond was set up. The next step would be to line up vendors, apply for credit with each, build the final menu, determine how they would market the operation, build a budget, have their website designed, establish a social media campaign, write job descriptions and determine staffing needs, interview and hire a staff, and finally, set up a training schedule. All this must be accomplished in the next six weeks. Suddenly, it began to look like an impossible task.

Carla took control; "We should spell everything out for the clerk of the works on kitchen layout and then give him full control of the process." She and Jake would work from a makeshift office set up in the restaurant so that they would be close at hand if needed. "Let's use our house for recipe testing in the evening when we can focus and not be interrupted." They would have dinner at Caffe' Rustica the following evening and ask Kevin if he knew of a local web designer to get the ball rolling on that project. "I think we should separate tasks and touch base for lunch each day to review progress on all of the details needing our attention." Finally, they would build job descriptions and place an ad in the Adirondack Enterprise, as well as post on www.adirondackhelpwanted.com so they could collect resumes and job applications for the positions needed. Both Carla and Jake would interview every candidate for each position so that they were in total agreement.

Knowing Chef Hirsch and crew would be with them for the final crunch week was comforting. He would be able to catch whatever they had missed and maybe correct mistakes she and Jake had made along the way. She asked Jake to contact Chef Hirsch and firm up dates for the second week in June. They would have one week of soft opening and then go full bore the last week in June when the Lake Placid Horseshow was in the area. There would be many sleepless nights between now and then.

That weekend, Jake's parents arrived with the van full of furniture, not much to fill a house. Although they knew they didn't have the time to entertain, Jake and Carla took them out to dinner at the Belvedere Restaurant, a local favorite, put them up in Gauthier's and sent them back home the following morning. Not the most gracious hosts, but their impossible timeline did not leave room for a day out of focus. Jake's parents said they would be back for the soft opening to help any way that they could.

Jake and Carla took the balance of Sunday to unpack and set up their house as best they could. After a shopping trip for supplies, they were able to cook meals at home. The couple lit a fire, cracked open a bottle of wine, held each other close and fell asleep on the old couch they moved from New Orleans. It was the only piece of furniture in their living room. Tomorrow was the beginning of madness.

CHAPTER TWENTY FOUR

FORTY-TWO DAYS AND COUNTING

In a perfect world, every piece of equipment would arrive on time and be intact, the furniture would be perfect, power and plumbing would be problem free and all the staff would be easy to find. But it is not a perfect world, as Jake and Carla were about to find out.

The first week in May with six more to go, the initial wave of problems reared up their ugly heads. The ranges and line equipment arrived: two six-burner Jades, a Plancha, two convective Friolaters and a Char-Grill, a tabletop Combi-Oven and a salamander broiler. They were beautiful, there was only one problem, they were set-up for natural gas, not available in the Adirondacks - instead of propane. Not a huge problem, but a delay never the less. New regulators could be sent within a week. But when the contractor reviewed the gas lines installed by the propane company, he realized that they weren't sufficient to handle the gas volume to create the BTU's required by the menu. Another delay.

With electrical work running behind and plumbing installation yet to begin, the general contractor told Jake it didn't look likely that everything would be complete by mid-June. This, of course was not acceptable. If Bayou was not operating by the last week in June they would miss out on some of the biggest volume weeks of the year and would find it difficult to catch up before the bottom fell out in November.

Jake called Gary and relayed the problem. Gary understood the dilemma Jake and Carla were facing and said he would be by that afternoon. He arrived with three other tradesmen he'd pulled from other jobs to give the restaurant top priority. In the meantime he had called the propane company and asked for a favor: the gas lines had to be revamped by the end of the week and they agreed. The value of living and running a business in Saranac Lake for decades was paying off, Gary brought things back under control.

Carla was focused on interviewing potential employees. She and Jake were looking for four line cooks, two prep people and one pastry assistant for Carla. Additionally, they needed a solid host who could coordinate the front of the house, ten servers and two bartenders. Ideally they would all be experienced, but realizing this was not likely, Carla was also working on a series of training sessions to implement the week before opening.

Each night Carla and Jake would shop for ingredients and test out recipes at home. They rarely finished before midnight and were back at it each morning before seven. They were getting exhausted after only two weeks into crunch time. Four more weeks till opening and the list of tasks did not seem to get any smaller.

Week three was much better. Carla had lined up quite a few interviews for potential staff members. Of particular interest would be the two key positions of sous chef and dining room host/supervisor. They were pleased with the candidates on paper and would be interviewing three candidates for the sous chef position as well as four for dining room host this week. One of the sous chef candidates had worked with Jake and Carla at the Cloister in Buffalo and would be driving up for the interview. All the interviewees had reasonable experience and considering the tight timeline faced, this seemed positive.

Construction was back on track with the gas company already on-site for a retrofit of the lines, and the plumbers scheduled to arrive the following day. Even though the equipment was fit for natural gas the process of converting to new regulators allowed them to position the equipment, and line up the Ansul system. The quarry tile floor in the kitchen was set and a mason was working on finishing the grout. It was starting to look like a kitchen.

This week Jake would be meeting with potential vendors to review their product line and prices. Painting in the dining room was almost finished, and a representative from Micros had arrived to install the point of sale system.

Carla would be working on the bar set-up since they had decided to knock down a useless wall in the restaurant waiting area. They converted the space to a larger bar with six taps for regional beers, and a back bar that would display their wine inventory. She hoped to have the entire system operational by the end of the week.

On Wednesday, interviews for key positions began. Two of the three sous chef candidates seemed well-aligned for the position, but Jake and Carla decided on Scott, the line cook they had worked with in Buffalo. It just seemed safer to go with someone they knew. Scott was offered the position and he accepted. He needed a couple weeks to give notice in Buffalo, pack and move to the area. The only downside for Jake was that he would have preferred to have him present during the interview process for line cooks, dishwashers, and prep people, but he understood. Carla spent time with the four candidates for dining room host - all were local. Jake and Carla agreed on a middle-aged woman who was born and raised in Saranac Lake. Lindsay was personable and confident, and she had actually worked at Casa del Sol during its heyday. Carla felt it was vital to have a dynamic personality in the front of the house since neither she nor Jake would be able to break away from the kitchen on busy nights. Lindsay was now responsible for selecting service staff and bartenders. With her knowledge of the area, it seemed obvious that she was better suited for this task than Carla or Jake.

Word got around quickly and by the end of the week Jake had a pile of applicants for the other kitchen positions. He would start interviews next week.

On Friday, the new propane regulators arrived, and were quickly installed. The electrician was finishing up, and the contractor had arranged for the building inspector to do a walk-through on Monday. If all went well they could fire up the line early next week and begin testing all of the equipment. The health inspection was the final hurdle, and the inspector would be there on Thursday.

Carla and Jake entered the weekend with a new sense of confidence. They had worked every evening on recipe testing and were ready to put together the final opening menu. All the recipes were done, as were order lists, inventory forms, prep sheets and vendor pricing. The goal was to have the menu to the printer by mid-week. They were now three weeks out and things were looking better than expected. They might actually be able to enjoy the weekend together. But, they did not want to be too optimistic because there were still many things that could go wrong. They woke on Saturday to the ring of a cell phone. It was the web designer, he was having some challenges with the site; the most significant was that he was unable to find a domain name not already taken. After some strategic marketing discussion, they all agreed on www.AdirondackBayou.com. He said that the beta test of the site would be up in a few days for them to review. The rest of the weekend was free for Jake and Carla to enjoy. They decided to pack a lunch and go for a late spring hike in the High Peaks.

They hiked up Noonmark Mountain off the Ausable Club property near Keene, ate their picnic lunch and took in the view - there was still snow on top of the mountain - and allowed everything to sink in. They were about to open their own restaurant in one of the most pristine areas of the country. This might even be the place that they would eventually raise a family.

CHAPTER TWENTY FIVE

PREPARING TO OPEN AND MURPHY'S LAW

On Monday the building inspector arrived, the electrician was finishing a few details, all of the ranges and ovens were in place, plumbing was complete and coolers were coming up to temperature. The inspector toured the facilities with Jake, Carla, the contractor, the clerk of the works and Gary. The electrical system passed with flying colors, gas lines were up to code, and accessibility and HVAC airflow met standards.

While touring the inspector turned on water at various locations to test plumbing capacity and as they rounded the corner back to the kitchen the floor drains began to overflow. The contractor turned off faucets and watched in horror as the overflow slowly receded. There was obviously a problem and the building inspector held off on granting an occupancy certificate until it could be rectified. Roto-Rooter was there within the hour and once the sewer lines were scoped it was determined that the main line from the restaurant to the town line was clogged with tree roots. It would need to be replaced. This meant digging up the front yard of the restaurant, hopefully not into the restaurant itself. They could be there with a backhoe later that day, but it would likely take two days and would leave the front of the restaurant property looking like a bomb went off.

Once again, Carla took control and said, "This won't move us away from the opening deadline. While the repairs are taking place every other task will still stay on track." Furniture was scheduled to arrive within a few days, china glassware and flatware the next day, and the website would be up and running shortly. Additionally, the health inspector would be in later in the week to give his blessing on the kitchen.

For the anticipated soft opening week Carla was planning a series of receptions for local dignitaries, the press, friends of the family and regional chefs. She thought to herself, "Although the restaurant won't be officially open, the pressure on the kitchen and dining room will be just as intense. There is some comfort in knowing that Chef Hirsch and his team will be here to help take off some of that pressure." Carla had reserved a bank of rooms at Gauthier's, and had rented a boat for their use during any free time over the course of their five-day support visit.

By Monday the land in front of the restaurant had been excavated, the clogged pipe removed and a new section put in place. The project would be completed the next day and Gary agreed to bring in a landscaper to do some cosmetic work. Painters would return on Wednesday to repaint the exterior of the building and on Thursday the exterior sign proclaiming, "Bayou, A Taste of New Orleans in the Adirondacks" would be installed.

Aside from the sewer problem the rest of the week went as planned. Once the painting and sign installation were done the restaurant looked like it was coming together. The beautiful furniture arrived, the website was a home run and would be going live on the following Monday, and on Friday morning the health and building inspectors would return to (hopefully) give their blessings on the property. Jake had been busy in the kitchen making sure that all of the ranges were calibrated, tables leveled, dish machine operating correctly, small equipment unwrapped and tested, and refrigeration racks in place ready to receive product.

Carla and Jake delayed some of the final interviews for kitchen staff, but their host/dining room supervisor carried on with front-of-the-house interviews using Jake and Carla's home for the process. Next week they would start training servers and bartenders in the restaurant. Kitchen employee interviews would resume on Monday and Tuesday - a week late - leaving Jake very nervous about timing.

Carla had the Webmaster post some tickler information about the restaurant referring to "coming soon" activities. Locals were already buzzing about the restaurant and trying to figure out what they could expect. Jake and Carla had learned about the 25th anniversary party Casa del Sol's original owner had thrown a few years back and decided to offer something similar for the general public on the last day of their soft opening. They booked two local bands, acquired a permit for outside activity and rented a tent for the parking lot. The kitchen would offer samples of their cuisine, the bar would be open and the mayor of Saranac Lake would be the official master of ceremonies. The amount of work Carla and Jake had been able to accomplish in six weeks was remarkable. Even Gary couldn't believe they were about to meet their deadlines.

By Wednesday of the next week Jake and Carla had selected the balance of their team members. Some would be ready to work the week before the soft opening, but nearly half would need to give more notice to their current employers. This meant that Jake and Carla would need to depend even more on Chef Hirsch' team to get them through the opening. Two newly-hired kitchen staff members would start that weekend, and everything in the kitchen needed to be scrubbed, china and glassware unpacked and cleaned, the dining room set, windows washed and coolers prepped to receive supplies.

Jake set up the kitchen office, fired up the computer and tested the point of sale system. Instruction on the system was scheduled for next week, as was the balance of server training. The printed menus arrived, as did the first wave of supplies for the bar. The liquor license had arrived that morning, something they had been concerned about, and now they would be in good shape with the front of the house.

Jake and Carla moved to kitchen preparation and final testing of recipes. They spent the next three days testing recipes again, preparing every dish on the menu, taking pictures of plate presentations and using this data to prepare training manuals for staff members. Jake set up his storeroom and coolers with labels that paralleled the inventory forms and began placing orders with select vendors. All supplies would start arriving on Thursday of next week, giving them four days to prep for the soft opening week. Chef Hirsch and his team would be arriving a week from Saturday and Jake and Carla wanted to be in good shape for them.

Everything was moving at breakneck speed and every night Jake and Carla made up new punch lists as the days seemed to get shorter and shorter. They both knew no matter how well they planned, some details would be missed. But, they were determined to minimize the impact of Murphy's Law. It was important to them that the soft opening week take place without a hitch. They crossed their fingers.

CHAPTER TWENTY SIX

THE NEW ORLEANS TEAM ARRIVES

Everything was in place, the recipes had been tested and plating pictures taken, the website and Facebook page were live, staff was in place (aside from those still working through their two-week notice), server training was complete and food supplies were in-house. Now it came down to execution.

Carla had opening week activities organized with a strategic plan of attack. Tuesday was dedicated to families of employees with a welcome from Jake and Carla before service, a sequence of small plates focused on getting every menu item on tables for guests to taste, service dry-runs including drink orders, and then a sit down with the restaurant audience afterward for a full critique. Wednesday was reserved for the key players in the community: the mayor, local school board members, the editor of the paper, prominent local business owners, vendors, motel owners and leaders of the Chamber of Commerce. This would be the first night the full menu would be tested offering guests an opportunity to order in a typical fashion, challenging the service staff and line cooks. Comment forms were handed out soliciting input on everything from ambience to choice of china, from food quality to service efficiency. Thursday was reserved for the press that Carla had invited, including: WPTZ Television, WNBZ Radio, The Press Republican Newspaper, The Lake Placid

News and even Adirondack Life. Their families were also invited with the same format as the night before. In all cases Carla had limited the number of guests to 50 so the staff could ease into a real-time environment. Friday would be a day to regroup with the restaurant closed and a chance to prep for the celebration on Saturday.

Chef Hirsch and his crew arrived the previous Saturday, having a chance to tour the restaurant, review the menu and systems Jake and Carla had developed and get a feel for the town. Over dinner, the New Orleans team fired questions at Jake and Carla - trying to find gaps in their plan and areas they should focus on in preparation for the week of testing. This was an invaluable process, pointing out a handful of simple, but critical details that had escaped Jake and Carla. The couple neglected to build in a standard approach for guests with allergies, a process for handling large parties over eight, and selling gift certificates. They were small issues, but could become significant if the restaurant was not prepared. Better to address challenges now than when the restaurant is fully operational.

It was agreed that Carla and Jake would work on their respective lines with the culinary team all week as they continued to train, and walk them through preparations, while clearly defining plate presentations and personally critiquing the system set in place. Chef Hirsch would help facilitate the dining room, serving as a liaison between front and back of the house while Scott, the sous chef, who had only arrived two days prior would expedite on the line. The Hirsch team would be troubleshooters and kitchen back up.

Sunday and Monday the team helped with final details and worked through all the menu items one more time, making a few minor adjustments along the way. Chef Hirsch was cautious to only support and not take over. This was Jake's and Carla's restaurant and they had done an outstanding job getting ready. Hirsch knew if this was an operation in Louisiana it would be a hit, but he did not have the same level of confidence in Saranac Lake.

Tuesday, Wednesday and Thursday went extremely well and although they originally intended to leave after Thursday, Chef Hirsch sent his team home and agreed to stay through the community event on Saturday. Friday he took Carla and Jake out for breakfast in Lake Placid and spent some time going through his assessment of the restaurant, the food, service and marketing. "I want you both to know, I am extremely proud of the way you have pulled this business together. The menu looks and sounds great, the place feels like it belongs in New Orleans, and your staff seem ready and able to meet the challenges ahead." Jake could sense the "however" that was coming. "There are a few things I see as potential problems. You will want to address them sooner, rather than later." His ability to see the full picture was amazing and Jake and Carla took notes on his observations. "As much as I love Cajun/Creole cooking and you have both adopted it as your own, I am always leery that people who are not accustomed to the food of the Bayou, may not enjoy it as much. To this end, I would suggest you tone down the spice just a bit and add a couple generic restaurant favorites to please those who are not adventurous. Maybe a typical steak or roast chicken dish." This made sense to Jake. "Finally, it will be important for your service staff to loosen up. The beauty of Louisiana food is its tone. Dining in this restaurant should be fun. Make sure the staff is having fun, and that this is obvious to the guest. This is what you should market, this is what will set your restaurant apart from the competition." Not everything could be corrected overnight, but they knew he was right on every point.

That day everyone was busy with mise en place for the community event on Saturday. There would be an official ribbon cutting by the mayor and their landlord, followed by three hours of tasting, drinking, handshaking and great local music. The weather forecast was perfect, not always the case in the Adirondacks, and by 8 p.m. they were ready. Jake and Chef Hirsch would be in at 5 a.m. to light the fire pit for outdoor grilling and Carla would be close behind to prepare a huge Kings Cake as the celebratory centerpiece for the ribbon cutting. The food would begin to flow at 2 p.m. and since the entire town was invited there was no telling how many would show up. Jake and Carla's parents arrived that evening from Buffalo and were assigned to be greeters at the Saturday festivities. They were given Bayou T-shirts so the people of Saranac Lake could easily identify them. Both sets of parents were bursting with pride.

The mayor had arranged to have two police officers at the restaurant to direct vehicular traffic and guests walking across the street.

At 5 a.m. Jake and Chef Hirsch were hard at work at the fire pit and Carla was already sliding the cakes into the oven. The full team arrived at 9 a.m. and everything was moving along nicely. All menu-tasting items would be prepared as single bites with disposable plates instead of china, due to the sheer number of servings anticipated. They planned for 800-1,000 based on predictions Gary, the landlord, offered.

Gary was very emphatic, "Whenever you say "free" in Saranac Lake and "party" in the same breath, you can expect people to come out of the woodwork. Add the passion locals had for the original Casa del Sol and you'll have a very big crowd."

As the start time crept up, the team began to fire the hot items, Andouille sausage on the grill, fried oysters for mini Po'boy sandwiches, Cajun grilled shrimp, pots of gumbo and special creole-style grilled goat served in tortilla. Carla kept it simple; aside from the 40 Kings Cakes (a New Orleans tradition) she had baked in the morning, she would spend most of her day frying beignets. Her goal was to make sure that every Saranac Laker left with powdered sugar rings around their mouths.

By 1:45 p.m. people were arriving, and by 2p.m., there were easily 200 people present for the ribbon cutting. The mayor offered a few words of welcome to Jake and Carla, cut the ribbon and signaled for the music to begin. Cooks offered samples of key items from the menu and the outdoor fire pit was burning at well over 600 degrees bringing out rivers of sweat from Jake and Chef Hirsch. They traded in their chef hats for sweatbands, and had to take a break every 15 minutes or so to clear the smoke from their eyes. By 2:30 the numbers had easily grown to over 400, and people had spread to both sides of the road, even the parking lot of the nearby Comfort Inn and Gauthier's Motel. Cocktails were sold in the restaurant (the only thing not given away that day), the music was lively and very loud, people were dancing outside and Jake and Carla sensed they were on their way to a successful start. By the end of the day they estimated Bayou had served over 1,200 - likely anyone and everyone in town on that day - and all indications pointed toward happy guests ready to support this returning landmark. The entire crew stayed around to clean up gathering in the restaurant at 8 p.m. to share a toast to Chef Hirsch, Jake and Carla, and the entire team.

Sunday was the official day of rest and then they would be off and running. Sunday morning Jake and Carla drove Chef Hirsch to the airport in Burlington, Vermont, hugged him like a member of their family and thanked him for all of his support and mentorship. "Chef, we will never forget your generosity and support. We owe our passion for Louisiana food to you and your business savvy for getting us to this point. All we know to say is thank you." Chef Hirsch smiled, "Jake and Carla, you are my friends and I am happy to help friends reach for their dreams. Best of luck."

Before they headed for Vermont, Jake and Carla's parents had left for the return trip to Buffalo. They would be back in Saranac Lake in the fall after the busy season was over. Based on their experience with people in the restaurant business they knew better than to suggest a visit during season.

Restaurant Bayou was christened.

CHAPTER TWENTY SEVEN

SEASON ONE AT BAYOU – SUMMER HAS ARRIVED

The first month at Bayou was terrific. After a few minor issues during week one, the team got into a rhythm and service problems seemed to melt away. Guest reaction was great, as people in Saranac Lake and surrounding communities adopted the restaurant as their local spot as they had the old Casa del Sol. It appeared that Louisiana cooking was well received, and with the pronounced flavors of this melting pot cuisine, people found many similarities to Mexican food.

On average, Bayou served nearly 1,000 guests each week. This was right on budget, and Jake and Carla were excited about how well the operation was doing. Since her pastry assistant was comfortable with the dessert menu Carla was able to step away from some of the daily production and spend a portion of each week on managing the business. She took care of scheduling, payroll, inventory and accounts payable. This allowed Jake to stay focused on food and oversight of service. Carla worked herself into a comfortable schedule, taking a day and a half off each week working a split shift on others. She arrived at 8 a.m., took a few hours off in the afternoon and returned for evening service. Jake, on the other hand, arrived before 7 a.m. each day and stayed until closing. Some weeks he worked seven days and was fine with that. He felt things would slow down once he was comfortable with the operation and his staff.

At service time, the kitchen and dining room were in sync. The best hire so far had been Lindsay, the host/front of the house supervisor. She ran a tight ship, trained her staff well, was very attentive to guest needs and quickly became the personality of the restaurant. Lindsay was always upbeat, great with names, able to remember guests from visit-to-visit. And something about them that made her greetings personal. There were very few issues between service staff and cooks, which was unusual in most restaurants. Lindsay seemed able to keep her cool even when challenges arose. Carla and Jake felt fortunate to have her on the team.

In the kitchen things were not as smooth as Jake had hoped. Carla's concern was less with the cooks than how Jake was unable to relinquish control to the sous chef and allow the staff to do their jobs. Jake was constantly critiquing the cooks and losing his temper when he felt a plate was not exactly as he wanted it. Carla thought she would talk with him at some point if he didn't cool down. She would often hear kitchen staff talking among themselves about the demeaning approach Jake took towards them. It was not uncommon for him to lash out with, "This gumbo sucks. How incompetent are you? Follow the damn recipe unless you can't read. Can you read, or would you like me to read it to you?"

Still, the most important thing at this point was that the guests of Bayou were happy and returning time and time again. Over 3,000 meals served in the first month! The question, of course, was whether or not they could continue this pattern of success through the summer months and into the fall. Even with a great opening, Carla and Jake were fully aware business levels in the Adirondacks would fall off after October. Aside from a few short bursts through the winter, business was not likely to pick up again until the following June. The success of Bayou would depend solely on the support they received from the local community and how well the restaurant was able to adjust expenses during the lean months.

By the time August arrived the restaurant had exceeded expectations. Business was fantastic and the locals had adopted the restaurant as their own. Lindsay had a following and was considered by many to be the key person at Bayou. Jake and Carla rarely made it into the dining room to interact with guests so they were, for all intents and purposes, invisible to the public.

The restaurant had been open for almost seven weeks, and Jake had not taken a single day off. Everyone in the restaurant, Carla included, were walking on eggshells around the chef. It looked like he could come unraveled at any moment, and no one wanted to be close when it happened. Jake began to mumble under his breath, slam doors and fling pots and pans into the sink. His vocabulary was reduced to a string of four-letter words directed at no one in particular, but everyone at the same time. What was most distressing was he didn't appear to be enjoying the success of the restaurant. Jake hadn't taken the time to appreciate their success.

That Saturday night after service Carla grabbed Jake, "You are done for the day my friend. You will be taking tomorrow off." On the walk home, Carla began, "You are becoming detrimental to the restaurant and the entire staff is not only concerned, they are downright afraid of you. If you don't get yourself under control and create some balance in your life, your team will start looking for other places to work." Jake was shocked because Carla never talked to him like this. At first he felt like she was not being understanding or supportive but as they entered the house she wrapped her arms around him, "Jake, I want you to enjoy this wonderful restaurant we have created, but you need to shape up first. I will not let you spiral out of control. The restaurant is doing well, customers are happy, the food is great and the community believes in what we are doing. Don't blow it."

Jake slept in until nine o'clock. He couldn't remember the last time this happened, but it felt good. When he walked into the kitchen Carla had made a Quiche Lorraine and fruit salad. They made some espresso and walked their food down to the edge of Turtle Pond, spread out a blanket and enjoyed the view and each other's company. Very little was said, they just relaxed and soaked up the mountain air. After breakfast they went for a walk in the woods, down parts of the Jack Rabbit Trail, and talked through all of the issues in the restaurant, many of which stemmed from Jake's dark attitude and the constant pressure he placed on the cooks. In the end, he agreed the staff at Bayou was doing a good job; he needed to recognize this and cut them some slack.

Carla had an idea. She turned to Jake, "On Monday I want you to go into work after the crew, spend some time with vendor salesmen, touch base with the crew on prep for the night and leave at 4 with me. We will return at 7 p.m. as guests for dinner in our own restaurant." She wanted him to relax and see just how good the food and service was. Jake reluctantly agreed, "I promise to approach my role differently."

The balance of Sunday was just fun time with his favorite person. They went to Caffe' Rustica for pizza and wine, just like they had early on, and caught a movie at the Palace Theater. Neither Jake nor Carla set foot in the restaurant.

Monday found both of them back in Bayou, Jake not arriving until an hour after the prep cooks. The crew didn't know what to think when they arrived - the chef wasn't around. When Jake did arrive, he had a smile on his face, said good morning, and then went into the office. He spent an hour on the computer reviewing financials from the past few weeks, and then time with the trail of salesman looking for this weeks orders. Around 11 he put on his chef coat and interacted with his prep cooks, tasting their food, reviewing recipes and cooking methods with them, and demonstrating some knife skill tricks. At 12:30 he took time to cook a light lunch for the staff. Shortly after, the evening crew began to arrive. Once again he smiled and gave each one a high five as they started their work. He reviewed prep for the night with Scott and at around 3 returned to the office to type up the menu insert of specials for the evening. He took off his chef coat, walked back to the kitchen and said, "You guys have been doing a great job so far, everyone in town is impressed and I want to thank you for taking our food seriously. Have a great night, I'll see you tomorrow." They were in shock. The chef was going home? The chef thanked them for doing great work. It took about an hour before everyone loosened up. Scott said, "OK, Chef is not here tonight but everything's the same. We have set a standard for this restaurant and it continues when the chef is here and when he's not. Let's knock it out of the park tonight."

The only person who knew that Carla and Jake were coming in for dinner was Lindsay. She was totally confident in the staff and felt at ease staying committed to treating the operators of this restaurant just like every other guest - exceptionally well.

Jake was nervous, but ten minutes into dinner he relaxed. The place looked great, the food was perfect and the service was warm, friendly and spot on. He suddenly felt a mix of relief and pride. He didn't see it, but Carla took him to school that night. Things would be different from this point on.

For the remainder of August and through the "leaf season," the restaurant continued firing on all cylinders. His approach with the staff had changed and everyone was extremely relieved. The kitchen crew looked forward to work and it showed in the food and how it was served. The Adirondack Enterprise and Plattsburgh Press Republican did wonderful reviews on the restaurant, pointing to Bayou as a new gem in the mountains.

As mid-October approached Jake and Carla were relieved they would be able to take a breath, but nervous about their first down season. They didn't have a real plan since they were shooting blind, but knew they'd have to either cut staff hours or lay off some of the employees they had come to appreciate and depend on. This would be a difficult education for the couple, something that in the past was always someone else's headache and heartache. Now it was theirs. If they did not play this right they could lose everything they had gained during an exceptional first summer.

CHAPTER TWENTY EIGHT

FALL-THE STRONG SURVIVE AND THE WEAK SHALL PERISH

Fall in the Adirondacks is truly spectacular. The colors from deep in the woods accented by the rocky crests of the high peaks, already covered by a dusting of snow, make for postcard pictures. The month of October draws visitors from all over the country, even overseas, to experience the vibrancy of the mountain paradise. It was difficult to deny some type of a grand design when you saw and felt the palate of colors, the sound of running water, morning fog nestled in the valleys, crisp mountain air, and an occasional family of deer darting through the woods looking for food and a safe haven from hunters. This part of the Adirondack experience made Carla and Jake feel truly alive and fortunate. By the third week in October the tourists were gone, and Northern New York was starting to settle in for a long winter.

As tourism begins to rest, so do the number of people in hotels and restaurants. The real test for Restaurant Bayou would be how well the locals supported this newcomer from November through May. The long stretch of sketchy business would receive a few short reprieves during Christmas Week, President's Week in February and weekends from December to March if enough snow fell for winter sports. Creating a steady diet of resident diners would be the focus of everything Jake and Carla did during this period of time.

Having talked with other area restaurateurs, the couple decided it would be best to close two nights per week instead of one. Sunday and Monday would be a reprieve for the staff of Bayou. Additionally, in preparation for the inevitable, Jake met with the kitchen staff and said, "We will try hard not to have any layoffs, but everyone should expect to have reduced hours." Many local kitchen employees are fine with this - more time to ski. Finally, even though many restaurants close for a period of time in April, Jake and Carla said they were going to hold off on a decision until they got a feel for how the winter looked. "Certain costs will continue whether we are open or not, so it might make sense to keep the doors open and generate some revenue, at least enough cash flow to pay our fixed expenses."

The last week in October saw restaurant sales drop considerably; nearly 50% less than the week prior. No one panicked, since it was the week everyone in the area caught their breath after tourists departed. When things didn't improve by mid-November, Jake and Carla became concerned. They'd accumulated some reserves over the summer and hadn't depleted their personal loan yet, but they could not foresee surviving if this lasted past December. They made an appointment with their bank to arrange a line of credit to help pull them through till June. The bank, based on their short-term positive sales picture, reluctantly agreed to a small line of $25,000 that the couple could draw from, and pay back at the current rate of interest. At least this gave the couple a bit of a cushion. They hoped not to use it, since it would need to be paid down fully within twelve months.

Thanksgiving was special in the Adirondacks. Jake and Carla's parents decided to come up to Saranac Lake to have dinner with their mountain restaurateurs. Bayou was closed for the day, leaving dining-out options to regional hotel restaurants that offered substantial buffets. Jake and Carla decided to have Thanksgiving at Bayou for their families and staff who were unable to go home for the holiday. The dining room was converted into a classic family table for 22 people to enjoy a Louisiana version of roast turkey dinner. The centerpiece was still American roast turkey and stuffing with Andouille sausage, but the complements included Cajun style planked salmon, spicy coleslaw, sweet potatoes with onions and jalapeno, Southern style hush puppies and fried green beans. Jake and Carla did all the cooking and the staff members, who were grateful for the invite, helped with set-up, service and cleanup afterward.

Jake spoke at the beginning of the meal, "This is a great day. I want to thank everyone for all of the support, hard work and patience you offered these past few months as Bayou got off the ground. We hit the ground running and haven't stopped. I know I have been difficult at times, and I am grateful you all put up with my nonsense. I know this restaurant has a great future with your continued help." He finished by raising his glass, "Most of all, I want to thank my incredible partner, and her family and mine for giving us this opportunity. Cheers." Everyone clinked glasses and passed around the substantial platters of incredible food.

The following day Bayou remained closed, not a great restaurant day anyway. After that, Carla and Jake were back at it.

As they approached the end of December Jake and Carla sat down with their accountant to review where the restaurant stood. Unfortunately, the news was not great. They had already depleted much of their reserves just trying to stay ahead of payroll, vendor invoices and rent. Taxes would be due and they would likely need to tap into their line of credit by the end of January. With five more slow months ahead of them, this news was disheartening. They had to make some difficult decisions as soon as possible, or face a financial hole that would be difficult to crawl out of.

After heart-wrenching discussions that evening they met with their staff to let them know there would be some layoffs at the end of January. Jake and Carla did not want to take any action over the holidays and thought giving staff some time to prepare would be a way to ease the blow.

Christmas week was a positive boost as sales were nearly as good as any week in August. This would buy them a little bit of time and maybe keep them away from the line of credit until February.

There hadn't been much snow activity yet, and Whiteface Mountain and local merchants were concerned. Little snow meant few skiers. No skiers meant an even softer off-season for sales. Compounding the problem was a somewhat warmer December than they'd had in recent years. When there was precipitation it was usually a mixture of light snow and freezing rain - not a good combination for a winter sports area.

What buffered the blow a bit was increased interest in Lake Placid due to the upcoming Winter Olympic Games in Sochi. Whenever the Winter Games took place, Lake Placid always received more interest from tourists and the press. Having hosted the 1932 and 1980 games, Placid was a place to feel the Olympic spirit without actually being where they were located.

By early January the weather had changed from unseasonably warm to bitter cold. The majority of days in January were below zero and often 20-30° below. Still, there was no sign of snow except a dusting on the sides of the road.

As the North Country continued to suffer through a deep freeze, the rest of the country was getting hit hard with snowstorm after snowstorm. During this early part of winter New York City, Philadelphia, Boston and as far south as Atlanta and Houston saw much colder temperatures (for them) and snow. It seemed as though weather patterns were turned upside down and inside out. The first week was written off as another anomaly, a pattern happening every few years, but by the third week in January it appeared this was something else. Could it be a result of the melting of polar ice caps, holes in the ozone layer and rising ocean levels? Right now, what was on Jake's mind was the fact that minimal snow meant even weaker business. People tend to be most concerned with what is right in front of them. The big picture of global weather change was not part of Jake's reality, at least not right now.

With weather patterns as they were, the domino effect took hold. Flights were canceled, making it even more difficult for people to travel on vacation, delivery of goods was delayed, making it challenging to get some of the supplies operators like Bayou required (especially the fresh fish from Florida and Louisiana), gasoline prices escalated again because stations had a difficult time getting deliveries, and the cost of keeping the restaurant heated, doubled. This was the proverbial perfect storm for business operators.

In spite of the weather, business at the restaurant was picking up. Carla attributed this to people tiring of being stuck in their homes trying to stay warm and wanting an opportunity to do something. The restaurant began offering more opportunities for neighbor gatherings by emphasizing their family table in the dining room. They hired Steve, a well-known local guitar player to keep people in the restaurant and were even toying with the idea of offering Bayou Meals-to-Go, if the gloomy weather patterns continued.

But one of the biggest events of the year was just around the corner. Saranac Lake hosts the oldest Winter Carnival in the country. The cold weather was good for preparations as volunteers built the annual Ice Palace with 300 pound blocks cut from the lake. It took dozens of dedicated workers to assemble thousands of blocks into the centerpiece of the Carnival. This year's building was spectacular with numerous carvings of dragons and armed Celtic soldiers. At night the Palace was lit with colored spots. At the beginning and end of Carnival week the castle would be stormed with fireworks.

This event was something Jake and Carla had no knowledge of before moving to Saranac Lake and it was a welcome lifesaver for the winter season. Carnival led right into President's week so February would turn out to be very strong for the restaurant. People came from all over the state to spend time in Saranac Lake and enjoy all of the local, and somewhat corny events, bringing the entire community out of their homes to watch or participate.

There was the coronation of the King and Queen of the Carnival, test of strength with the frying pan toss, curling, racing on snowshoes, rugby in knee-deep snow, snowshoe volleyball and of course, lining the streets of Saranac Lake for the foolish, but wonderful Winter Carnival Parade. Floats, fire trucks, marching bands and the famous Lawn Chair Ladies would entertain thousands of people from one end of town to the next.

The restaurant was packed almost every night from the last day of January until the third week in February. This, accompanied by the first real snowstorm of the season for the Adirondacks, made it possible for Bayou to avoid touching their line of credit; at least for now.

Carla was masterful at managing the finances of the operation and had decided to spend most of her time juggling funds to ensure vendors were paid fairly, payroll was met and rent was paid. She was even able to save some for the even slower times to come and managed to start paying her and Jake's parents back for their loan. So far, they were keeping their head above water.

Jake, with all of the increased stress of keeping the restaurant operational, was beginning to slip back to his dark side. He was again working six days per week, 15 hours a day, and had lost the balance Carla had helped to create. He kept thinking: if we can just hold on until June.

Carla decided to promote the opportunity for some in-house catered events, and offered these services to local organizations. This resulted in a few banquets in March allowing them to close the operation for a private dinner. Jake invited some chef friends to do guest spots and marketed them on the website and a newly started blog that Lindsay managed. These special dinners were well received and as a result March held its' own. They still had not touched the line of credit, and thus far, had been able to pay all their bills even though vendors were held at bay for 60 days.

In an effort to fight off any significant losses in the worst month of the year, Carla and Jake decided to close for three weeks in April. This gave their staff a chance for a much-needed vacation, and Carla and Jake time to regroup. At Carla's suggestion, Jake joined her for a week of rest and relaxation in New Orleans. They needed a break from the cold and knew Chef Hirsch would be a great advisor as they assessed what should be done to prepare for their second round at Bayou. April would be the first time they tapped into their line of credit just to keep the heat on and pay rent. They told Scott and Lindsay they would not be able to offer them a paid vacation this year, but hopefully that would change next year.

The tax accountant they were using offered them some good news, "With first year expenses in mind, the business won't owe any additional taxes for 2013 and your abysmal personal income was low enough to warrant a sizeable tax refund." They could use this to pay for their time in Louisiana. All things considered, the couple was happy with their survival skills during this very nerve-wracking off-season. Now they could relax a bit on their old New Orleans turf, enjoy some Zydeco music, break bread with their culinary friends and maybe even catch an early tan on the Gulf beaches.

When they returned it would be time to set a path for the future, build on their loose business plan from last year and map out a strategy for another year of ups and downs.

Jake and Carla had some deep discussions with Chef Hirsch about the restaurant's performance and even Jake's attitude. Chef Hirsch was again very helpful analyzing their performance and offering some personal stories about his own attitude adjustment as a restaurateur. Of real concern to Jake and Carla was the fear that Chef Hirsch expressed regarding the integrity of fresh fish supplies. He felt that restaurants would soon be feeling the pain of escalating prices for quality seafood.

After numerous great Louisiana dinners with many of their old co-workers, including a trip down memory lane at the Gumbo Shack, an informal concert by Aaron Neville at a bar in the French

Quarter, and a good dose of sunshine at the beach, the couple was refreshed and ready for round two in Saranac Lake.

CHAPTER TWENTY NINE

FISH STORIES

Something alarming had been occurring over the past few months to vendors and chefs. The Monterey Bay Aquarium was now recommending that any fish from the Pacific Northwest, Florida Gulf and some parts of the Northeastern waters near Nova Scotia be classified as inedible, all for different reasons. Recent tests disclosed high levels of cesium present in ocean fish common to waters between Northern Japan and the Pacific Northwest. This was a result of the nuclear disaster at Fukushima and the tsunami in 2011. Although there were mixed reactions to the data collected, the recommendation was strong enough that consumers began to shy away from Pacific fish of all types and inquire about the source before they ordered seafood in restaurants.

"There is evidence the radioactive water emanating from the plants starting two years ago has made its way into the ocean currents and will soon start to affect the ecosystems in North America as early as the spring of 2014.

Some say it is already here.

Reports are coming in that the North American food supply is already being affected by Fukushima.

Bluefin tuna caught off the San Diego coast is showing evidence of radioactive contamination. This is the first time that a migrating fish has been shown to carry radioactivity 3,000 miles from Fukushima to the U.S. Pacific coast. It is a nutrition source that accounts for approximately 20,000 tons of the world's food supply each year.

According to the <u>report</u> published by the National Academy of Sciences, 'We report unequivocal evidence that Pacific Bluefin tuna, Thunnus orientalis, transported Fukushima-derived radionuclides across the entire North Pacific Ocean.'"

The National Academy of Science

Adding to this was a new surge of oil tar washing up on the beaches of Louisiana and northwestern Florida. Since this oil spill residue was still present in the Gulf water, many feared it had not yet worked its way out of the ecosystem supporting the fishing industry. Finally, adding insult to injury, on-going concerns about mercury levels in fish off the coast of Nova Scotia continued to point to the need for consumers to modify consumption of fish from those waters.

This was devastating to restaurants focused on fresh seafood since they were now limited in availability of safe fish for their menus and prices surged due to demand that was greater than supply. Once the media took hold of the potential dangers of fish consumption, perceptions were set. Fear, even if it was proven to be over-blown, was always fueled by perception and not fact.

The supply and price issues created challenges for Jake and Carla who were in the process of preparing a new menu for the summer season. The new customer climate around fresh fish would not keep them from offering seafood, but they would need to be careful about sourcing. Carla and Jake would need to spend extra time and effort sharing factual information with their customers.

Carla did the research and was committed to being totally upfront with customers, and a trusted source of public information. The more she read, the more she wondered if this seafood problem was just the tip of the iceberg. Regardless of which side of the discussion you were on, there was enough scientific data to point to some areas of real concern when it came to American and world food supplies.

May business was OK, but nothing to brag about. They were barely paying their bills, and operating with a very small staff. Jake worked every shift, and Carla was doubling up with handling the finances and covering two shifts a week in the bakery working from 7 a.m. till close. They still had $8,000 of their credit line available and they desperately wanted to make it to the second week in June without dipping into that reserve again. Starting in June business would pick up substantially and Carla wanted to rebuild their reserves, finish paying back their parents, and pay the line of credit down to zero before the fall of 2014.

A key to maximizing sales during the summer months was to plan a menu that struck a positive chord with both locals and visitors. Last year's menu was well received, but emphasized many of the seafood items now imbedded in customer's minds as unfit. Carla decided to use the restaurant blog as a source of information for the menu that she and Jake would develop. She brought Lindsay into the fold since the blog was a piece of the business she managed. Collectively, they designed a campaign to be implemented in June. This would include the blog, press releases to local papers, a banner on the restaurant website, key designations on the menu referring to the source of fish, and the words, "Bayou Safe Fish". All of the servers and bartenders were to wear buttons that proclaimed, "Safe Fish – Ask Us."

As a public interest piece, WPTZ Television picked up on the campaign through a press release Carla sent to the media and did a cover story on how the local restaurant was approaching the issue of safe fish. This played very well into Carla's strategy. The stage was set for a very busy summer and as May was winding down, Carla and Jake began to build confidence.

Now, they had just one more significant issue to face; since staff hours had been cut dramatically over the past three months, a handful of quality team members had found new jobs in the area and told Jake they would be leaving before the end of June. Jake and his sous chef had to scramble to find replacements at the last minute. All told, they lost three of their five line cooks and two terrific servers. Lindsay said, "I am confident front of the house replacements will be found, but line cooks will be difficult, so close to the beginning of season." Jake decided to turn to regional schools and look for interns. In a last-minute scramble they were able to find two eager interns from the New England Culinary Institute in Vermont and one local line cook who was frustrated with his current employer. It would take some effort, but Jake felt they could train everyone and get the new staff up to speed fairly quickly. In the meantime, Jake would return to working the line with his staff during a time when the learning curve was steep.

It was now early June, the menu was complete, the marketing strategy in place, staff hired and last years remaining crew back to full-time. Financially, the line of credit had not been touched since early May and all vendors were current. Carla and Jake were ready to rock the food world in the Adirondacks.

CHAPTER THIRTY

SEASON TWO – LOADED FOR BEAR

What's most unsettling in the restaurant business are the fluctuations in business and customer volume. Once a restaurant team finds their rhythm, it is easier to be very busy than slow. The Adirondacks, like any other seasonal tourist community dependent on weather does not ease into its' busy season. One day, it is painfully slow, and the next day you're beyond capacity.

June in the Adirondacks kicks off with two events: first, the Lake Placid Horseshow arrives, bringing a thousand horses and all the people who support the animals in competition, and school lets out for summer. During the first week of June, Bayou was serving, on average, around 40 dinners each night, the third weekend in June that number jumped to 175. From this point on, every night would be as busy as they could handle.

The seafood campaign Carla and Lindsay had developed seemed to be working. They also printed takeaway menus for guests who wanted them, with links to their blog and website, as well as for the Monterey Bay Aquarium site. Lindsay's new service staff hit the ground running and her skill at training was evident. Back of the house was a little sloppy at first as Jake quickly realized that although the interns he hired had great attitudes and solid foundational skills, they needed considerable coaching when it came to handling serious numbers on the line. They would come around, but in the meantime Jake would need to stay on the line a bit longer. His typical shift was back to when the restaurant first opened. He arrived at 7 a.m. and worked until close six days per week. At first, he was fine with this; in fact, after suffering through the slow season, this seemed like fun.

Aside from some timing issues with getting the food out guests were again happy with the menu, and the attentiveness of the service staff. Lindsay was pleased to see her regulars return for dinner, sometimes every week. Everything had come together, and everyone was confident season two would be even better.

One thing that was disconcerting was the price paid for the fresh fish that fit the restaurant's guidelines as safe. In some cases the restaurant was paying prices 50% higher than the previous season. The dilemma all restaurants face in this situation is how to approach the problem. They could raise prices, cut quality, reduce portion sizes, eliminate the costly items, or grin and bear it, leaving everything as it was and hoping prices would eventually go down. Since Jake and Carla were not ready to gamble, they chose to raise prices and explain the reason on their blog.

The result was almost instantaneous. Guests stopped buying the items priced higher, and began complaining about a greedy pricing structure. This, of course, could unravel everything the restaurant had worked to build. So, Carla came up with a radical idea to keep from losing the trust and support of their steady customers.

Bayou immediately offered a neighborhood discount card. All residents of Saranac Lake, Lake Placid and the surrounding region were offered an opportunity to join the Bayou Neighbor Program, entitling them to a 10% discount at the restaurant without limitations. Members simply had to visit the restaurant and fill out a short form including their email address, name and town of residence. A member card would be sent to them within ten days. In addition, there would be a handful of events throughout the year including beer and wine tastings and even new menu item testing receptions. All members would be invited to attend free-of -charge. As the program was introduced at

Bayou, on their website, and blog, Carla also included an apology, not for the price increase, but for the way it was handled.

"To our loyal guests: in recent months the cost of fresh seafood has increased dramatically. This is due to recent scares about the safe consumption of certain species and the supply and demand of those considered safe. Bayou did not want to sacrifice quality so we decided to raise our prices. We now feel the manner with which we made this change was a mistake and for that, we apologize. Your business is very important to us so Jake and I have decided to reward your loyalty with this discount program. There are no immediate limitations on this, as long as you are a local resident, the discount applies. Again, please accept our apology and stick with us through this challenging time."

After a few weeks of lackluster business (something they could not afford) guests returned in even larger numbers to become members, thank the restaurant for their response, and to enjoy the great food and service Bayou had a reputation for. What started as a significant problem turned into a positive step in solidifying community support.

Over time, Jake had managed to train the staff and although he could now step off the line, continued to put in the same mind-numbing, backbreaking hours.

The summer was much hotter than usual in the Adirondacks. Typically, the area might see a week or two of temperatures in the eighties, but rarely more, and rarely much hotter. July's average temperature was 91 and it hadn't rained in over three weeks. The Department of Environmental Conservation (DEC) issued a high fire warning, instituted a ban on campfires, and even suggested people refrain from hiking in areas that were bone dry.

People in the Adirondacks were not used to these temperatures, so everyone's demeanor was pretty gritty. Temperatures and humidity in the kitchen made working conditions close to unbearable and tempers were always on edge.

Customers still flocked to the restaurant but did not seem as friendly as in the past. The saving grace was the air conditioning Carla had insisted upon in the dining room, something very rare in the Adirondacks. Carla wasn't sure if guests were coming for the food or for the cool dining room. Either way, they were busy.

The temperature, change in the staff's attitude, long hours, and constant worries about finances were taking a toll on Jake. Everyone could see it, especially Carla. The kitchen staff sensed Jake had slipped back to the dark side, and was even closer to flipping out than he was the previous year. Gone were the mornings when he would arrive with a smile and greeting for his staff. The compliments didn't come any more and quite often Jake would pound his fist on the table or throw a hot pan across the kitchen bouncing it off the wall as it splashed into the pot sink. Jake even berated vendors to the point where they didn't want to stop in unless Carla was there.

Jake lost 15 pounds from the heat and lack of a reasonable diet, more often than not didn't bother to shave, or comb his hair. His uniforms, once a source of pride for Jake, began to look like they had been slept in. It was just a matter of time before he would melt down.

The restaurant continued to break budget expectations, and Carla was able to build a nice cushion in the bank. By the end of July she had paid back her and Jake's parents and, as hoped, the line of credit was paid back in full, allowing them to access the full line again (if necessary) when the slow season was upon them. One glimmer of positive energy happened in early August when Carla told Jake they had already exceeded budget by $75,000, and she felt that it was time to reward the staff. The two agreed to split $15,000 of their reserve among the 23 employees on the payroll. Rather than use any complicated formula they decided to treat everyone as an important member of the team and split the money equally. During the second week of August each staff member from sous chef to dishwasher, bartender to server received a bonus check for $650. This caught everyone by surprise as Carla handed out the checks, saying, "We're in this together and Jake and I are so grateful for your contribution." The entire crew broke into applause, giving each other high fives and some even hugging Carla (no one felt comfortable offering the same type of affection to Jake). Additionally, Jake and Carla called their sous chef and Lindsay into the office and told them each would receive two weeks paid vacation this year once the season had settled down.

But the euphoric feeling in the operation only lasted a few days when Jake finally lost control and caused everyone to question his or her tolerance of this behavior.

CHAPTER THIRTY ONE

THE CHEF LOSES CONTROL

The following weekend started normally. Bayou did not take reservations, neither had the original Casa del Sol, however, business had been so consistent lately that the kitchen and dining room were confident Friday and Saturday would push near 200 covers. Everyone in the kitchen was busy with mise en place: mincing shallots and scallions, slicing garlic, peeling and deveining shrimp, making remoulade, simmering stock for gumbo and filleting fish for the evening's features. As was always the case, the early shift took care of the heavy prep and the evening crew worked on details.

Jake had arrived at 7 a.m. just like every other day. Deliveries had been arriving since the back door opened and Jake was checking quality on everything. He would check the eyes and gills on whole fish, weigh every piece of meat, open cases of vegetables and fruit and look at the bottom layer, cut open a sample orange or lime to make sure they were moist and not suffering from storage burn and even count the potatoes that were sold by case count. Drivers hated him, but respected his attention to detail. They always made sure the product delivered to Bayou was in good shape; if they didn't, Jake could be relentless.

Nobody knew exactly what set him off, but out the corner of her eye Carla saw Jake pick up a case of produce and throw it at the driver. The driver gave Jake the finger and drove off. Jake returned to the kitchen with eyes on fire. From that moment on, nothing in the kitchen was right. He turned to the prep cooks, "I want all of this vegetable prep re-done. All of your vegetable cuts are crap." He tasted the stock, "This is shit!" Jake even lit into the dishwasher when he picked up a pan that still had some visible carbon on the bottom. Everyone kept their head down and Carla simply rolled her eyes and kept working on payroll for the end of the week.

When the evening crew arrived, he started in on them. "I can't believe you are working with dull knives. I thought you guys knew what you were doing. Your stations are a mess and nowhere near as clean as they should be." Jake went after the sous chef for the way he was mincing shallots and slicing garlic and even how fast he and his staff were walking from point A to point B. When Carla told him to lighten up, he looked at her with daggers in his eyes, "Mind your own business, Carla, this is my kitchen." She stormed back to the office rather than get into a confrontation in front of the staff.

As service began he was still walking around like a man obsessed with anything and everything. Then it happened, an early order was returned from the dining room. The fish was overcooked. He barked at the line cook, pointing his finger at him, "I'll fire you if you don't shape up." When a second order came back it looked as if he was going to leap over the line and grab the very distressed cook. When the sous chef tried to hold

Jake back he was physically pushed aside. The kitchen became very silent. Jake looked at his sous chef with gritted teeth and finally turned and walked towards the office. He was in a rage and walked to the office area, cocked his fist and slammed it into the wall. He yelled in pain and fell to his knees. Carla ran from the office only to find Jake with a bright red face, grimacing in pain. His fist was already swollen to twice its size as the kitchen looked on in disbelief.

Carla asked one of the cooks to help her get Jake in the car. She drove to the Emergency Room of Adirondack Medical Center. Carla didn't say a word on the way, while Jake held his hand and wept in pain. They waited a few minutes in the Emergency Room while a bed became free and then after a quick exam Jake was sent for X-Rays. It was quickly determined that his hand was indeed broken. They gave him painkillers, set-up an IV and proceeded to set his hand in a cast. The hospital would keep him overnight and the doctor told Carla he would be in the cast for at least eight weeks, and then would likely need physical therapy to regain full use.

The next day when Carla took him home, Jake remained silent. "Jake, I am extremely disappointed in you and your staff is in shock. You will need to think about how to approach them." He agreed to stay home for the day after Carla told him the restaurant was operating just fine without him. She even added, "Right now it's functioning better without you."

That day Carla worked a full shift. She found it telling that no one asked her how he was doing. It was as if they didn't care. When she arrived home after closing, Jake was asleep in the living room with an empty bottle of wine by his side.

The following day he was awake at his normal time and had already left for the restaurant before Carla had even gotten out of bed. The two had not talked since driving home from the hospital. Carla walked to the kitchen, and saw that Jake had left without a word. After a few minutes of reflection, Carla picked up a piece of paper and a pen.

Jake arrived at the restaurant before anyone else and parked himself in the office. No one acknowledged him when they arrived for work, even when he walked around the kitchen and quietly inspected their work. He never said a word to the staff except his sous chef, to whom he said, "Sorry for the other day." Jake spent most of the day and night in the office wondering when Carla would arrive. He knew he had to talk with her, but didn't know what to say. His performance was inappropriate at best. He hoped she would understand and forgive him.

CHAPTER THIRTY TWO

CARLA

As Jake arrived at the house he noticed all the lights were out and Carla's car was gone. He wondered where she might be as he turned the key in the locked door. Jake flipped on the light and went to the kitchen to make a cup of coffee. On the counter was a note from Carla.

"Dear Jake, I want you to know that I love you dearly, more than I ever thought possible. We have experienced many wonderful things together, but I see a terrible change in you. I cannot face watching you spiral down, alienating your staff, and turning on me and ruining all of those great memories. I have thought long and hard about this and have decided to leave. Lindsay is fully capable of taking care of the financial parts of the business and the pastry team is quite independent. Don't bother trying to find me. I hope you are able to turn yourself around and find peace and enjoyment in your wonderful skill as a chef. Be well. Love, Carla."

His knees got weak and he grabbed a chair before collapsing. This couldn't be, Carla would never leave him. How could she do this? What am I going to do? Oh, my God, Carla is gone. A wave of emotions gripped him at that moment and be began to sob uncontrollably. She was the most important person in his life, the person who gave waking up in the morning meaning, his partner in business and in life, his best friend. What had he done? This was his fault. How can he go on? He must get her back, somehow.

Jake paced for hours trying to figure out what to do. There must be a way. As he worked things over in his mind he began to realize that nothing was important without her. The restaurant was meaningless, the details consuming his every minute at work seemed trivial, his professional dreams as a chef all but melted away. It was, and always would be about Carla. Now, she was gone. Where could she have gone? How can I find her?

At some point Jake fell asleep for a few hours. When he woke his hand was throbbing, as was his head. It took a few moments before the reality hit once again. It was the first time in years that he woke up without Carla beside him. The house was so lonely, so empty. Jake needed to make a plan; he must do whatever he could to find Carla. With a sense of urgency and an adrenaline boost he jumped into the shower, careful not to get his cast wet, shaved and threw on some clothes. It was 6:30 in the morning and he was prepared to search for the love of his life. He was starting to think clearly and knew he would have to take care of some business at the restaurant first. He called Scott and Lindsay and asked them to meet at the restaurant as soon as they could. They arrived at 8 a.m. to find Jake in the dining room with his cellphone and a half empty cup of coffee. They sat at the table with him and waited.

Jake looked up and thanked them for coming. He began, "First I've had time to reflect and want to apologize as sincerely as possible for my behavior, for creating undo stress in the restaurant, for not showing the right level of respect for you both and for putting you in a terrible position with our staff. I know it will be difficult for everyone to accept what I say, but I hope we can start to mend our relationship. I do have enormous respect for both of you and for our staff and want to stress once again how sorry I am." He went on for another moment trying to paint a picture of the stress he brought on himself and how it consumed his every moment, to the point where he lost control. Scott interjected, "Chef, we understand how difficult it is to operate a restaurant and you need to know everyone wants to meet your expectations." In his heart Jake knew this, "Thanks Scott, but nothing can justify how I acted."

Jake went on, "Now I need to ask for your understanding, patience and help. Because of my stupidity and insensitive behavior, the most important person in my life has left. When I returned home last night I found a note from Carla stating she was leaving me, the restaurant, and the Adirondacks behind." He paused for a moment to keep his emotions in check, "I don't know where she is and I feel my life has suddenly lost all meaning. I am afraid that I do not know how to go on without her and must, even if I fail, do everything I can to find her, make amends and bring her back. So, I need to ask you a question and for a monumental favor." Scott and Lindsay were not prepared for what Jake was about to say, "First, if either of you have any idea where she might be, I beg you to share the information. Secondly, I have decided to dedicate my time to finding her and winning her back, so I am asking the two of you to operate the restaurant for as long as this might take."

They looked on as Jake continued, "Lindsay, Carla mentioned in her note that you have an understanding of the financial aspect of running the restaurant. And Scott, I know your standards for our food are as solid as mine, so I fully trust that you can both handle things. I will have my cellphone and can be reached if you need advice, but my time will be spent looking for Carla. I hope you accept this challenge and understand where my efforts need to be."

Lindsay began, "Jake, you have been a complete ass for months, but you must know that we love and respect you, at least the old you, and will do whatever you need. I don't have any idea where Carla is, she didn't share this decision with me. I am shocked, but not surprised based on how much she cared for you and how hard it has been for her to watch you fall apart." Scott jumped in, "Chef, I have known and worked with you since Buffalo. I'm with you through thick and thin. Go find Carla and don't worry about the restaurant; we'll give it our heart and soul and maintain your standards for as long as it takes." They both rose and gave Jake a hug. "Please explain things to the staff any way you feel comfortable. I will stop by the landlord's house and let him know what is going on, and tell him that any communication regarding the restaurant should be directed to both of you."

Jake picked up a few items from the office, returned to his apartment and started making some calls. First, he contacted Carla's parents. They were rather cold on the phone, "Jake, we know of Carla's decision, and understand she is safe, but she didn't even tell us where she is." He called Carla's cellphone but it went automatically to a voice mail message. Jake called his parents and once again cried as he explained what he'd done to drive Carla away and how much she meant to him. His parents were supportive and told him they would do whatever they could to help.

Jake no longer had a car. He sold his when they were in New Orleans and never felt the need to have two cars in Saranac Lake since their apartment was so close to the restaurant. Driving would be very difficult anyway with his cast, but he needed to try. He asked Lindsay to drive him to the Saranac Lake/Lake Clear airport to rent a car, gave her a key to the apartment, packed his bags and computer, took a few thousand dollars out of his bank account (noting that Carla had only taken a small amount of money herself and left the rest for him), took the address book Carla had left, and set out to visit with her friends on the east coast to see if he could find her.

Over the next three weeks Jake traveled to Western New York and stopped in on friends in Buffalo and Rochester, touched base again with her parents, drove on to Albany and Hyde Park to visit a few of her old friends from the CIA and looped through Connecticut and Pennsylvania to touch base with a few of her uncles and cousins in hopes they would know something. In the end, he was no further ahead than he was the day she left. Carla was gone and apparently did not want to be found. Jake's life was changed, this time not for the better. For the first time in years he would need to find his way without Carla.

After three weeks on the road Jake returned to Saranac Lake. Lindsay had only called once regarding an issue with the bank, but otherwise he hadn't heard a thing from his two key players. When Jake walked into the restaurant, his staff turned one-by-one and said, "Good morning Chef." Whatever Scott had told them the unspoken understanding was that he was forgiven. His employees were glad he was back. Lindsay met him in the office and spent an hour updating him on the business. The restaurant was doing great. Sales were even better than before and guest comments continued to be very positive. When she finished, Jake opened up, "I will be dedicating the next few months to ensuring all bills are paid, the initial loan with the bank is satisfied, and a solid strategy put in place for the fall, winter and spring when business will drop off." When that was done he said, "I would like to offer you and Scott the opportunity to take over the business." He would be walking away one-way or the other. His heart was not in it now that Carla was gone from his life. "I hope you will accept and if so, I will spend time with the landlord and the bank to make the legal arrangements for transfer of business ownership." If they did not want Bayou, he would understand, but he would look for someone else. Jake was mentally and emotionally gone from the business already.

Lindsay hugged him as a dear friend, "I am sorry this has happened. I will talk with Scott and we will need to give your offer some thought." Jake only spent a few hours in the office pulling together all of their contracts, loans, and legal papers to work on back at the apartment. His mind was made up; within a couple of months he would be leaving Saranac Lake and this chapter of his life.

PART FIVE

THE ONLY THING CERTAIN IN LIFE IS CHANGE

"Time passes, things change, but memories will
always stay where they are, in the heart."
Sarah Moores

CHAPTER THIRTY THREE

TRANSITIONING OWNERSHIP AND MOVING ON

The next two months passed quickly as the second season for Bayou was winding down. Jake made sure all outstanding debt from the original personal loan was cleared, and accounts payable with vendors was up to date. It was a great summer for the restaurant, providing a sizeable cushion for the operation to help carry them through the winter. Lindsay and Scott took Jake up on his offer, with one stipulation; "Jake, we insist you hang on to a ten percent equity position in the operation. This was, after all, your and Carla's dream that brought the restaurant to fruition."

Jake worked with the new partners, the bank and landlord to ensure the transition was seamless. The bank even agreed to continue a line of credit so Lindsay could access funds to carry the operation through the slow season (if needed). By the end of October it was done. Jake was free to move on with his life and decide what was next.

The crew of the restaurant threw a big party for Jake on his last day. He was grateful for their caring thoughts, but his heart was not in it. His heart ached for Carla and the life they had together. Since his focus on the restaurant was done he needed to think about what he would do and where he would go.

The next day he took a hike through a portion of the Adirondack High Peaks, winding up at the top of Algonquin Mountain. As he looked out at the magnificent vista of mountaintops and colorful leaves, he had a fleeting thought of just getting lost in the woods and simply letting nature take its course. The feeling passed quickly as the survival instincts that had carried him this far in life took control. He would move on, and somehow find his way.

Back at the apartment he began to pack without a clue as to where he might end up. As he mindlessly packed, he mulled over his options. He could go back to Buffalo, but that just seemed too much like giving up. He could certainly go back to New Orleans, but he couldn't face the thought of feeling like a failure. In the end, Jake knew it was important to break away from his history and go in another direction. He knew he could always get a job in a kitchen, so it was not an issue of income. The real question was where he would go to try and forget.

Jake sat down and pulled out a pad (he always thought better when he itemized pros and cons of a decision). As he made a list of potential destinations it became clear to him that a large city would be a good place to get lost. Cities always had jobs for cooks, and would take him far away from the experience of being in the Adirondacks, where his memories were so painful. He chose New York City, the center of the universe, and a place so large, everyone became anonymous. He remembered the stories of many celebrities who said New York was the place where all people were equal and no one stood out in a crowd.

He would travel to New York by train, spend a few days looking for an apartment and job and then ask some friends to bring down his possessions. He gave away most of his furniture, feeling it was important to travel light. His Saranac Lake apartment was paid for through the end of the year and thanks to Carla he had a few thousand dollars in his savings account - enough to get settled in the city. A few days later he was en route to Penn Station and the next phase of his life.

Jake had only been to New York twice before. He wasn't sure where to start, but picked up a copy of the New York Post and started looking for apartments. He spent the next two days taking the subway from apartment to apartment until he landed a tiny studio in Lower Manhattan. The apartment was furnished, so it was easy to settle in.

After paying his first month's rent and security deposit, Jake still had enough money to survive, maybe a month, so he hit the streets looking for a job. As down as he was, the thought of working in a great NYC restaurant was exciting. He bought a copy of the Zagat Guide and read through the book, circling those restaurants close to his apartment rated as "up and coming." He knew enough about these name restaurants to realize that there would be a waiting list of great cooks hoping to land a job there. Jake thought it was best to look at ones that had potential, but weren't there yet. As he started the cold call process of dropping off resumes, he conditioned himself to only look for a job as a line cook. Jake did not have any desire to be a chef again, at least not for quite some time.

On his second day of job hunting, Jake walked into a restaurant called Lust. It was a relative newcomer, but had received very high ratings in Zagat from guests. The food was rated 25 and service a 24. These were the same marks you would find in operations like Le Bernadin and Aquavit, so Jake was intrigued. Lust was only open for dinner, so when he walked in the back door (chefs are accustomed to always using the staff entrance) he ran into the chef. Jake introduced himself, "Chef, I just moved to the city, have substantial experience and really want to find a restaurant on the move where the food is of consummate importance." Jake just wanted to cook with people as passionate as him. The chef pointed Jake in the direction of the espresso machine, "Help yourself to an espresso. We can meet in the dining room in a few minutes." Since Jake was pretty much addicted to espresso, this was a welcome start to the interview process.

The dining room had the feel of an old world, Wall Street male with lots of wood and brass. A bistro complete with a mural behind the bar depicting the lust for food, two hundred dollar bottles of wine, 12-year single malt scotch, beautiful women and money. Jake could picture lots of Brooks Brothers suits, expensive dresses from Saks, illegal Cuban cigars, and American Express Black Cards when the restaurant was in full operation.

The important thing to Jake would be the food. He gazed at the menu while waiting for the chef and was pleased to see a mix of high- quality steakhouse fare, and contemporary items similar to what he worked with at Spice in New Orleans. He could be comfortable working with this menu.

The chef arrived, "Sorry to keep you waiting. It's a pleasure to meet you Jake, my name is Andre." The chef was a towering figure, easily six-foot three, broad shoulders like a Rugby player, long hair for a chef in New York, and a contemporary ponytail. Jake guessed that he was probably in his late thirties.

Andre looked over Jake's resume and asked a few questions about working with Chef Hirsch and the dynamic of being so close to the great seafood of the Bayou. Then came the big question, "Why would you leave your own restaurant, that according to the info on your resume was successful, to come and work in NYC as a line cook?" Jake didn't hold back; he told his story. One thing that heartbreak leaves you with is a "what the hell, here you have it" feeling when talking with others. He felt this was the only logical answer to the chef's question anyway.

Chef Andre nodded and said, "It's ironic, just yesterday one of my key line people left without notice. I have an immediate opening." The chef went on, "Normally, I would ask someone to trail before hiring, but I am willing to offer you a trial-by-fire if you can start tonight." Jake said, "Sure thing chef, I can be back in an hour with my uniform and knives. I'm comfortable with the menu items, but will likely struggle a bit until I learn your system." The chef understood, and was staffed enough for the next two nights to allow Jake to shadow, more than own a station. Jake would be starting on grill, handling the important steak and chop portion of the menu. Most of the steaks were Wagyu beef, product that cost over $35 per pound, and due to extensive marbling of fat, a little different to cook than USDA Prime. Jake shook the chef's hand, "Thanks for the opportunity."

Jake literally ran back to his apartment to change, put a quick edge on his knives and returned to the kitchen within the hour.

This was a good sign - things might just turn out OK for him in the Big Apple.

CHAPTER THIRTY FOUR

BACK IN THE SADDLE – THE LINE COOK IS REBORN

Jake quickly picked up on the mise en place for his station. His first night was a Wednesday and unlike some places where he had worked, in New York, well-received restaurants like Lust couldn't tell the difference between a Wednesday and a Friday night. In fact, if there was a slower night in the city it would be Saturday since many of the office workers were home for the weekend. On this particular night, he had the luxury of shadowing a line cook who had been at Lust for over a year, and was fairly adept at the grill station. Jake took notes on the mise en place for future reference, watched plate presentations early on and the "order-fire" system used by the chef. By 7:30, Jake had taken over the grill without the operation losing a step. This, of course, impressed the other cooks and the chef. His first night in a new kitchen, with new menu, grilling Wagyu beef that was more challenging to cook just right, but not a single order came back. It was obvious Jake had his act together, and had enough confidence in his abilities, that the chef knew he was a great hire.

By the end of that first week, Jake was a solid performer, and had the menu and plate presentations imbedded in his subconscious. It felt good to be back on a line cooking, because the great thing about line work is that you can't think about anything else. The orders and timing demand your full attention.

For the first time in months, Jake was able to take his mind off of Carla and become totally wrapped up in his second love: cooking.

The routine of the line was just what Jake needed. The menu was excellent, but the cooking was pretty straightforward stuff. His shift began at 2:30, and wound up ending around midnight. As in the past, Jake was usually at work by 1 p.m. (off the clock) so he could get a feel for the kitchen on any given day, ensure his product was ready and help out wherever he could. His day began around 7 a.m. when he woke up, showered, took care of basics like laundry and bill paying, drank a few cups of coffee from his Keurig, watched a bit of CNN and went for a walk around lower Manhattan. Inevitably he wound up at Abraco, a place where many restaurant workers hung out for their espresso fix. He might pick up a sandwich or soup at a local deli and then walk into work shortly after. His shift typically ended at around midnight with station cleanup, although in New York he found people had a different interpretation of "dinner hour" and might meander in to Lust as late as 11 p.m. looking to start their dinner. Whatever time he finished he would shuffle down the street to an open bar for a late night drink before hitting his pillow by 1 a.m. – give or take. There was less and less time to think about anything but work except on his day off, which was typically Monday, and if the chef was feeling generous, maybe a Sunday as well.

Jake was not fond of days off since he always wound up thinking about Carla. The first month he was in New York he tried calling her cell a couple times each week, but it always went to voicemail. It was obvious she was screening him out. He had tried to stay in touch with her parents, but they also rarely picked up and when they did he received the same lack of information, "Sorry Jake, we don't know where she is, but she is fine. No need to worry. Maybe it is time for you to let her go and move on."

There had been some sporadic communication with Lindsay at Bayou. They were struggling through the off-season, but making ends meet. Locals were still happy with the food. She and Scott had not tapped into the line of credit yet, and even though hours had been cut, their entire crew was still intact. By Christmas time those phone calls from Saranac Lake had all but ended.

Christmas in New York was busier than normal. Shoppers lined the streets from Central Park South to Macy's on 34th street, and throughout SoHo and the Village. The restaurant was cranking every night, which Jake enjoyed. It took his mind off the holidays and the fact that he would be spending them alone, without Carla. Every night the restaurant would turn the dining room two to three times, hitting 200-plus covers. It was relentless.

Christmas Day, the restaurant was closed, giving staff a chance to be with family. One day off was not enough for Jake to travel to Buffalo and he had not been at the restaurant long enough to ask for three or four days off to visit family. Jake was alone in his apartment for Christmas. He made the cursory call to his parents, tried Carla again with no response, and wound up inviting a bottle of good wine as his only guest. A movie marathon pulled him through the night.

Back to the restaurant the day after, Jake was so grateful to be at work and out of that lonely apartment. It was a slow night so the chef left early and asked Jake to expedite while the last handful of customers was served. Jake asked if he could stay after service and work on a couple of new entrée ideas he had. The chef agreed and tossed Jake a key to lock up when he was done. This was a good restaurant, not one that would be setting the tone for food in the next year, but a solid operation with consistently good food and service. The chef was respectful of the staff, not a yeller/screamer and always a good listener. Jake was content, if only he didn't have to go back to that apartment.

Line skills are something a cook builds with time. Jake already had his chops and knew what it took to be successful at the position. First and foremost a line cook needed to be organized.

A cook's mise en place is everything. Everything has a place and everything in its place is part of every cook's daily routine. This goes down to how many side towels they have and how they are folded. If you are sufficiently prepped and organized you can handle any crowd. Second, the cook must know every step of how each menu item is prepared and exactly how it should taste. He or she must, through the process of cooking, ALWAYS taste as they work to ensure they trigger the flavor memory appropriately. Finally, the line cook must be totally in the zone. They must listen for everything: the chef's order-call, the sizzle of the pan (you can hear when a pan is ready), the communication with other cooks and the clink of a plate that is ready to receive the components of a menu item. If a cook gets out of the "zone," all is lost. If they allow themselves to be distracted, then the system will unravel. Jake knew this, it was part of his being, and he didn't need to think about it anymore than he needed to think about breathing.

Jake loved to watch the kitchen gear up and kick into motion when the orders started flying in. "Ordering; Three Wagyu, two mid-rare, one black and blue; two fillets, one rare, one medium." Jake would call back, "Yes, Chef." The cadence would continue; "Fire- Two pork chops, medium; one veal chop, mid-rare; one lamb rack for two, rare." Again he replied: "Yes, chef." Similar directives would fly to the appetizer station and sauté, as the printer seemed to spit out orders in rapid succession. This would start around 6 p.m. and not cease until well after 10 p.m.

When on the line, time would either stand still on the occasional slow night, or fly by, as was the case during Christmas week. Before they knew it, it would be 10:30 and nearly time to start breaking down, making tomorrow's prep lists, and cleaning up. Jake loved this. He enjoyed the banter, the military-style organization, the sense of team that was so necessary, the sweat streaming down his back, a clatter of plates, the chef's cadence and control over timing, and even the occasional burn; it made him feel alive. The adrenaline high that came from working a line was like nothing else. Those who have never experienced it are definitely missing out. Jake's only drug, unlike some of his fellow cooks, was the natural high of the kitchen tempo and way too many double espressos.

Jake spent another hour in the kitchen that night, working through two new entrees he wanted to pitch to the chef. Obviously, they had a New Orleans influence because it was what he knew so well. If not on the menu, maybe the chef would at least try them as a nightly feature. Anyway, he was grateful for the opportunity to spend some time alone in the kitchen, just him and the stove. An open flame was his best friend now, something that did not judge, was there whenever he needed it allowing Jake to express himself through his craft.

Slowly, very slowly, Jake was beginning to come out of his terrible funk. Maybe he could someday forget and move on, just not yet.

CHAPTER THIRTY FIVE

OPPORTUNITY COMES WHETHER YOU WANT IT OR NOT

Jake had been at Lust Restaurant for six months. During this time he had moved from Grill to Sauté, and from Garde Manger to Butchering. In a short period of time, he demonstrated the capability to do just about anything in the restaurant. His skills were as strong as Chef Andre had seen in anyone who worked at

Lust, and the rest of the staff liked and respected him. Jake won everybody over in a short period of time.

Jake was content and began spending even more time in the restaurant. He wasn't sure whether it was because he was needed or the simple fact he did not want to be alone in his apartment. The restaurant was gaining even more recognition for not only their standard menu, but also the new creative New Orleans style influence creeping into their repertoire. In mid-June the chef called Jake into his office and asked him to have a seat.

Up to this point Jake had been an hourly employee. This was fine with him since he made enough money to pay his bills. He had no intention of seeking a raise. The chef began, "Jake, you are doing a great job. I am impressed with your commitment to the restaurant, and the contributions to the diversity of our menu. I will be placing you on salary with a benefit package including health care and a two-week paid vacation." Jake was surprised but grateful. The chef went on, "Jake, what is most significant to me is the level of respect the rest of the staff has for you, and the way you handle yourself. The kitchen crew looks up to you as a leader." The restaurant was getting busier all of the time and Chef Andre had been thinking seriously about creating a sous chef position. "I would like to offer a sous chef position to you. Whether you accept it or not, the salary and benefits will still apply, but I would really like to have you serve as my restaurant partner in crime." Jake was quiet for a moment. He had not wanted to do anything but cook. He had mixed feelings about taking on the responsibility of a supervisor of others again. It hadn't worked out well for him in Saranac Lake and he was fearful he might find himself in a downward spiral once again. He looked at the chef and explained, "Chef, I am honored, but have some concerns about jumping into management after my last series of challenges in Saranac Lake." He finished with a handshake and told the chef he just wanted to think about it for a couple days. The chef understood and said, "I would like your answer by the end of the week or I will need to start looking for other candidates."

Once again, Jake used his foolproof method of decision-making. He pulled out a legal pad, a pencil, and began to list the pros and cons. On the negative side, his fear of seeing dark Jake appear again was strong. His experiences in Saranac Lake had left a bitter taste in his mouth and he wasn't sure he was ready to take another stab at supervising others. Otherwise, the positives were evident; he would have a chance to help the restaurant move forward, his style of cooking would find another portal for expression, he would be able to learn from yet another chef about how to operate a successful restaurant. After all, he would not be the person with final decisions on his shoulders - that was the chef's job.

The following day Jake arrived at work and went right to the chef's office. "Chef, I gave it plenty of thought and decided I would be honored to work with you as a sous chef, if the offer still stands." The chef responded with a smile, "Jake, I am happy you have decided to accept my offer. Please, from now on when we are in my office you can call me Andre. We can reserve the formalities for the face we put on in the kitchen. Let's say that this will go into effect next week. In the meantime, I will let the staff know. Welcome on board, Chef Jake!"

Jake's new role would require managing the kitchen schedule, setting-up prep sheets for each station, placing orders with salesmen and regional farmers and taking weekly inventories. This would be in addition to his work as evening expeditor, trainer, and occasional fill-in on a cook's days off. He was familiar with all of these tasks so the learning curve would be short. Most important to Jake was the ability to work seasonally with the chef on building new menus, creating dishes and finalizing recipes. He was ready, more than ready.

Once a cook has a taste of running the show it is very difficult to give it up. Jake was starting to realize this as he began his new position. It felt good to be a decision maker and a leader. He wrote a crisis plan for himself and modeled it after a story he heard about the great chef Escoffier. As the tale goes, Escoffier (known as the king of chefs and chef of kings) had a pretty serious temper, and was a perfectionist with little patience for anyone not as serious about food as he. Whenever he felt his temper rising to the boiling point, Escoffier would walk away, step outside, count to ten and take a deep breath. If need be, he would walk a few blocks to loosen up and put things in perspective. Jake was determined to keep himself in check.

When he walked into the kitchen on that first day as sous chef he already knew things had changed. As he approached the prep station the morning cook looked up and instead of saying "Hey Jake" he smiled and said "Good morning chef." Jake patted him on the back and simply nodded.

Jake pulled up a cutting board and asked the cook what he could help with. Jake picked up fabricating the steaks and chops for the night, doing so with the touch of a professional butcher. Every steak he put on the scale was on the money even after trim. He tasted the soup and made a few suggestions, turned down the steam on the stock to keep it from agitating too much, scrubbed down his station and told the cook to let him know if he needed any more help. Jake then moved over to the dish area, gave the dishwasher a high five, removed his chef coat and began stacking clean plates and moving them to the right location on the line. It only took ten minutes, but the dishwasher was grateful and surprised a chef would jump in. Finally, he picked up the clipboard with the night's reservations to determine when the line could expect crunch time. He pulled out his pad and made some notes on how to approach any potential bottlenecks. It had only been an hour since he began his new position and already staff members were giving him a thumbs-up. Jake spent the next few hours with the chef getting up to speed on the computer software he would be using, any project timelines coming up and the template the chef used for building weekly schedules. When they finished the evening crew was beginning to arrive.

As the line cooks, the masters of the restaurant universe, keepers of the adrenaline key, and frustrated plate artists of Lust, arrived, each one stopped to shake Jake's hand and congratulate him on the position. As much as they liked Jake, they would be watching to see how he handled the role, whether or not his attitude and altitude would change, and most importantly, if they could trust him since he moved "to the other side". Jake was familiar with this drill, it was the right of passage existing in every restaurant. He had been on both sides before, he knew exactly how to handle it.

It wouldn't take long for caution to be converted to total trust. Jake reviewed the pattern of reservations for the night and pointed out 8:15 as a problem. He proceeded to use his method of problem solving to show the cooks how to physically and mentally prepare for it. "We will need the grill to pre-mark some steaks, sauté must blanch and shock vegetables so they can quickly be re-heated at plating, sauces can be reduced in advance and set aside until the 8:15 crunch and finishing herbs will be moved to my expeditor station." Jake talked with the service staff about adjusting order timing and pick-up as the witching hour approached. He explained that there would be no chatter between line cooks and servers. "Any communication will come through me." He then informed the cooks, "My voice will be the only one that you listen to as we get busy."

As the evening progressed from a slow start up until around 8 p.m., everything seemed smooth. When 8:15 arrived, the orders began coming in at a rapid pace, cooks began to tap into their crunch time reserves (kind of like in football when an offensive switches to the two-minute drill as they are running behind with little time left), servers did not panic because Jake kept talking with them, keeping the line of communication open. At one point the sauté station was really getting stressed and Jake could see the deer-in-the-headlights look come across the line cook's face. He got his attention and simply and calmly said, "Look at me, I've got your back and will walk you through this. Everything will be fine, we are in this together." This was masterful and instantly put the cook at ease. They were getting through this just fine.

The chef, as was his plan on a busy night, was playing host and mediator by working the dining room as the face of the restaurant. He talked with guests, made recommendations, occasionally asked the kitchen to send out a free tasting portion to a table he deemed very important, and served as a support mechanism for the host. Prior to this move with Jake, the chef would have been trying to keep things together as the expeditor, the role his new sous chef had taken on. He could see right away how much this was going to help and how remarkably good Jake was at it.

They made it through the night with flying colors. The restaurant served 240 guests and nearly half of them between 8 and 9:30 p.m.. The line cooks were pumped. They had never clicked so well and had risen above the potential panic of more orders than they could handle. Jake was the man!

Jake asked Chef Andre if he could buy them all a shift drink when they were cleaning up. It didn't happen often, but the chef agreed. This was a moment for the staff and a huge moment for the new sous chef.

Initiation over, mission accomplished.

PART SIX

THE EVENT

"Natural disasters are terrifying – that loss of control, this feeling that something is going to randomly end your life for absolutely no reason is terrifying. But, what scares me is the human reaction to it and how people behave when the rules of civility and society are obliterated."

Eli Roth

CHAPTER THIRTY SIX

"SOMETHING'S HAPPENING HERE, WHAT IT IS AIN'T EXACTLY CLEAR"
STEVEN STILLS
THE EVENT THAT CHANGED EVERYTHING – BEGINS
(2015)

Things had been changing for quite some time. Everyone had talked about it when unusual things happened and then they would quickly forget. There would be fear and loathing for a period of time, and then pretended ignorance of the signs. Ignorance may be bliss on paper, but it isn't an excuse that holds up with time. Somehow the signs became standards of political dissention rather than facts to contend with. It was like finding black mold on your walls and simply covering it up with a coat of paint hoping it would just go away. The thing is, it doesn't go away, and it just gets worse.

There were many signs, namely increased tornado activity, many of which were close to category four or higher, and incredibly destructive hurricanes targeting areas unaccustomed to them. In relation to the food supply, Mad Cow Disease from feeding animals other animal protein, Salmonella, E.coli, and Listeria outbreaks were capturing headlines in newspapers. The Novo Virus appeared all too often on Cruise Liners creating a lack of trust among cruise line tourists. Ecologically, the country was experiencing a rapid loss of bee colonies, diminishing clusters of monarch butterflies, thousands of acres of burnt forests, increased volcanic activity and earthquakes to rival the destruction of the worst in history. The results were depleted farm crop yields, weeklong spells of below-zero weather in the Northeast and frost and snow below the Mason-Dixon Line. The list went on and on.

Everyone debated global warming or rightfully called, climate change, and failed to approach any strategic solution. Some denied the melting of polar ice caps, yet time-lapse photography showed just how alarmingly fast this was happening and evidence clearly pointed to rising ocean water levels as a result. Yet, after a few days out of the media, the American people would forget. Not anymore.

The most dramatic changes began to occur in the winter of 2015. Unlike the previous winter when temperatures hovered below zero in the Northeast and Midwest for over three weeks, in 2015 sub–zero temperatures of 25 below zero and lower began in December of 2014 and lasted until March. Some parts of the country saw the thermometer dip to 50 below. A series of ice storms attacked the Northeastern seaboard causing power outages that kept major cities in the dark for weeks on end. Two weeks of frost in Florida combined with spreading citrus canker had left the orange crop damaged beyond recovery.

On the West Coast, the drought continued from 2013, with ongoing forest fires destroying millions of acres in just over a year. As a result grape agriculture was decimated putting the California and Oregon wine industry in jeopardy.

As spring turned the corner, Mid-Western wheat became infested with a fungus, which was yet to be identified. More than 20% of the wheat crop was destroyed, putting a huge dent in the flour industry and impacting the cost of bread and pastry products. The declining bee population was taking its toll on pollination of other crops across the country, and something was happening with corn crops. The genetically modified seed used to stabilize corn production and yield appeared to be backfiring, and this year's growth produced dark brown, inedible corn. The only salvation for farmers was that it still seemed to be useable for ethanol production.

Everything seemed to be coming undone, but aside from some inconvenience and increasing prices, business carried on across the U.S. This is the way Americans dealt with disasters, a bit of denial, cross your fingers, move on, and don't look back. It will get better if we just carry on. Unfortunately, these calamities were just the tip of the iceberg.

The real issues began in June. It started in Texas and quickly moved up through Colorado and on to Montana. A small herd of Black Angus steers in Texas showed signs of Mad Cow Disease (Bovine Spongiform Encephalopathy). This hadn't happened at this level since a decade prior in England. The USDA (US Department of Agriculture) and the CDC (Center for Disease Control) were concerned. The herd was quarantined and destroyed, but it was too late. Within a month, the United States had been forced to kill more than 250,000 head of cattle, and the number was growing. Beef prices rose quickly, then they doubled and by the end of July beef was, for all intents and purposes, unavailable. Even McDonald's was unable to meet their needs, and started offering turkey and pork burgers in some locations.

The warning on Pacific fish from Monterey Bay Aquarium evolved into a ban until radiation levels decreased to an acceptable level. Gulf Coast waters seemed to be improving, so at least Gulf fishing was recovering.

Restaurateurs were at a loss for any reasonable solution. Menus moved from stationary documents to fluid lists of whatever chefs could get in the marketplace on any given day. Failure rates among restaurants had always been high but now the National Restaurant Association conducted a survey revealing a 15% increase in failure and bankruptcy rates since January of 2015. The prognosis was not good.

Jake had been reading about this series of connected events referred to by the media as *The Event*, even though it was more than that. What was really happening was Mother Nature's

Revolution. Since Jake was responsible for ordering product in the restaurant, his job had become exponentially more difficult and menus were now planned each night after confirmation on product from vendors.

In August, a hurricane took a quick right turn up the Gulf of Mexico, skirted the western edge of Florida, and landed on New Orleans. It was a Category Three, and although the new levee system in the city held, the hurricane churned up the Gulf waters and flooded the Bayou, essentially wiping out schools of fish the area, and the country depended on.

Menu choices were getting few and far between. Chefs were tearing their hair out just trying to figure out how to survive.

In many areas, especially urban centers, restaurants were a way of life. People had busy lives with little time to cook, and in many cases they just didn't know how. No matter what was happening, people still went to restaurants, but with little patience for menu gaps and changes. Restaurants were getting flak from vendors and guests.

Jake was doing the best he could. The commitment to quality was still there, but without the right raw materials it was becoming more challenging to maintain standards. Business was still good with numbers holding at previous levels. Prices could only go up so far, so in many similar cases, sales were yielding lower profit. Restaurant Lust, like many others in New York, just couldn't raise prices any higher. Everyone was walking a tightrope when it came to profit.

It was a particularly busy weekend and the restaurant was humming. The food looked and tasted great, customers were letting their hair down. Regular guests were laughing, buying expensive bottles of wine, and ordering multiple course dinners. Every line cook was on his/her game and the chef was beaming as he worked the dining room, checking in on guests and making wine recommendations to accompany the food Jake was helping to orchestrate. The sign of a great restaurant: it can thrive even during tough times. Times were very tough at the moment.

By the end of the night, a Sunday to boot, the restaurant had served 272 dinners, a record for this time of year. Given the current state of chaos from coast-to-coast, and the difficulty everyone was having getting their hands on quality raw materials, these numbers were astonishing. At 1 a.m. the crew was finishing up with cleaning and making plans to stop at Gramercy Tavern for a drink before closing. Everyone quickly washed up and changed (you didn't go to Gramercy looking like an after work cook), and grabbing cabs en route to the bar. One drink turned into two and then the bartender said, "Last call." Everyone said good night and left for their respective apartments. When Jake got home it was almost 3 a.m. He was beat and fell asleep almost before his head hit the pillow.

Cooks are creatures of habit and although Monday was his day off, actually the restaurant was closed on Monday, he still woke up at 7 a.m., crawled out of bed and headed for his Keurig. He had a headache, but as long as he was up he might as well get on with his day. Jake was unaware at this point, but of all the challenges he faced over the past few years, none would compare with what he would face today. As the normal day ticked away, his boredom settled in to a simple lazy afternoon and evening.

*Fast forward to Friday, October 18, 2015

CHAPTER THIRTY SEVEN

THINGS COULDN'T GET WORSE – OR COULD THEY? OCTOBER 18, 2015

Jake opened his eyes, and after just a minute of personal reflection that seemed like an eternity, the recent change came back to him.

The phone call; *"Jake, this is Chef Andre. I would normally take care of this face-to-face, but given the seriousness of the situation I wanted to call you right away. Let me get right to the point: there's been a suspected outbreak of E.coli traced back to our restaurant. Jake, I don't know how to say this, but four people have died and six others are in the hospital as a result."*

The silence that followed was haunting. Jake was in shock and gradually felt a series of emotions creep up from the depths of his soul. He began to weep without really knowing why. Was he weeping for the poor individuals who died? Was he panicked for the restaurant, his crew and his own potential responsibility for this? Was Jake just in shock and this was a way to keep from passing out?

What came next left him alone and confused. "Jake, I'm calling to let you know that I'll have to let you and your team go in an effort to save the restaurant. Someone needs to be responsible for this. You can pick up your last check any time this week or we'll send it in the mail. Take care Jake, you're a great cook, I'm sorry this happened." Jake ended the call and set down his iPhone. For the first time since he was 16, Jake was without a job, alone in New York, and possibly responsible for the death of four restaurant guests. How did this happen?

So much had changed since he first received that phone call on Monday morning, the death of restaurant guests, losing his job only to regain it after he and his team were exonerated, meeting with Chef and overhearing the scary revelation from the Health Department - everything seemed to be falling apart. Shelly was still beside him on a bench in the Green Market. Once again, he opened the newspaper she had placed in his hands.

He could hardly believe what he just read in the Daily News. In a matter of 24 hours, the weather changes and odd food supply issues had moved from front page news to an afterthought. The headline said it all, "People Want to Know; Is This the Beginning of the Apocalypse?" Leafing further he was shocked to read the extent of the problem since news of the four deaths just a few days ago. What the Health Inspector at Lust had alluded to when Jake talked with him yesterday was far worse than he had dreamed. As of the release of the paper just a few hours ago, more than 20,000 people in the U.S. alone had died from an unknown cause. Although it had yet to be fully identified, it appeared there was some type of bacterial infection striking without warning, killing almost 100% of the time within 48 hours. What was even worse was that nothing, including typical treatments with antibiotics, was working to slow down the damaging impact of the infection. The story went on to state there were early indications that similar issues were beginning to appear in China, Africa and certain parts of Europe.

The doomsday advocates were having a field day. This was it in their minds, the beginning of the end. God and Mother Nature had had enough. Man was incapable of making the right decisions and taking care of the planet, so it must be time to start over.

Although full disclosure of information was sketchy, either because it was too early to collect or our government was trying to keep the extent of the issue under wraps, there were some indications of safe areas in the United States, Canada and the Northeastern parts of Europe. No one knew why, but at this point there were no reported cases of infection in Vermont, New Hampshire, Maine, Northern New York State, Washington State, Wisconsin, and Alaska, all of Canada, Scandinavian Countries,

Nova Scotia, Iceland, Greenland, Northern Great Britain, France, New Zealand and Australia. The rest of the world had not been so lucky.

The CDC refrained from any detailed comments except to state the cause was renegade, did not show any consistent pattern, and was one of the most deadly diseases since the early 20th Century polio outbreaks. It was quickly becoming a world problem, a pandemic of epic proportions. Early estimates from an American research institution predicted that unless the world could find the cause and cure quickly, fatalities could easily wind up in the millions.

Jake shared the article with his friends, who all had the same reaction. It was similar to 2001 when terrorists had attacked the Twin Towers in New York City. The first reaction was deep panic. No one knew what to say, what do, or even where to go. Everything was cloudy. You cannot think straight. You may even feel the need to coax your body to take the next breath. Your palms are sweaty, your heart beats faster, you want to cry but can't find the tears, and you just want to get up and run somewhere, anywhere.

So much for Jake's methodical approach to problem solving. Suddenly jotting down what they knew and what to do next on a pad seemed meaningless. Jake had nothing, no ideas, no solutions, nothing. Suddenly he wondered, "Could this be an act of terrorism? Was someone or some group responsible for this? Might this worldwide catastrophe be part of some design, a statement of some sorts? Did the government know more, but was trying to keep information away from the American people? Was there an end game and what would it look like?"

Jake did not share these thoughts with his friends, although he was sure some would eventually come up with a similar conspiracy theory. He quickly put it out of his mind, realizing that if this were the case, then there would be absolutely nothing he or his friends could do. He turned to his friends, deciding someone needed to take the lead and said, "We should go to a place where we feel safe, a place affected by all of this, but where we can get our heads together and calmly try to think things through. We need a place where we might be able to learn more about what is happening. We need to go to Lust, we can use it as our home base." They all agreed, because they didn't have any better ideas. They took off for Lust, their home-away-from-home, a place where they might find answers.

They arrived at the restaurant to find the news crews were gone (the story was much bigger than one restaurant in New York now) but the chef, owner and a few service staff were sitting in the empty bar area watching CNN on the big screen TV. The chef unlocked the door and invited them in. He said nothing, but simply went back to watching the news. They all grabbed a cup of coffee and joined the group while Anderson Cooper spoke of the rising death toll from coast-to-coast. An interview with the Surgeon General was taking place, and he described what was know at this time. "What we know is this; the disease is bacterial, not viral. It is not transmitted through the air, but through physical contact with another infected person, especially through exchange of any bodily fluids. We have not been able to find anyway of slowing down the spread of the infection, and at this point, have seen an almost 100% fatality rate. When the first symptoms become visible, coughing up blood, severe rash, bleeding from the eyes, loose teeth. Death comes within 48 hours. Although it is impossible to control 100%, we are declaring Marshall Law in all major cities. Everyone must stay inside except for extreme emergencies. If you notice symptoms in yourself or others do not, I repeat, do not go to the hospital. Right now all hospitals in major cities are filled to capacity and are not allowing any more infected patients inside. This is as serious a situation as the world has ever seen and we are adamant about these warnings. The U.S. Military is being deployed as well as all State National Guard Units to control hospitals and the streets of our cities. Do not leave wherever you are. Stay inside! All businesses will be closed and streets will be cleared until we get to the bottom of this. Transportation centers are closed. There will be no flights, trains or traffic allowed in any of our major cities. If you have an emergency please do not use 911 in your local area for there is little they can do and the lines will likely be flooded with unnecessary calls. I am sorry to be so blunt, but we must slow the spread of this infection quickly so we can take a breath and come up with a solution." The President of the United States followed the Surgeon General and reiterated the warnings ending with, "The United States is the greatest nation on earth. We have the best doctors, research scientists and problem solvers in the world, and given the necessary control in a crisis situation like this, I am confident we will find a solution. Please take care, be vigilant and support your families during these very difficult times. God Bless America."

Anderson Cooper returned with red eyes and a shaking voice; "These are the most challenging times to ever face our country and the rest of the world. We at CNN are committed to working around the clock to keep everyone informed, to be a source of comfort and do whatever we can to help America through this. Our coverage will continue from coast-to-coast without interruption from this point on. If you have questions, please use the Internet. We have attendants online 24 hours a day to try and answer your questions or relay your concerns to the proper authorities."

Jake looked at the chef and their eyes said it all. A mystery assailant who was determined to take no prisoners was holding America captive. Whatever system that was in place to handle disasters would be ineffective this time. All they could do was sit back, wait, hope and pray. The only thing certain was that everyone in the bar would be camping out in the restaurant for some time.

CHAPTER THIRTY EIGHT

THE BEAT GOES ON, BUT WHAT IS THE SONG?
OCTOBER 19, 2015

Chef Andre was a bit older than the others sitting at the bar watching the news on the TV. What came to mind was a song from his parent's youth. It seemed so applicable now. He could not get the lyrics out of his head:

"But you tell me
Over and over and over again, my friend
Ah, you don't believe
We're on the eve of destruction."

It was Barry McGuire who talked about the impending doom of mankind in his 60's anthem: *The Eve of Destruction*. Is this where we were headed? Everything pointed to a doomsday scenario. The food supply in America was tainted, weather patterns were out of control, antibiotics, the wonder drug, were no longer effective, restaurants were closing left and right, the Stock Market was taking a dive, and people had little faith in their government to solve the massive problems the country was facing.

As the crew continued watching the dire news on CNN (there was literally nothing else to do), their only solace was sharing stories of their youth and talking about the good old days. Jake took it upon himself to keep everyone nourished, relying primarily on canned goods since it was uncertain whether or not the fresh food supply was infected. They had locked the door and pulled down the shades to discourage anyone from breaking in (a protectionist attitude was always pervasive in times of crisis), and determined they could probably survive for quite some time on what they had in stock. Jake and his line crew returned to taking notes. This was, after all, the way they functioned. The team hoped at some point to make sense of what was happening, help resolve the situation, or contribute to a solution. It was a way to keep their minds off the severity of the situation.

Reporters on the TV began to focus on micro issues cropping up as the real information from the government was sparse. There had been a run on grocery stores as soon as the Surgeon General declared Marshall Law. Crowds were out of control and didn't bother paying for what they could grab. Survival of the fittest was the call to arms.

Survivalist groups in the South and Mid-West had hunkered down in their compounds with arsenals of weapons stockpiled for just this type of situation. They had already declared independence from any government action to control their movement. Looting in major cities had transitioned into all-out riots with broken windows, overturned cars, fires, and even scattered fatalities as America's right to bear arms showed its ugly side. Shelters in every city were filled to capacity and food reserves were running very low. People wore masks and shied away from physical contact with anyone else. It was a paradise for reporters who were always looking for a crisis to exploit. The problem was now there were so many crises that people were no longer shocked. Everyone was glued to the TV, void of emotion. All of the tears had been shed, fear had turned to hopelessness and it looked like American society had lost faith. And it only took a few, short days.

Anderson Cooper would occasionally show a depressing graph of America with color-coded areas representing the spread of infection, and death tolls by state. Figures were often computer projections since hospitals were closed to infected individuals and everyone was relying on first-hand reports from communities. The map looked like the typical election results graphic except that the information was not a tally of votes, but rather a tally of destruction and despair. Three days after the start of this disaster, it was estimated more than 200,000 Americans were dead. One could only guess of the worldwide toll. The devastation continued until on the sixth day, something interesting began to occur.

Reports were coming in of people who had severe symptoms similar to what the Surgeon General had warned of, but these people weren't dying as they previously would have. More and more, people were recovering after what amounted to their worst case of flu in memory. Death tolls were dropping dramatically and those original folks who had flooded hospitals were regaining strength. By day ten, Marshall Law had been lifted with a 7 p.m. curfew still in effect. Americans were beginning to return to their homes, to work, and to some semblance of order. Two weeks after the original outbreak it appeared that the worst was over and the bacterial infection, although still not identified, was mutating into a fairly harmless stomach bug.

Eighteen days after the first reported deaths, America was back to work, the curfew had been lifted and the President of the United States claimed victory over the worst foe the U.S. had faced in its history. All said and done, more than 225,000 Americans had died in less than two weeks and worldwide numbers totaled nearly one million. It was a modern version of the Black Plague.

Although American's were breathing a sigh of relief, the CDC was still in a panic because they were no closer to finding out what had caused the infection, and had not discovered how to combat it in the future. Many at the CDC felt that the world was living on borrowed time, and that something would rear up its ugly head again in some fashion. Would it be next month or ten years from now? This was clearly a warning in their minds; something the world should pay close attention to.

President Obama, nearing the final year of his second term, was not oblivious to the dangers, and formed a taskforce to look at the cause. Many believed *The Event* was connected to global weather changes, and was the cumulative effect of the abuse Mother Nature had undergone, which Americans had ignored the signs of for decades. Michael Bloomberg, in his new role as UN liaison for issues relating to Global Climate Change, was designated as the taskforce leader, which included icons of industry such as Tim Cook from Apple; Michael Dell from Dell Computers; Bill Gates from Microsoft; representatives from agriculture, the cattle industry, chefs and teachers, high ranking members of Homeland Security sub organizations, and the CDC. The goal was to find the cause, build a portfolio of scenarios, and come up with solutions to protect America from future outbreaks. Michael Bloomberg would bring findings to the UN and hopefully begin a world movement toward solving this problem.

Back in New York, it was clear, like in so many cities, that it would take time to regain momentum. The Stock Market had taken its greatest dip since the drop in 2008 and was weary of any false sense of euphoria. The restaurant business had been devastated and many operations would likely never open again. The favorable climb in employment over the past few years was in a state of flux as businesses didn't know where to start in terms of recovery, and people were just downright scared.

As the weeks passed there were fewer and fewer mentions of *The Event* on the news, in papers, and on-line. As was usually the case in America, especially if it didn't impact the daily lives of anyone, everything must be fine. People either quickly forgot about the earth's near-miss at the Apocalypse, or simply wanted to move on and not think about the horror they experienced those few weeks in October. It was clearly a moment right out of *Gone with the Wind* when Scarlett O'Hara said, "I'll worry about that tomorrow." Except, no one had any desire to worry about it anymore. The news channels returned to covering nonsense stories about Justin Bieber throwing eggs at his neighbor, sports figures denying charges of steroid use, who would make the final four on American Idol, and details of Dennis Rodman's next trip to North Korea.

The Event came and went, as far as most people were concerned. Time to return to business as usual.

CHAPTER THIRTY NINE

BUSINESS AS USUAL FOR OTHERS, BUT NOT FOR CHEF JAKE

Restaurant Lust reopened and Jake and his crew were called back into action. If the temperament of the general public was any indication, the chef anticipated normal business volume to return shortly. New York was, after all, New York, and life must go on. Jake tried pretending everything was back to normal, but he just couldn't. He reflected on the days when he and Carla had felt like they had a cause. They stood for something important, the connections with real farming and real cooking, protecting the environment and making sure that they only used fish still in ample supply, and free of toxins. That special time in his past was now resurfacing. Those beliefs and practices were important now, even more so than in the past.

In his heart, Jake believed *The Event* was a warning. He was sure that there was a connection between how people treated the environment, dealt with crop management, and how animals were cared for and prepared for use in his kitchens. He knew that what had happened just a few short weeks ago was avoidable. Sensible people needed to help their country, and the world, change before this warning went way beyond what everyone had just experienced. Jake had difficulty sleeping whenever he thought about those innocent people who had died as a result of society's ignorance, and the families who continued to suffer the loss of loved ones.

Jake wondered where and when it all went wrong. Why did people continue to smoke cigarettes when it was an absolute fact that tens of thousands of people died every year from inhaling tar-laced smoke? Why did people continue to eat garbage convenience foods full of chemicals, high fructose corn syrup, excessive sodium and preservatives; the root cause of many cancers, diabetes, heart disease and obesity? Why were people ignoring signs pointing to human's abusive nature, and refusing to deal with the problems us, as a people, cause? Why, why, why? He must do something. He couldn't continue to ignore all of this. To avoid this change would be hypocritical, and a violation of everything he stood for.

Jake was a cook with integrity, he like many others, knew what the real story was and knew what could and must be done. As much as he cared for his new crew and appreciated the opportunities that Chef Andre had provided, he had to make a move and stand up for what was right. New York was not the place to find the answers and was way too large and complex to effect change. He knew he had to leave, but the question was where to? He had only been in New York for a little over a year, and realized leaving would likely not look great on a resume, but right now what good was a resume?

Jake wrestled with a decision for weeks, but just before Christmas, he determined it was time. He spent his day off sifting through options, but it wasn't until he sat down at Abraco for his daily espresso fix that the light bulb went off. He was paging through some food magazines up for grabs and came across one called *Vermont Life*. He had heard interesting things about Vermont, the lifestyle there, their politics and most importantly their dedication to farmers and the food they produced. As he paged through the magazine he came across an article about chefs who took a step back, opened small bistros in Vermont and provided many of the ingredients used from their own gardens as well as farms and producers within a stone's throw of their operations. As he turned the page he came across a picture that stopped him cold and brought a smile to his face. It was Chef Philippe, his old boss from the Cloister in Buffalo. So, he thought, this was where he wound up. The article talked about his philosophy of cooking, his love of growing vegetables and commitment to buying local and regional goods only. Philippe pointed to the problems with centralized farming, the use of GMO's, feeding animals corn they weren't meant to digest, and growth hormones used to add bulk to animals before slaughter. The article went on referring to the issue surrounding menus that did not reflect what was in season, but rather put stress on a system of single-focus farms, and a distribution system partially responsible for carbon emissions, and the connection to global climate change. It was an eye-opening article reflecting the same feelings Jake had been mulling over. The article ended with the name of his bistro, a website, and email address.

Without a moment's pause, Jake fired off an email reflecting on how much he missed Philippe. The message briefly reviewed what Jake had done professionally over the past few years and how he would like to move to Vermont if Philippe could use his help.

After a few glasses of wine, Jake was able to fall asleep. When he woke the next morning he found a message from Chef Philippe. It was short and to the point. "Great to hear from you, when can you be here?" Jake quickly responded, "Let me give notice at work. I will be there by the end of the first week in January." That day when Jake went to work, he told Chef Andre of his decision and why he had to leave New York and focus on making a contribution to change. Chef Andre was disappointed, but like Chef Hirsch in the past, he understood Jake's position. "Good luck Jake, I hope you make a difference."

Jake worked until early January, paid his last month's rent, packed two suitcases, and grabbed the train from Penn Station to Burlington, Vermont. Philippe was living and working in a town called Richmond, a short 20-minute car ride. Jake rented a car and was off to see his mentor.

PART SEVEN

RENEWAL IN VERMONT
THE EPICENTER OF A
RETURN TO REASON

Getting to the Source, Helping to Make a Difference
"The best learning experiences happened when we were
weeding. We would start talking about the plants we
were cultivating. It was truly learning by doing."
Author - unknown

CHAPTER FORTY

CHEF PHILIPPE AND THE VERMONT CULINARY LANDSCAPE
JANUARY 2016

The train arrived in Burlington and Jake went immediately to the Hertz Rent-a-Car booth. He picked a Jeep Renegade with four-wheel drive since he was in snow country.

Burlington is a great city with multiple colleges, great restaurants, boutique shops and a feel unlike any other city he had visited, but today he would just be passing through. There would be plenty of time to get back to Vermont's largest city. His focus was driving to see his friend, and start on a mission he truly felt was right.

Turning on to Route 89 South, he saw it was only 10 miles to the Richmond Exit and according to Philippe about a 10 minute ride from there. The roads were snow covered, but passable and even though he had not driven in snow, or for that matter a car, for quite some time, he did just fine. He turned off Exit 11 and continued on to the Town of Richmond. Just past the city limits was a sign for Chez Philippe, a restaurant in the middle of farm country. Jake was excited, this just seemed right.

As he turned into the driveway Jake was impressed by the view of a restaurant resembling a classic farm house with traditional red barn in the back, acres of farm land, and a fenced in area with chicken coop and a few pigs. He parked the car and opened the door to a greeting from two full-grown golden labs. They enthusiastically escorted Jake to the front entrance. Before Jake made it up the five steps to the wrap-around porch, Chef Philippe was there with open arms. His ear-to-ear smile was contagious. They kissed on each cheek in traditional French fashion, and immediately broke into the kind of laughter only friends understood.

Chef Philippe quickly removed his apron and told Jake he needed to see his plantation in Vermont. They toured the barn where hay had been put up for winter animal feed, walked the perimeter of what would be the chef's summer garden where most of his restaurant vegetables would be grown, the chicken coop with a dozen hens and a royal rooster holding court, and his five pigs called pig one, two, three, four and five (original). "Giving them real names Jake would make it much more difficult to turn them into chops, roasts and sausage."

The dining room was right out of a French Countryside version of Better Homes and Gardens. Hand-cut beams, hardwood floors, craftsman style tables and chairs, and Provençale-style curtains and table runners. The tabletop featured quality Riedl glassware, Simon Pearce china, and sterling silverware. The highlights were panoramic views of the farm, rolling Vermont hills and the warm and inviting beautiful stone fireplace. The dining room sat a mere 32 guests, "Just enough," Philippe chimed in.

The kitchen was quaint, but more than adequate with a small Aga Range, wood-fired oven, enough refrigeration (old-style with wooden doors) and a fantastic twelve-foot-long hard rock maple work table. There was one employee, Tom, who was 20 years old. He was working on peeling winter carrots and pulling leaves off Brussels sprouts. Tom looked up and said "hello". Philippe said, "Tom is my only employee during winter and spring. In the summer I will add a dishwasher and one other talented cook," here he looked at Jake.

Chef Philippe made some French press coffee, and they sat in the dining room to catch up. Jake told him his entire story including his revelation after *The Event* in New York. Philippe responded, "Vermont and other New England States avoided the bacterial infection that devastated the country and aside from snow, cold and some brutal fall storms we weren't touched by the calamities of the past year. Vermont is special."

Philippe's plans for the future included farmer dinners every week of the summer and fall. He hoped to feature their crops on a menu served on long tables in the middle of his garden, or barn, if the weather did not cooperate. This addition to the normal restaurant was something he could certainly use Jake's help with. In addition, "I hope to get approval to begin making and selling my own charcuterie in a retail butcher shop in Richmond proper." Philippe already signed a lease on a storefront, and was in the process of converting the space. "If you are handy, I could use an assistant carpenter, electrician and plumber. I couldn't pay you very much at first, but we do have a nice spare apartment on the farm that you could use. All your meals will be included, and after you turn in the rented Jeep, feel free to use the farm pick-up truck whenever you need it." Jake would be a Jack-of-all-trades working on the farm, converting the storefront, cooking and even serving in the restaurant. Philippe's wife Martha took care of the dining room, but occasionally needed an extra server. In the summer they would add a second waiter to take care of business.

It sounded great, just what Jake needed and was looking for. Philippe finished by talking about his involvement with the Vermont Fresh Network (VFN) connecting farmers and chefs, the Vermont Slow Food Movement, Chef's Collaborative and a new group being formed to provide input to President Obama and Michael Bloomberg on *The Event*. "Jake, this group will represent farmers, ranchers, producers and private restaurants, especially those who were able to avoid many of the issues associated with the devastating impact on the food supply. At this time, the group is comprised of a few prominent local chefs and farmers as well as big names like Alice Waters, Ann Cooper, Thomas Keller, Rick Bayless, Danny Meyer and Drew Nieporent." This was the group that interested Jake the most. This could be his avenue for making a difference.

Jake settled into the farm apartment, stoked up the wood stove, the only source of heat and joined Philippe and Martha for a country-style dinner with a French twist. Philippe mentioned they were eating food from producers within 10 miles of their farm. "This is the case most of the time at my restaurant and is the norm at many other restaurants throughout the state."

Philippe said, "As soon as spring arrives, I will take you around to visit farms and chefs I consider of like mind. Tomorrow we will tour the storefront in Richmond, take a longer ride to Waterbury to visit my friend Mane at Vermont Artisan Coffee and then a special trip to see the best bread baker in the western world." The food was wonderful and as he retired with a warm cup of Vermont Artisan Coffee, Jake opened his journal and made note of the things Philippe had shared. He started his list of things to do, including becoming a member of the organizations he had been introduced to.

Jake slept like a proverbial log, and woke up refreshed, even as the rooster crowed and startled him awake. He looked at his clock, it was 5:45 a.m. and there was barely a hint of sunlight on the horizon. There was frost on the single pane windows, and the inside thermometer read 52 degrees. Outside it was below zero. He stoked the coals in the wood stove and within minutes a roaring fire had increased the temperature in the room above 60. He showered, shaved and dressed in jeans and a couple layers of sweatshirts. He only had kitchen shoes and sneakers from his trip, but knew that at some point he would need to pick up a pair of good boots.

Martha had set Jake up with a pair of cross country skis and snowshoes. He would try them out later on. As he walked from the apartment to the main farmhouse he could smell bacon cooking. Cooks never get tired of the smell of bacon. In the kitchen, Chef Philippe was already at work. It was before 7 a.m. and the kitchen table was set with poached eggs, bacon, and fresh apples from cold storage. Rich, hot coffee, local cream and the most fantastic bread Jake had ever tasted made the meal complete. The bread was crusty on the outside, full-flavored with undertones of walnut oil and a chewiness that was hard to describe. "Is this the bread you were talking about?" Philippe nodded: "Incredible isn't it?" Yes, it was.

Philippe and Jake traveled to Richmond and unlocked the storefront space. It was small and reminiscent of a butcher shop from Jake's grandmother's era. The refrigerated meat cases had been purchased from a general store, circa 1940, the ceiling was tin, the floors hardwood, and the walls covered in stainless sheets. There were blackboards behind the coolers for listing products and prices, an old- fashion brass cash register, hanging industrial lights and a full picture window with an etched logo proclaiming Richmond Butchery.

The kitchen still needed work, although there was an ancient wooden walk-in cooler that Philippe had rebuilt from the same general store where he found the meat cases. Sinks were in place, but no plumbing was evident. The floors were stripped, and piles of used quarry tile were stacked in the corner waiting for adhesive and grout. There was a ban saw that would be positioned in the walk-in, another beautiful hard rock maple butcher block, stainless tables, a six-burner range with an appropriate hood in place, a reach-in freezer, sausage stuffer, 60-quart Hobart mixer with meat grinder, boxes of small equipment, and a tiny office in the back. The back door opened to a loading dock for deliveries.

It was perfect, and Jake could feel the positive vibe. This place had great bones. There was still plenty of work to be done, but Jake could envision the business ready to open before the summer season.

Next, they were off to Waterbury. Chef Philippe talked about the flood of 2011 and how it devastated this quaint town. He talked with pride about the growth of Green Mountain Coffee into a global company, the Ben and Jerry's plant and their unique style of management, and of course Heady Topper, the award-winning beer from the old Alchemist bar. They stopped at a much smaller plant, the home of Vermont Artisan Coffee and met one of the world's most influential coffee tasters, Mane. He was to coffee what Helen Turley was to Zinfandel. His palate was as sophisticated as they come, and people traveled from all corners to learn his craft and buy his coffee. Philippe could have the coffee delivered to his restaurant but he liked coming here, smelling the roasting coffee, tasting with Mane, and chatting with Renee who managed accounts for the roasting company. They loaded up a few cases of coffee, roasted just minutes before, and took off for the bread experience. "The car smells like coffee and I swear I have a caffeine high just from breathing."

Finding the bread bakers shop would be something that would take Jake some time to master. It was well off the beaten path, behind a farm similar to Philippe's. The chef explained the baker only made one type of bread, a limited amount, baked fresh every day and only those people who he respected were among the privileged allowed to purchase it.

They walked into a shop resembling a barn more than a bakery. The aroma was heavenly. Baking bread is one of those smells that, once imbedded in your aroma memory, is hard to forget. As they walked in, Jake noticed that the far wall was solid, with windows overlooking the flowing Vermont hills, now covered with snow. Everything, each cooling rack, the bowl for the poolish, walls, chairs and ceiling were made of wood. Philippe explained that the baker made everything himself, and believed that the natural feel of wood was important to the process of baking. There were two wood burning ovens, one when you first entered and in plain sight, the other around the corner, out of view. The baker. Gerard, and a mason who lived next door, had built both ovens. Gerard greeted the visitors with a smile. Jake guessed he was in his seventies, and still continued to work every day. He explained he had one person helping, but it was someone different each day working simply to learn the craft. Gerard's schedule was unique. He would start fires in the ovens at 5p.m and combine his dry ingredients for a batch. Then he slept for four hours. When he returned he would mix the ingredients with his starter and allow it to sit and bowl proof. The next step was to cut and round the loaves, set them on wooden boards and on the racks he had made by hand. The loaves would need 4-6 additional hours of proof time. The fires would be tamped down into coals, then he would sleep for another four hours while the bread went through proof, and the ovens cooled to the right temperature. On this final stage, he would add some more wood to the fires, test the loaves, and when ready begin the process of baking. Each loaf would take around 50 minutes in the oven, but due to the sensitivity of temperature, he always needed help at this stage. This was where his apprentices were invaluable. In fact, his apprentice that day was a woman who was pulling breads from the oven. Gerard said: "Let me introduce you."

Philippe pretended to be checking out the equipment as Jake was escorted around the corner to the other oven. When he rounded the corner he came to an abrupt stop, his jaw dropped and he stood there speechless. The baker pulled a dozen loaves from the oven and turned to acknowledge the visitor. At that moment, time seemed to stand still, and Philippe joined Jake and put his arm around his shoulder.

It was Carla.

CHAPTER FORTY ONE

A REUNION

Jake's eyes met Carla's for the first time in nearly 18 months. There was an immediate rush of feelings from excitement to wonder, from anger to disappointment, from understanding to even a bit of fear, but most importantly, love. A slight smile came over Carla's face and tears began to flow. They had not said a word; their eyes spoke chapters. Carla dropped the bread peel she had been holding on to as a crutch and eased toward Jake. She extended her arms and the two embraced, and held on like their lives depended on it. Both began to weep not out of sadness, but with a sense of joy only they could understand. After a moment, Jake looked into her eyes and simply said, "I'm sorry." He had been waiting for 18 months to say this to her if he only had a chance. As much as he tried to move on, even with the all-consuming events of the past few months, even when he was pumped up with adrenaline working on the line at Lust, Jake never forgot Carla; not for one moment.

Carla responded, "Jake, I love you and have missed you, but after I left I just didn't know how to return to where we were." They hugged and kissed and then suddenly realized they were not alone. Philippe and Gerard were standing behind them, smiling. Jake turned to Philippe, "You knew! Was this a plan to get us together?" Philippe tried to present a look of confusion, but once again smiled and shrugged his shoulders. "Jake, you two are meant for each other and it made me very sad to know you had separated. When Carla was in need of a friend, she contacted me and asked if she could find a temporary home in Vermont. She has been here since leaving the Adirondacks. Martha and I were happy to help her out, but were torn between helping her and knowing you were in pain. I had made a decision from the day she arrived, I would not violate her trust and contact you, however, if you ever got in touch with me, I would do whatever I could to bring you back together."

Carla finished up her last batch of bread while Jake waited and watched. Philippe returned to his farm and left the couple alone. When Carla finished she asked Jake, "Do you want to return to Philippe's farm or spend some time at my apartment in Richmond." He cautiously said, "I would love to spend time with you, if it is all right." Carla smiled and took his hand. On the way back to Richmond in her car they talked as easily as they had all those months ago in the Adirondacks. "I have spent many hours reflecting on the way I was in Saranac Lake and how much I have changed since then. Carla, I am a different person now." He talked about New York, his time back on the line, *The Event* and how it brought him back to his beliefs; those beliefs they both shared when in New Orleans, and his decision to try and make a difference beyond cooking great food.

Carla pulled into the driveway of an apartment building in downtown Richmond and said, "Philippe owns the building and was kind enough to set me up when I arrived in Vermont. I work four days a week at a very nice bakeshop in Burlington and one day at Gerard's in exchange for bread and knowledge about artisan baking." She was getting by and loving her life of balance. They walked up to her apartment, Carla opened the door and let Jake in. "Make yourself at home, I have to visit with my neighbor for a moment and then I have something important to tell you."

The apartment was comfortable without many pieces of furniture. He recognized a few items from their place in Saranac Lake and her touch in the kitchen. His eyes fell on the coffee maker, so he made a pot while waiting for Carla. The door to the apartment opened and he heard Carla enter. When he turned, his eyes opened wide as Carla stood with a young child in her arms. "Jake, I want you to meet Shawn, your son." Carla's eyes were inquiring, wondering how Jake would react. Jake stood there holding on to the kitchen counter for balance. "My son? I, we, have a son?" Carla looked at Jake and simply said, "Yes, Shawn is 10 months old."

At first Jake didn't know whether to sit down, jump for joy or run like hell. He repeated, "We have a son?" Carla could see he was overwhelmed. She stepped closer to Jake and said, "Jake, would you like to hold him?" Jake extended his arms and pulled his son close to his chest. He had never held a baby before, and probably held him a bit too tight. He could feel Shawn's heartbeat, smell the fresh aroma of baby scent, and sense the electricity of a father-son bond. Jake held Shawn at arms- length; the baby smiled and then threw up on his shirt. Carla laughed, the baby smiled, and Jake began to tear up once again. He ignored the mess on his shirt and hugged his son again and began to dance around the kitchen. Wonderment and fear transitioned very quickly to incredible joy. Finally, he handed the baby to Carla who went into the bedroom to clean Shawn up, pointing Jake towards the bathroom to do the same. It had not fully sunk in yet.

Carla cleaned up the baby and set him down for a nap. When she returned to the kitchen, Jake was sitting at the table with a cup of coffee. He looked up at Carla and said, "How could you have held this back from me? I was a father and you didn't try to contact me or even answer one of the calls I made over these months? Carla, I don't know what to say." Jake paused to catch his breath. Carla could only hang her head as he continued, "I know I was wrong in Saranac Lake and my actions hurt you, but this is inexcusable. My God, I am a father and didn't even know. I missed helping you through your pregnancy, missed the birth of our son, and missed sharing this wonderful news with my parents. I am in shock."

Carla knew he would rightfully ask these questions, and for 18 months she had struggled with how to answer them. She needed to proceed carefully. She had made the initial move causing this separation, and did not want to lose Jake again. Carla felt he was different now, and hoped, really hoped, they could get back together. "Jake, I know no matter what I say won't be totally satisfactory. When I left you in Saranac Lake I saw a man I loved who was beginning to self-destruct and I didn't know how to stop you. I could not bear watching you spiral downward and although I sensed I might be pregnant, thoughts of us being together while you continued to turn from Dr. Jekyll to Mr. Hyde was something that didn't make sense." Now it was Carla who paused to let Jake take it all in. "I have seen too many families stick it out just for a child, and watched as their relationships turned from love to hate. I couldn't have this happen to us, so I left. Was it the right thing to do? I am not sure that there is a clear answer to that. When Philippe and Martha took me in, I felt safe, and wanted some time to think. Within weeks it was confirmed I was pregnant with your child." Her words were flowing freely now. Carla had waited 18 months for this conversation. "I let my parents know I was safe but did not want them to come after me, so initially I didn't let them know where I was. They were very angry with you, and I suppose felt it was best to them that you and I not get back together. They told me you called, but would not relay any other information. As a result communications with my parents were, for a time, few and far between. When you would call and leave messages I just couldn't bring myself to answer or return them, although I came close so many times. I did not know what I would say."

"When Shawn was born, Martha was there with me and called my parents to let them know. I returned to Buffalo for three weeks while I was getting accustomed to being a mother. My parents were great, but insisted calling you was not in the best interest of the baby. After three weeks, I returned to Vermont with Philippe and Martha's help." Carla explained how she managed to get the job in Burlington, and found some day care with Martha's help. "I had no idea you were coming to Vermont, but always hoped I would build the courage to find you and set things right. Please forgive me Jake, you know I love you, and more than anything else I want, I need you to love your baby."

Jake suddenly relaxed, and began to talk about how much he thought about Carla over these months. How he regretted the way that he was in Saranac Lake, and how his life became inconsequential without her by his side. "I wanted deeply to make things right given the chance and decided if I ever found you the first thing I would do is ask you to marry me." He then got down on one knee and said, "Carla, I don't have a ring at this time, I know I have made mistakes and I want you to know this is not an act of responsibility because we now have a child, this is absolutely out of love. Carla, will you marry me?" Carla literally knocked him over as she wrapped her entire body around his, kissed him and looked him in the eyes; "Yes, Jake the cook, I will marry you. You are the love of my life."

Jake and Carla called their parents to relay the news. Jake's parents were surprised but thrilled, Carla's parents, not so much, but they wished them well. They spent the night together at Carla's apartment and had a very special breakfast the next morning: Jake, Carla and Shawn.

Having waited so long for this reunion, Jake and Carla did not want to plan a large wedding or one that was months away. They decided to get married in Vermont in May on Philippe and Martha's farm. The guest list would be relatively small with both sets of parents, Philippe and Martha, Chef Hirsch and his guest, Lindsay and Scott from Bayou in Saranac Lake and a handful of cousins and uncles. In total, there were around fifty people. Chef Philippe prepared the food, a local bluegrass band played and as the sun was beginning to set, Jake, Carla and Shawn became a family. This was the best day of their lives.

CHAPTER FORTY TWO

LIFE IN VERMONT – FOOD WITH PURPOSE

Carla and Shawn moved into the apartment on Philippe's farm, and began to settle into their new life together. As much as Jake and Carla thought they knew about food, they quickly discovered how limited their knowledge was. The beauty of Vermont, and in particular Chef Philippe's restaurant, was its closeness to the source of ingredients.

As spring approached, Jake and Carla became involved with planning the restaurant menu with Chef Philippe, as well as designing the summer garden. What they planted and sowed would become the core of the menu. The flavor profile of the items from the farm would dictate how they cooked, and the connections they made with other regional producers would drive the format of the evolving restaurant focus. If Philippe were to build a strong alliance with a local grass-fed beef producer, then that would play a strong role in how the menu evolved; if he purchased extra piglets to be raised for slaughter, then that would be a direction to follow. What is special about Vermont is people get it. They understood the way to avoid many of the issues that lead up to *The Event*, was to radically change the way people lived.

The concept of centralized farms, although very effective in increasing yields and accessibility to ingredients, did not maximize the quality of soil and failed to appreciate the beauty of flavorful ingredients in their appropriate season. Centralized farming was also extremely susceptible to climate changes and the impact of acts of God such as drought, tornadoes, floods, hurricanes and frost. One freak frost in Florida could wipe out orange production in the United States for an entire season or longer. A drought in California would dramatically impact the price and availability of iceberg and romaine lettuce, and tornadoes and drought could devastate wheat and corn production and in-turn, cattle yield. The decentralized approach to farming practiced in much of Vermont, although unlikely to make many products available year-round, did yield products of peak flavor and quality. This process allowed farmers to rotate fields to regenerate soil nutrients, give those in surrounding communities a chance to buy local and minimize the carbon footprint associated with packaging and shipping.

Carla continued to work part-time at the bakery in Burlington, and one day a week baked artisan breads outside of Richmond. Her bread baking skills were improving exponentially, and as a result, this was quickly becoming her passion. Martha offered to take care of Shawn on those days when Carla was working. In exchange, Jake and Carla agreed to take care of the garden and farm in addition to helping Philippe in the restaurant. It was a family of like-minded, energetic, passionate partners in a business and a lifestyle agreeable to all.

Jake visited High Mowing Seeds in Hardwick, Vermont, the second largest organic seed source in the country, and purchased GMO-free seeds. Their growing process would also be void of any chemical pesticide penetration. He learned about organic farming through High Mowing and by spending time at Pete's Greens, also in Hardwick. He marveled at the quality of Vermont cheese by spending time in the affinage caves at Jasper Hill, and helping with goat milking at Vermont Butter and Cheese. Jake made a mental note to add cheese-making skills to his repertoire at some point in the future. Most importantly, Jake was learning about the benefits of foraging and partnering with other producers. The quality of his personal cooking would improve simply by raising the bar with the raw materials he used.

Jake and Carla discovered cooking in Vermont was less about what you added, and more about how you treated the raw materials you had the privilege to work with. Coaxing flavors already there was a more important role for chefs, than adding ingredients that would mask natural flavor.

As April became May Jake found himself tilling the garden with Philippe's tractor, adding manure as a natural fertilizer, testing the PH of the soil and making natural adjustments to ensure the ground would support the crops he chose for the garden. He and Philippe planted, labeled, weeded, trimmed and nurtured the crops as they began to grow and produce the first vegetables in early June. First to arrive were peas and salad greens. These crops became a focal point on the restaurant's menu. Next were strawberries and early raspberries from returning bush growth, as well as zucchini blossoms and petite summer squash. Fresh herbs were available early on and would remain throughout the season. Jake planted herb beds surrounding the restaurant. These beautiful and fragrant items became the center of the landscaping plan serving both as a source of flavor and a visual appointment to the building. Later in the season would be the root vegetables and hearty greens, carrots, beets, turnips, sun chokes, kale, mustard greens, cauliflower and broccoli. Salad greens were harvested throughout the summer as growth after growth matured.

Jake would wake at 5 a.m. every morning and tend the garden until noon. He, Martha, Philippe and Shawn would have lunch, and then Jake would shower and prepare to work in the kitchen for dinner. Seven days a week in the garden, and five days in the restaurant. Two afternoons and evenings per week he, Carla and Shawn would spend every minute together, either relaxing on the farm or exploring other parts of Vermont.

The restaurant did very well, staying open Tuesday-Saturday, filling each night. Jake, Philippe, an intern cook and dishwasher made up the entire crew. There were no big salaries to contend with and even though Carla and Jake made very little money, they did not need very much. Philippe and Martha provided them with the apartment. The farm provided their food, Carla brought home bread she baked and Shawn was taken care of by Martha when needed. There was enough money to cover their health care costs, a small amount for fun, and a steady stream into their savings account.

Bayou Restaurant in Saranac Lake seemed to keep chugging along since the Adirondacks were not impacted directly by *The Event*. The 10% equity stake Jake retained in the restaurant did pay a small, but steady dividend and if they ever sold the business Jake felt it might yield a nice addition to their nest egg.

By the summer, Shawn had his first birthday, and was heading quickly towards a time when he would be walking, learning, and getting into trouble around the farm. Jake and Carla had been talking about the need to relieve Martha from some of the responsibility for Shawn, and how this might impact on their professional roles. They agreed this might be the last year Carla would be able to work full-time away from the farm. They would need to come up with an alternative plan. Life was really great, and now that Jake had nearly one season under his belt, it was time to start looking toward his involvement in the national change movement. A movement, like the one in Vermont, leading America in a new direction to help avoid a disaster far more significant than *The Event* had been.

Jake loved the connections he made with food from the farm. Pulling carrots from the ground, brushing off the dirt, washing them, placing them on the stove to simmer in stock, and finishing with cultured butter and sea salt produced a product rivaling any steak. Roasted beets in the fall, fresh shucked peas and lightly sautéed fava beans served with fresh herbs became central to the food Jake and Philippe were cooking. The beautifully creamy Capoule and Bijou goat's cheese from Vermont Butter and Cheese, and the deep, smooth and creamy texture of Bayley Hazen Bleu from Jasper Hill defined quality cheese in Jake's mind. Grass fed beef vs. corn fed, no comparison in flavor. Grass feed is natural for the animal, and allowed the diner to taste the meadow where the animal matured. The bread Carla was now producing was the American equivalent to Poilane from France, considered by many to be the finest bread in the world. The food Jake, Carla and Philippe were making involved honest cooking, paying homage to the farmer, and the land. This was cooking as it was meant to be.

Vermont and a few other areas of the country were spared the wrath of *The Event,* and once Jake looked into probable links he was fascinated to discover each of those areas followed similar practices in farming. There was a universal respect for the environment in these parts of the country. Many would deny any connection, but to Jake, the connection was vivid.

If it wasn't apparent in the summer, fall brought home the reason why Vermont was so spectacular. The colors of the leaves were something Jake was familiar with since Western New York and the Adirondacks were meccas for leaf peepers, but Vermont with rolling hills, morning fog settling in the valleys, and crisp blue skies, made the passing of summer seem just fine. Although they didn't grow many fall vegetables such as pumpkin, Hubbard, acorn squash and Brussels sprouts, there were enough local farmers who did. The menus at the restaurant could feature these lush flavors. Jake incorporated many of the less than prime cuts of meat like lamb shanks, short ribs and shoulder of beef, kept frozen for the fall season. These delicious items were now braised with garden onions, the wonderful carrots kept in cold storage, and one of Jake's favorites, parsnips. The hearty braising liquid made a soulful accompanying sauce to pot roast, lamb Osso Buco, and braised short ribs jardinière.

Soon, the restaurant would revert to its winter schedule of four nights per week, and with the garden in hibernation, Jake would have plenty of time to work on pickling and curing items to be put up for next season. This was definitely a back to foundations experience that both Carla and Jake fell into quite easily. Winter would also be the time when Jake would be able to step back and become actively involved in those organizations focused on driving substantive change for the future.

Vermont Fresh Network, Slow Food USA, and Chef's Collaborative were organizations benefiting from Jake's involvement, but he felt it would be most important to invest the majority of his free time with the Michael Bloomberg taskforce. He asked Philippe to try and open some doors for his involvement.

CHAPTER FORTY THREE

A TIME FOR ACTIVISM – IGNORANCE IS NOT BLISS

WASHINGTON, DC – The Food and Drug Administration on Wednesday put in place a major policy to phase out the indiscriminate use of antibiotics in cows, pigs and chickens raised for meat, a practice that experts say has endangered human health by fueling the growing epidemic of antibiotic resistance.

The change, which is to take effect over the next three years, will eventually make it illegal for farmers and ranchers to use antibiotics to make animals grow bigger. The producers had found that feeding low doses of antibiotics to animals throughout their lives let them to grow plumper and larger.

Federal officials said the new policy would improve health in the United States by tightening the use of classes of antibiotics that save human lives, including penicillin, azithromycin and tetracycline. Food producers said they would abide by the rules.

December 12, 2013 (NY Times – Sabrina Tavernise)

Jake met with local representatives on a taskforce that included chefs, representatives from the State Department of Agriculture, cheese makers and farmers. Additionally, the group communicated via Skype with Alice Waters, Danny Meyer and Drew Nieporent, to draft a comprehensive recommendation to Michael Bloomberg. In assessing the FDA requirement for farmers to cease using antibiotics throughout an animal's life cycle, the general conclusion was that even though this was a very good initiative it was too late to help those impacted by the bacterial infection, associated with *The Event*. The general consensus was even though the CDC hadn't been able to isolate the bacterial infection everyone knew it was antibiotic resistant. This was probably the result of antibiotic overuse for decades. In the eyes of the research group this was a blatant example of legislators influenced by industry without considering the long-term impact of their inaction.

Global climate change is, as demonstrated with scientific data, a reality. Surface temperatures and carbon dioxide levels are increasing radically, more dramatically than at any other period of time in history. There is little doubt this is a result of two primary factors: increased burning of fossil fuels, and deforestation in areas such as the rainforest area of South America. The results are evident on the West Coast of the United States. California produces almost half of all the vegetables and fruit consumed in the U.S., and the extended drought they have been experiencing puts those crops in jeopardy. Some denied the existence of climate change, the impact of melting polar ice caps, the potential dangers of genetically modified seed and excessive use of antibiotics to mask issues surrounding how livestock is prepared for the food supply, but more and more those denials were proven wrong.

This same denial and lack of vision allowed other aspects of *The Event* to ravage the United States. Increased greenhouse gases, global weather change, depletion of the ozone layer, use of GMO's to purportedly protect crop integrity, and the use of pesticides has, at some level, contributed to the crisis America and the rest of the world is trying to recover from. There was scientific data to support the group's assessment, and they knew in their hearts this chain reaction of avoidance had contributed to the collapse of a very sophisticated food system. It was important for the group to not only point to concerns, or even produce more supporting facts, but to offer suggestions for change. The end game was to avoid another crisis, one that would likely be on an even grander scale than *The Event*.

Jake and those conscientious individuals who were fact-finding and problem- solving with the presidential taskforce were committed to the important job at hand. Although they knew a quick fix was no longer a possibility, they felt that over time, with enough statistical proof and continued media attention, a change could be made. There had been historical examples of this same approach: cigarette smoking had once been so commonplace in America that from the 1940's until the late 1990's it had become part of the culture. Behaviors can be changed, but culture is nearly impossible. Yet, with undeniable data about the dangers of smoking, constant media attention, support from the Surgeon General, and hundreds of grass root groups promoting awareness, smoking had become socially unacceptable. People made a change, and in turn, the impact of smoking on respiratory problems, heart disease and cancer was reduced.

This group of advocates knew they were part of a change, in how people lived, with a new definition of acceptable practices, and pushing for a change in culture. The questions were: how much time did they have, and was it already too late? The group would not allow a "too late" feeling deter them from their charge. Jake and others knew they would need to be in it for the long haul, and they were prepared.

Jake, Carla and Shawn were part of a test case in Vermont. Their lives were a benchmark for others to follow. This life in Vermont was idyllic, a life they felt very fortunate to have.

CHAPTER FORTY FOUR

A FUTURE IN VERMONT

Philippe and Martha had built a wonderful life in Vermont. Their restaurant was successful enough to provide a comfortable living for them, the farm was a labor of love, the new charcuterie and butcher shop in Richmond was up and running and they had set the stage for future change in how Americans looked at their food system. They had not been back to France, Philippe and Martha's home, for nearly 20 years and, as much as they loved Vermont, they missed their homeland.

What struck Chef Philippe was his great fortune in having brought Jake to Vermont, helping to bring Jake and Carla back together. Philippe and Martha cared for Jake, Carla and Shawn as if they were family, and trusted them completely with the operation of the farm, restaurant, and new butcher shop. It was only natural that Philippe looked to this opportunity to step back, solidify Jake and Carla's presence in Vermont, and take the time to return, for an indefinite period of time, to France.

Philippe called a family meeting with Martha, Jake and Carla. He prepared a classic meal of Cog au Vin, and opened a special bottle of French Pinot Noir. The aroma of braised chicken in red wine with lardons of bacon from their own smokehouse, a rich pan sauce that married the fat from the chicken, the smoky richness of the bacon, and root vegetables from the garden, was intoxicating. The fire was tempered down to coals, and the sun was setting as everyone sat down for an evening together. Martha started with a toast, "Sante - to our friendship, the farm, Vermont, and great food." Everyone raised glasses in agreement. Philippe began, "Jake and Carla, we feel so blessed to count you as friends and allowing us to be a part of your lives. You are both accomplished cooks, as well as damn good farmers. Vermont seems to sit well with you. I have personally watched both of you grow since we first met in Buffalo, quite a few years ago." Philippe seemed to glow like a proud father. "It has been a pleasure to sit back and learn of your commitment to the real issues around food, and learn of your willingness to sacrifice for the betterment of the whole. I am proud of you both."

The aging chef went on, "Carla, you have become a world-class bread baker and I think this is now your real calling. It doesn't make sense for you to work for others when we could benefit from your skills here, enjoy using your bread in the restaurant, and probably sell even more through the butcher shop. I am willing to invest the money to build an appropriate bakery for you to practice your craft and, if you are game, I would empower you to work with local artisans to build the wood-fired oven needed for the task." Martha was nodding in agreement. "There is space in the back section of the butcher shop for this to happen. Jake, Martha and I would like to return for a period to France, spend time with our families and enjoy life in the French countryside. We will return to Vermont at some point, but really just want to enjoy life. To this end, we would like to sell you and Carla a 60% stake in our restaurant, farm, butcher shop and bakery."

Jake and Carla were taken off guard by this incredible offer. "I understand you don't have the funds to do this, so we would hold the mortgage on the businesses in exchange for a comfortable monthly payment from business operations. As controlling partners, you would have total autonomy in deciding what to do with the businesses. We are confident your decisions would parallel the same ones Martha and I would make. This is certainly a lot to digest, and we do not expect an immediate answer, but do hope you will take this opportunity. It is a perfect match for both of you, and it will allow Martha and me to take time away and enjoy life."

After dinner, Jake and Carla said they would discuss this wonderful offer, and let Philippe know in a few days. This was an incredible opportunity, but both Carla and Jake could not help reflect on their last experience as owners of a restaurant, and how their new priority was, and must continue to be, their relationship and new life with Shawn.

Over the next few days, the couple continued with their normal business and only talked about the opportunity before them in casual conversation over dinner. On the third day they decided it was time to address the offer. It was Jake who began, "Carla, I have never been happier than I am with you and Shawn, right now. We have found each other, are now man and wife and have a wonderful child who is more important to me than anything. This is a great opportunity before us, yet I find myself thinking less about it than about the impact it could have on our family. I am a different person today. Food is still extremely important to me and the farm has become a new passion. Vermont is such a wonderful place to operate a restaurant and my involvement in helping to make potential policy changes to help future generations is invigorating. Yet, everything pales in comparison to what we now have as a family. If we decide to accept Philippe's offer I feel it must be with some comfortable escape if we sense any infringement on our lives together." Jake took a deep breath, "To this end, I am not advocating one way or the other, this is not my decision, it is ours and your feelings are more significant in this matter than mine. It was my zealous approach towards being in business and lack of self-assessment that almost signaled the end of our relationship. I will never allow us to be in a similar position again."

Carla looked Jake squarely in the eyes and calmly said, "Jake, you are a different person than you were, but not as much as you think. The person I fell in love with way back in the Buffalo days was the proud cook with visions of creating something special. You were so passionate about cooking, and would spend every waking moment planning, preparing, finishing and self-critiquing what you did. You are my husband and the father of Shawn, but you will also always be a great cook who needs an avenue for expression. To deny this would be to deny a very large portion of who you are. Besides, the opportunity for me to spend my professional time baking bread in a dedicated space of my design and having everything we do flow together from farm to plate is very exciting. My vote is YES for this opportunity. There will be days when things don't go right and there may even be times when we don't agree, but it will always wind up being what is best for the business and best for our family. I think we are strong enough now to weather any storm, and smart enough to know when to back away if things start to go sideways."

This was a discussion based on history, mutual respect, understanding of how important it is to support each other's dreams, and a real love for each other. Don't make the same mistakes twice, would always ring clear in their minds as they moved forward with a small amount of trepidation. But move forward they would. The next morning they had breakfast with Philippe and Martha (Jake cooked this time) and told them, "YES!" Everyone shook hands, and Philippe said he would have his lawyer draw up the documents. In the meantime, Carla should begin the design of her bakeshop. Philippe had already secured a loan for construction, and a contractor was ready to start as soon as Carla had her plan in place. And so, another chapter in the life of two cooks had begun.

THIS IS THE END OF THE BEGINNING.

EPILOGUE
AN OPPORTUNITY AND CHALLENGE
FOR THE FUTURE

It may be hard to imagine the scenario depicted in *The Event* as credible, yet in 2014 we are acutely aware that the components leading up to this disaster have been building over the past few decades. Though some may argue about the credibility of the doomsday approach many scientists have taken in describing the current path the human race is taking, there is growing evidence they are correct.

America's food supply is the envy of the world. We are able (although far too many Americans go to sleep hungry each night) to produce enough food to feed those who live in the U.S., and many more throughout the world. Our distribution system for food is amazing, and prices, in comparison to other countries, are very low. We have grown to depend on this system, the network of production and distribution, to provide for us what just a century ago we provided for ourselves. This dependence may be considered a right, and progress for a civilized society, but to some it signals a grave danger for our future. It would not take much for any crop, seafood or type of livestock to be priced out of the market or removed from the consumption chain through disease, chemical alteration, over-consumption or mishandling. A frost in Florida changes the citrus picture for the country. Drought in the Midwest impacts grain production and drives prices and availability in the wrong direction. This same crop depletion impacts the price of feed for our livestock and in turn drives prices beyond what the market can bear. The use of GMO's and antibiotics may threaten the integrity of our food supply and our ability to fight various infections for generations to come.

All of this is real. So, is The Event unrealistic?

This is a time for people to wake up and question what, why, and how our food is brought to market. This is a time to question the long-term negative implications our practices will have on the environment. This is a time to question the concept of centralized farming and consider the value derived from a more decentralized approach. This is a time to become advocates for change. It is never too late to change our ways.

Jake and Carla are examples of a growing number of chefs who understand what is taking place, and are committed to doing their part. They, like every food professional, have learned to balance the need to build a successful career with the conscientious need to no longer accept the way it is, to do the right thing. Their relationship, and the challenges they worked through, are typical of many couples, and likely greater among creative folks who work with food. Restaurant work is incredibly challenging, extremely gratifying, but unbelievably stressful. Many couples do not make it, those who do will typically reach a point where priorities change in favor of a lasting relationship.

Hopefully, there are some lessons to be learned within the pages of this book, lessons for cooks, chefs, restaurateurs and every American consumer with an open mind and a desire to do the right thing.

LIFE LESSONS FROM A LINE COOK
WWW.CULINARYCUESBLOG.WORDPRESS.COM

This was a post from Culinary Clue Blog in 2014. At the time of this printing nearly 75,000 people have read the article. It is a snapshot of the people who work in restaurants; those people who show respect for the farmer through their cooking; those people who dedicate their careers to making beautiful, healthy and wonderful tasting food for our enjoyment.

I may be a showing a bit of bias, but I do believe that there are many lessons that anyone can learn from observing the daily activities and mindset of a typical restaurant line cook. These seasoned disciples of the range, maniac adrenaline junkies, talented players in the kitchen orchestra and salty dogs sailing pans across the flat top range are models to be followed through life. Here are some examples of the line cook curriculum for an organized life:

[] BE PREPARED:
In life, as in the kitchen – those who anticipate, run through potential scenarios, methodically build the skills and aptitudes necessary for success are the ones who do, in fact, succeed.

[] EVERYTHING HAS A PLACE AND EVERYTHING SHOULD BE IN ITS PLACE:
In a foodservice operation we refer to this as "mise en place". It is a focus on all of the minute details that go into the make-up of a plate of food and establishing the precise location for

those details (ingredients) so they can be imbedded in memory. This can also apply to playing a musical instrument, flying an airplane, driving a car or functioning effectively in an office cubicle.

[] DO NOT RE-ARRANGE ANOTHER PERSONS FURNITURE:
Once a line cook has determined the precise set-up of his or her station and has designed a process by which he or she cooks and assembles plates – any disruption to the "plan" will result in chaos. If another cook steps into a line cooks domain he or she must respect the established mise en place. This is why many line cooks do not appreciate it when the chef steps in thinking that he or she is helping out. As in the previous statement about mise en place, this need for organizational respect applies to all other trades or professional work environments.

[] CLEAN AS YOU GO:
Maintaining a clean kitchen is only difficult when line cooks do not stay on top of cleaning constantly – even when they are busy. This trait, maybe above all others, is applicable in any person's everyday life.

[] IF YOU CAN LEAN, YOU CAN CLEAN:
Line cooks realize they are never paid to stand around. There is always something to clean in a kitchen. Once again, it is easy to see how this lesson can be applied elsewhere.

[] DO UNTO OTHERS AS YOU WOULD HAVE THEM DO UNTO YOU:
What goes around comes around. If you ignore the needs of others, fail to jump in when someone else is having a difficult time, choose to constantly focus on yourself, then you (line cooks in this case) will eventually face a time when your

needs will be ignored by others. If you are disrespectful, insubordinate or condescending – then you should be prepared for payback. This is not exclusive to kitchen life.

[] LISTEN MORE, TALK LESS:
On the line it becomes essential to keep the communication focused and relevant. "Yes, chef" says it all. To divert attention to trivial chatter is to disrupt the concentration and problem solving abilities of those who are under the gun. Line cooks cannot afford distractions.

[] STAY FOCUSED:
Once that first ticket arrives in the kitchen, all attention must be on the process a line cook has prepared him or herself for. Nothing else is important during the time of service. Apply this, as you desire to anything and everything. Focus is critical in life.

[] BEND YOUR KNESS BEFORE YOU LIFT:
Macho and smart do not always coexist. Smart people lift with their knees, not their backs. An interesting statistic points to a reality that the majority of all workmen's compensation claims are for back injuries.

[] ON TIME IS 15 MINUTES EARLY:
Everyone needs those 15 minutes to make sure they are properly dressed, groomed and mentally focused to start work. Restaurants do not pay people for this adjustment time, nor should any other employer.

[] STAY HYDRATED:
Your body does not warn you of hydration needs until it is often too late - especially in a kitchen where cooks may be

working with ambient temperatures well over 100 degrees, staying hydrated is essential. Line cooks (most of them) also realize the best source of hydration is water.

[] WE ARE ALL DISHWASHERS IN GOD'S EYES:
No one in a kitchen is above doing what dishwashers do day in and day out. You have a minute – jump in and help the dishwasher. Apply this to any position, in any business: help those who help you – we are all equal in life.

[] PLAN AHEAD:
No excuses. Better planning = fewer problems, happier employees and better results.

[] DON'T RUN OUT OF MISE EN PLACE:
The kiss of death on a kitchen line. Run out of mise en place and it is all downhill from there.

[] MAKE SURE THE PAN IS HOT:
In life, always follow the steps that you know are important to success. Do not compromise or take short cuts when you know the results will not be acceptable. On the line a hot pan will allow fish to slide smoothly during sauté or the meat to properly caramelize and add wonderful color and flavor to the dish.

[] A DULL KNIFE IS MORE DANGEROUS THAN A SHARP ONE:
Respect your tools! A sharp knife will slice cleanly and effortlessly through a product. If it is dull you will need to apply more pressure, the product may slip from a solid position on the cutting board and find one of your fingers as a target. Additionally, that dull knife will bruise the food unnecessarily.

[] WATER AND OIL DON'T MIX:
Many of the kitchen injuries on the line are burns. Hot oil will push water away and spit in all directions. Whether it is in a sauté pan or friolater – cooks need to pay attention to and respect this rule. In cold cooking we also realize that many liquids and oil will not stay in suspension without the addition of an emulsifying agent to bind the liquid and the oil.

[] THE NOSE DOESN'T LIE:
Fish that smells fishy is not fresh, meat that smells off – usually is, and vegetables that have the offensive odor of rot cannot be brought back to life. There are far more olfactory senses that taste buds – respect what your nose is telling you.

[] SNEAKERS ARE NOT SHOES – PROTECT YOUR FEET:
Your feet are the most important part of your body if you are a line cook. Sneakers may seem comfortable but they do not provide enough support or protection in a kitchen. Pick the right shoes for the job.

[] WET TOWEL/DRY TOWEL – DON'T MIX THEM UP:
Wet towels (in a sanitizing solution) are for cleaning, not for holding hot pans. Enough said.

[] TASTE-SEASON-TASTE:
My friend Chef Michel LeBorgne held this close to his heart as the mantra for all cooks. Know where the flavor is, adjust it and taste again before it winds up on a guests plate.

[] IF YOU DON'T HAVE TIME TO DO IT RIGHT, WHEN WILL YOU FIND THE TIME TO DO IT OVER:
Before it leaves the kitchen it must be right. Plan and take the time to do it right the first time. There is no room for beta testing with your restaurant guests or for that matter

with any product that consumers choose to purchase. The customer is no longer as forgiving as they may have been in the past – they are not interested in downloading "fixes" simply to allow the manufacturer the privilege of getting it out to market quicker.

The next time you are looking for worldly advice, check in with your favorite restaurant and watch how line cooks treat their jobs, their responsibilities and their peers.

A SAMPLING OF ORGANIZATIONS FOCUSED ON ISSUES
RELATED TO THE INTEGRITY OF OUR FOOD SUPPLY,
ENVIRONMENTAL CHANGE and CONSCIOUSNESS
and THE ROLE OF COOKS IN OUR SOCIETY

Chef's Collaborative
www.chefscollaborative.org

Slow Food, USA
www.slowfoodusa.org

Vermont Fresh Network
www.vermontfresh.net

The American Culinary Federation
www.acfchefs.org

Union of Concerned Scientists
www.ucsusa.org

The Sierra Club
www.sierraclub.org

Greenpeace
www.greenpeace.org

The Center for Food Integrity
www.foodintegrity.org

American Public Health Association
www.apha.org

Monterey Bay Aquarium Seafood Watch
www.montereybayaquarium.org

World Health Organization
www.who.int

Center for Food Safety
www.centerforfoodsafety.org

The Ecological Farming Association
www.eco-farm.org

CHEF JAKE'S LOUISIANA GUMBO
From Bayou Restaurant

Olive Oil –	1/3 cup
Onions – Small Dice –	2 large
Celery - Small Dice-	½ bunch
Green Bell Pepper – Small Dice-	2 large
Garlic – Minced -	8 cloves
Okra – Sliced –	1 pound
Roma Tomatoes Shells – Julienne –	3 each
Shrimp – Peel, Devein and Medium Dice –	½ pound
Seafood Stock –	2 quarts
Grouper – Medium Dice –	½ pound
Crayfish –	1 pound (tail meat)
Long Grain Rice –	½ cup
Fresh Oregano Leaves –	¼ cup
File Powder –	3 T.
Fresh Thyme Leaves –	3 T.
Old Bay Seasoning –	2 T.
Salt –	To taste
Black Pepper –	To Taste

Saute the onions, celery and green pepper in olive oil till translucent, add the garlic and okra and continue to sauté for 1 minute.

Add the raw rice and seafood stock and bring to a boil.

Reduce to a simmer and add the seafood and all seasoning except salt and pepper.

Simmer for 30 minutes or until the rice is fully cooked.

Adjust seasoning and add the tomatoes.

Simmer for 10 additional minutes and serve with a dusting of fresh herbs.

Add Tabasco if you want more heat.

CHEF CARLA'S BEIGNETS – STRAIGHT FROM THE FRENCH QUARTER

Granulated Sugar-	½ cup
Salt-	1 tsp.
Soft butter-	¼ cup
Warm Water-	2 cups
Whole Milk-	1 cup
Whole Eggs-	2 – beaten
Bread Flour-	4 cups
All Purpose Flour-	4 cups
Dry Yeast-	2 Tablespoons
Oil for deep-frying	enough to cover

Dissolve the yeast in the warm water.

Combine sugar, salt, butter, milk, water, yeast, eggs, and flour in a mixer. Using a dough hook, mix everything until the batter is smooth.

Transfer to a lightly oiled bowl, cover and refrigerate for 3 hours.

Roll out on floured board to about ½ to ¾ inch thickness. Cut with a biscuit cutter.

Heat the oil for frying in a deep, heavy pot using a high temp thermometer. Bring to around 370 degrees. Fry the beignets a few at a time until they have puffed and golden brown on both sides (turn when one side is brown).

Drain and serve warm with powdered sugar (be generous with the sugar).

A BIT OF IRONY

This book, although a work of fiction, is based on many experiences in my own life. I was born, raised and trained as a cook in Buffalo, worked at the original Cloister and Statler Hilton Hotel, attended college in the Adirondacks and eventually moved to Saranac Lake. I raised a wonderful family in this town that is as close to a perfect place to live as I can imagine.

I worked in Vermont for a number of years and became committed to the philosophy of farm to table, built an understanding of the issues facing farmers and our system of food production and distribution. As a result, this book and its underlying topics are very close and important to me.

I have been a cook, chef, restaurant manager and culinary educator since the late 1960's. Having invested my time building a fairly extensive base of knowledge, I started a restaurant and culinary school consulting and training business in 2012.

When I began writing this book, Casa del Sol (a real restaurant in Saranac Lake) was closed. This once popular landmark in our town simply couldn't survive. As a focal point in the book, I thought, resurrecting this operation would be enjoyable, on paper. While the book was in the initial editing phase, Casa del Sol went up for auction. I was there as a bystander. A prominent local contractor bought the building with the promise of finding the right operator and bringing Casa back to its old glory. He found Walter McClure.

Walter has a very long history of restaurant development and management, holding key positions with significant restaurant companies such as Morton's Steak House and the Palm Restaurant Chain. The town was very excited about the prospect.

Here comes the irony. Walter brought me on board, as a consultant, to help develop the kitchen, build and train the team, refresh the historic menu of Casa and work with him to reintroduce the neighborhood restaurant to Saranac Lake. This all took place, after I had written the book.

Many of the challenges and opportunities Walter faced in the process were similar to what I presented in the chapters of The Event. In June of 2014, Casa del Sol reopened to standing room only crowds and continues to do so. I wish Walter well, feel he is on the right course for success, and thank him for the opportunity to bring The Event to life in Saranac Lake. Jake and Carla would have been proud.

When you visit Saranac Lake, stop into Casa for a great meal and a Margarita. Tell Walter I sent you.

<u>www.casadelsolsaranac.com</u>

GLOSSARY OF TERMS – THE EVENT

Affinage:
   The artful and scientific process of aging cheese.

American Culinary Federation (ACF):
   The largest professional chefs organization in the United States and the only one authorized to certify chefs at various levels.

Ansul System:
   A fire protection system for restaurants with pressurized chemicals designed to smother a fire.

Barista:
   A coffee brewing and dispensing artist.

Beignets:
   A deep fried donut containing ingredients similar to choux paste (cream puff batter), served warm with powdered sugar.

Blanch:
   To partially cook in liquid or fat.

Burnishing Machine:
   A tumbler using stainless ball bearings and a polishing powder to restore, and polish sterling silver.

Caramelization:
   An end result of the Maillard Reaction: "The Maillard reaction is a culinary phenomenon that occurs when proteins in meat are heated to temperatures of 310°F or higher, causing them to brown." www.culinaryarts.about.com

CDC (Center for Disease Control):
 The United States Center for Disease Control.
 www.cdc.gov

Centralized Farming:
 The process of maximizing production in farming by limiting
 the number of crops in an area or on a farm. Farmers rely on
 elaborate distribution systems to move the product to all
 parts of a region or country.

Chef's Collaborative:
 "Chefs Collaborative works to fix our broken food system by
 engaging chefs in a network that inspires and educates them
 to change how they source, cook and serve food."
 www.chefscollaborative.org

Chafer:
 Chafing dish. A warm water bath for holding food at the
 proper serving temperature.

Chain (from tenderloin):
 The narrow side muscle on beef tenderloin.

Char-Grill:
 A grill, typically an open flame with heat radiating from
 under the meat rather than above as in a broiler.

Chimichurri:
 A South or Central American sauce for grilled meats. Typically,
 a Chimichurri contains garlic, olive oil, vinegar, parsley and
 dried chili.

Crawfish:
 Small, freshwater crustaceans similar in appearance to and
 related to, lobster. Also referred to as crawdads or mudbugs.
 The tail meat is treasured in Cajun/Creole cooking.

Crème Anglaise:

A custard sauce of cream, milk, egg yolks and sugar. Also, the foundation for most ice creams.

Crème Brule:

Egg yolk custard, baked in a water bath and served with caramelized sugar on top. The sugar forms a thin candy crust.

Cutter's Glove:

A glove of either Kevlar or chain mail worn to protect butchers from the sharp edge of a knife.

De-Centralized Farming:

Farming that integrates a variety of crops, works within the seasonal nature of crops grown and crop rotation to build the nutritional value of the soil.

Deglaze:

Lifting flavor from the fond of a roasting or sauté pan by adding an acidic liquid (citrus, wine or vinegar) to the pan while still hot.

Dishpit:

Slang name for the area in a kitchen designated for dish, glassware and pot and pan washing.

Dorado:

A fish from Caribbean and Mediterranean waters. This is a shallow feeding fish that is also known as Mahi Mahi or Dolphin Fish.

E.coli:

Escherichia coli is normally found in the gut of mammals (including humans). Many strains are relatively harmless; some, however, can cause serious food related illness, even death. E.coli is found in the feces of animals and due to the process of slaughter, meat can be contaminated. E.coli can be effectively killed with the application of sufficient heat. When meat that is contaminated is ground, then the bacteria can be spread throughout the product requiring full cooking to destroy the organism. Fertilizer made from animal feces can impart E.coli on vegetables as well.

Etouffee:

A Cajun/Creole dish made with crawfish, shrimp or sometimes langoustines. The broth is made from the shellfish stock, sometimes with the addition of tomato, seasoned with pepper, onions, garlic, and thickened with either a light or darker brown roux.

Executive Chef:

In a classic kitchen organization, the Executive Chef is the manager of the kitchen with overall responsibility for hiring, training, and coaching staff, building a menu concept and kitchen philosophy and managing the operational and financial performance of the kitchen.

FEMA:

Federal Emergency Management Agency. Provides disaster planning and relief to groups, communities and individuals impacted by acts of God and unforeseen disasters.

File:

Ground powder from the Sassafras plant. This is used in gumbo (also called gumbo file) as a flavoring and thickening agent. It gives the dish structure and an earthy or musty undertone.

Fishmonger:

The person responsible for collecting, dressing and distributing the fish that restaurant chefs and end consumers seek.

French Knife:

The workhorse knife of the kitchen. Offered in a variety of lengths, some with riveted wood handles, and others with molded plastic. Used for chopping, dicing, julienne, and mincing fruit, vegetables and various meats. This knife is the most important to a chef, and in many cases his or her most prized possession.

French Top:

The polished steel flat top of this range is heated in a manner that allows the entire surface to be utilized as a cooking surface. Gas units are typically heated with rings of fire under the top resulting in more intense heat on the flat top in the center with less intensity as the cook surface reaches its outer extremities.

Friolater (Fryolater):

A controlled (gas or electric) unit that is deep enough to accommodate gallons of fat or oil used in deep-frying.

Garde Manger:

The person in a kitchen who is responsible for primarily cold foods: salads, appetizers, relishes, fruits, crudité, cold meats and cheeses. In larger properties this cook will also play an important role in elaborate displays of food for banquets, ice carvings and other edible centerpieces.

GMO (Genetically Modified Organism):

"A GMO is a **plant** developed through a process in which a copy of a desired gene or section of genetic material from one plant or organism is placed in another plant. The only GMOs commercially available in the U.S. are the following eight crops: soybeans, corn (field and sweet), papaya, canola, cotton, alfalfa, sugar beets and summer squash." *Wikipedia*

Green Market:

A section in the Union Square area of New York City that is set to attract regional farmers and producers to sell their crops and products to restaurants and the general public.

Gumbo:

The Louisiana version of bouillabaisse, a classic French dish with some similar characteristics. A fish stew with a rich stock and typically - onions, garlic, okra, seafood such as crayfish or shrimp, occasionally a meaty fillet fish and often times with the addition of Chorizo or Andouille sausage. Gumbo is thickened with file powder and the waxy maize from okra. There are different variations depending on the section of Louisiana and the availability of raw materials.

HACCP:

Hazard Analysis and Critical Control Points. One of the most significant causes of food borne illness stems from poor control of temperatures during storage, production and service of food. HACCP control points require vendors and restaurants to track temperatures during these processes to ensure product safety.

Irradiation:

"Food irradiation is the process of exposing foods to a source of energy capable of stripping electrons from individual atoms in the targeted material. The radiation can be emitted by a radioactive substance or generated electricity. This treatment is used to preserve food, reduce the risk of food borne illness, prevent the spread of invasive pests, and delay or eliminate sprouting or ripening." *Wikipedia*

Jambalaya:

A dish that reflects back to the traditions of Southern France and Spain. Jambalaya is a Louisiana version of Paella with the core components of meat, vegetables, stock and rice. As in Spain and Southern France, this is a peasant dish made from those ingredients that the consumer can access and/or afford. Typically, Jambalaya would include ham (preferably Tasso), Andouille of Chorizo, Chicken and sometimes shrimp.

Onions, garlic, celery would balance out the flavors. The rice becomes the thickening agent.

Kings Cake:

Served pre-Lent during Mardi Gras in New Orleans, the Kings Cake is "a sweet and sugary iced Danish dough that is braided with cinnamon inside and a place doll representing baby Jesus inside or underneath. The top is glazed with icing and colored sugar. Hundreds of thousands of Kings Cakes are eaten in New Orleans during Carnival." *Wikipedia*

Lowboy:

A refrigerated unit under work tables or counters holding a cook's mise en place.

Mad Cow Disease:

"BSE (bovine spongiform encephalopathy) is a progressive neurological disorder of cattle that results from infection by an unusual transmissible agent called a prion. The nature of the transmissible agent is not well understood. Currently, the most accepted theory is that the agent is a modified form of a normal protein known as prion protein. For reasons that are not yet understood, the normal prion protein changes into a pathogenic (harmful) form that then damages the central nervous system of cattle." *Center for Disease Control (CDC)*

Mirepoix:

The foundation of flavor in stock, soups and sauces and a product that helps to coagulate the protein in these liquids. Comprised of two parts chopped onion, one part carrot and one part celery. When preparing fish stock, the carrots may be replaced by mushroom stems and even fennel.

Mise en Place:

Everything has a place and everything is in its place. Organization and ingredients preparation for cooking in a professional kitchen.

Mole:

A generic term for many varietal sauces in Mexico. There are many different versions, however the more common used in authentic Mexican cooking and creeping into some preparations in the Bayou may include as many as 40 different ingredients. Some will include a variety of chiles, peanuts, pepitas, garlic and onions and a somewhat bitter Mexican chocolate.

Monterey Bay Aquarium Seafood Watch:

This is the definitive resource for information about sustainable seafood as well as those species that should be avoided. The Watch is broken down by geographic region of the country and season.

Murphy's Law:

If anything is left to go wrong, it will.

One by One Strip (1 x 1):

A distinction for a strip loin of beef (the cut used for NY style strip steaks) that offers a 1" tail on the loin from end to end. Typically, the tail is almost entirely fat, but the plate presence of the steak on a plate is enhanced.

Plancha:

A heavy metal plate for grilling. The best are made of cast iron.

Point of Sale:

Touch screen computers programmed for a restaurant's specific menu. Servers tap in orders using nameplates or icons, the order is saved for guest checks and the list of items and details is printed in the kitchen for production.

Polar Vortex (Arctic Vortex):

Southerly shift in severe cold fronts emanating from the Artic, causing long, harsh cold snaps in areas unaccustomed to such prolonged artic activity.

Polenta:

Slow cooked, fine ground, cornmeal porridge, typically made with chicken stock, butter, salt and cheese (grated parmigiana and mascarpone or the French version with goat's cheese).

Poolish:

A pre-ferment sponge used for bread baking that adds complexity to the products flavor and helps to extend the breads shelf life.

Pommes Frites:

Thin Cut French Fries.

Pompano:

A Gulf and Southern Atlantic fish with sweet flesh and a firm, silvery skin.

Praline:

Almonds typically cooked in sugar.

Queen Snapper:

"In a family of beautiful fishes, the queen snapper, Etilis oculatus, is undoubtedly the most beautiful and the most unusual. Her color can only be described as candy apple red, far redder then even the vermilion snapper and completely eclipsing the pinkish-orange of red snapper." *Louisiana Sportsman*

Remoulade:

A French style tartar sauce that includes capers, cornichons, paprika, and sometimes anchovies in Louisiana.

Roundsman:

A versatile cook in kitchen operations who has the skill to work any station.

Roux:

A thickening agent that uses equal parts by weight of fat (butter, oil, chicken or duck fat, etc.) and flour. The roux is typically cooked with stovetop or in the oven to various degrees from blond to dark brown and even darker in some cases. The longer the roux cooks the more flavor it imparts, but the longer it cooks it loses its thickening capacity.

Russet Potatoes:

A deep brown skinned, white potato that is ideal for Baking, Mashing and French fries. Also known as the Burbank potato, this tuber grows in various locations, but one of the largest sources is the state of Idaho.

Salmonella:

"Salmoneliosis is an infection with bacteria called Salmonella. Salmonella germs have been known to cause illness for over 100 years. They were discovered by an American scientist named Salmon for whom they are named. Most persons infected with Salmonella develop diarrhea, fever, and abdominal cramps 12 to 72 hours after infection. The illness usually lasts 4 to 7 days, and most persons recover without treatment." *The CDC – Center for Disease Control*

Santa Anna Winds:

Very strong, down slope winds in Southern California, also known as "Devil Winds" because they tend to fan fires during the hottest part of the fall.

Saute:

A process of cooking in fat (usually clarified butter) where the product is kept in motion to encourage gentle browning through the Maillard Reaction.

ServeSafe:

A program developed and managed by the National Restaurant Association and recognized by the Public Health

Service as the standard for teaching safe food handling practices for restaurant employees.

Skirt Steak:
A long, thin cut of meat from the plate of a steer (between the brisket and flank),

Silver Skin:
Elastin connective tissue that separates the muscles on meat. This tissue does not break down during cooking so it is typically removed.

Slow Food:
An organization originally founded by Carlo Petrini in 1986. There are now over 150,000 members worldwide. "The future of food is the future of the planet. A better, cleaner and fairer world begins with what we put on our plates and our daily choices determine the future of the environment, economy and society." *Slow Food, USA*

Sous Chef:
Second in command in the kitchen. Typically, the person who oversees production.

Zydeco:
"A musical genre evolved in southwest Louisiana by French Creole speaking people. Zydeco blends blues, rhythm and blues, and music indigenous to the Ivory Coast and the native people of Louisiana." *Wikipedia*